The
Third
Messiah

Also by Christopher West

FICTION

Death of a Blue Lantern

Death on Black Dragon River

Death of a Red Mandarin

NONFICTION

Journey to the Middle Kingdom

The Third Messiah

Christopher West

St. Martin's Minotaur New York

www.minotaurbooks.com

Design by Heidi V. O. Eriksen

Library of Congress Cataloging-in-Publication Data

West, Christopher
    The third Messiah / by Christopher West.—1st ed.
        p. cm.
    ISBN 0-312-26665-0
    1. Police—China—Beijing—Fiction. 2. Beijing (China)—
Fiction. 3. Cults—Fiction. I. Title.

PR6073.E76245 T48 2000
823'.914—dc21   00-033308

First Edition: October 2000

10 9 8 7 6 5 4 3 2 1

For Tony and Nini

The whole world is one family, and all its people brethren.

—HONG XIUQUAN

The
Third
Messiah

The Holy City is ablaze.

I can hear the crackle of flames, the crash of buildings, the boom of distant guns, the yells of the blood-crazed enemy soldiers and the screams of their victims. And my nose is full of the smells of death and destruction: rank, bitter, and choking, but strangely intoxicating, too. I know what I have to do.

It cannot be far now. I turn a corner, and I know that is it. The palace of Hong Xiuquan, Emperor of the Heavenly Kingdom of Great Peace, Living Brother of the Master Ye Su, Second Son of the One True God Ye Huo Hua. I run down the cobbled street—somewhere behind me a shell lands; there is a loud *whump* and I feel a blast of hot air rip at my back—and stagger up to the huge, crimson, lion-faced gates. For a moment I am at a loss what to do, then I push at them and they open, as simple as that!

Inside the palace, I again know where to go. I walk through the outer gardens and courtyards to a magnificent dragon archway that announces the inner, Imperial quarters. A year ago—I've been here before, of course—this place was seething with soldiers and officials and ambassadors and humble citizens of the Taiping Heavenly Kingdom. Now nobody challenges me. Nobody is here who might challenge me. Is it totally deserted?

No, I know *he* will be here.

And as I enter an anteroom, I find him, seated at a desk, reading, nodding his head in quiet satisfaction. I pause for a moment, and he looks up and gives a simple smile.

The Son of God.

"At last," he says.

"Holy One..." I begin, but he holds up a hand.

"We must hurry," he says. He gets to his feet and walks, swiftly but never lowering his dignity to a run, down a long corridor emblazoned with scenes from his own life—his humble origins, his reception of the Holy Text, his dream, his early preaching, his first battle with the demons . . . Then we enter a chamber with a ceiling of intricate, interlocking beams. Captured Manchu banners line the walls, leading the eye to a stone dais at the end, upon which is a simple wooden seat.

"The Heavenly Throne," says Hong, pointing at this latter. "It is only before men that you have to impress. Before the Lord Ye Huo Hua, there is no need."

I nod. Hong Xiuquan goes to this throne, and I see that on it is a book. The western Bible, of course. His own translation.

"Take this, and change it into the speech of your time."

I resist the overpowering temptation to fall to the floor and kowtow, and walk over and accept the book from him. I feel its weight in my hands, and its coldness: while all around the air is growing hotter and hotter, this sacred volume retains its temperature perfectly. I cannot find words to express what I feel.

Hong then reaches behind the throne, produces a sword, and begins to buckle it to his waist. "You'll not need this as I have," he tells me.

I must appear puzzled, for he continues, "When the Time is truly come, it will be the simple power of truth that will convince the world."

"The Time?"

"You will know. It will be obvious." Then he gives a tired sigh. "My Heavenly Father is calling: I have done my work. Yours is about to begin."

There is a crash behind me: a shell has landed in the Imperial palace.

"You must go," says Hong. "Out of that door behind me is the future, your century, one that many will call accursed, but which is truly the gateway to the Kingdom."

I nod agreement, but do not move. Must I leave him? An idea

occurs to me. "Come with me, then, Holy One. If I can escape to
the new century, why can't you? Together we will be invincible!"

There is another crash, this time of beams falling. Smoke begins swirling into the far end of the chamber, and a flame stabs though the same doorway that, a few minutes ago, Hong Xiuquan and I entered.

He shakes his head. "I told you, my work is done. You will find other mortals to help you, and you will always have the guiding hand of my Father to show you the right course of action."

The far end of the ancient wooden hall is ablaze now. Smoke is beginning to fill the place.

"Go now. I command you!" says Hong.

One does not disobey the commands of an emperor. Let alone a Son of God.

But as I reach the door I turn, and see that Hong has climbed up onto his throne and is sitting there, impassive—as the fire flares up to the ceiling and begins to rip at the blistering paint, as the smoke comes swirling up from the marble floor and, in a sudden, terrifying moment, engulfs him. He is gone: Hong Xiuquan, Emperor of the Heavenly Kingdom of Great Peace, Living Brother of the Master Ye Su, Second Son of the Lord Ye Huo Hua.

I turn away, my eyes streaming from the smoke as well as the emotion; I pull the door open; I step through it and begin to fall, fall, fall through years, through decades, through a century and more of our land's history. I hear the cries of opium addicts and the shells of foreign gunboats; I hear the cackle of a witch-empress and the tears of a boy emperor; I hear the screams of raped Nanjing and the relentless marching song of Mao Zedong; I hear steam trains and automobiles and airplanes, the chant of Red Guards and the echo of Kalashnikovs on Tiananmen Square.

1

The peasants stood by the statue of Colonel Sanders and grinned. One of them put an arm around the white plastic waist; another tickled the Colonel's white plastic beard. The one with the camera stepped back, fiddled with the machine—he'd just bought it today, off a market stall, and still wasn't sure how it worked.

"Big smile!" he told them, and pressed the button. Several times.

"Tamade!" he cursed.

"Take it back!"

"No, let Lao Wu have a go." Lao Wu, Old Wu, the expert on everything.

"I want to be in the picture," a man in a bright red jacket protested—but in vain. If anyone could make the thing work, he could.

So they all changed places, and while Lao Wu was examining the camera it gave a great flash of light, almost blinding him.

"Ai, we'll get a big photograph of your nose now!" said one member of the group.

"That's not the worst we could get," said another.

Inside the KFC, which had been the first in China—they were now springing up in every city—a young woman stared out at the scene with distaste. "Julie" Lin was as urban and late-nineties as the peasants were rural and timeless. She was thin and nervous-looking; she wore makeup and a fashionably short skirt; every now and then she glanced down at her slim, shiny watch—*Carter, Genève*, it said on the face—or dug into her *Guci, Milano* handbag. From the latter she would produce a prop to both show her status and hide her nervousness: a mirror, or an embroidered handkerchief, or a "neon light" romantic novel, of which she would read a few pages before getting agitated again.

"This is too humiliating," she muttered.

Julie—an assumed Western name, of course: her real name was Xianghua, Fragrant Flower—got to her feet and clacked downstairs, her high-heeled shoes sounding uncannily like peasant clogs. She ordered a second low-fat chocolate shake, which she took back up to her table and sat drinking as slowly as she could. When she could consume no more without making embarrassing sucking noises, she pushed the carton aside, glanced yet again at her *Carter, Genève* watch, fiddled with the handle of her *Guci, Milano* handbag, and grimaced.

"Five more minutes," she told herself.

"Miss Lin?"

A young man, looking even more nervous than she did, was approaching her. He wore a suit, brown shoes, and a shiny silver tie.

"Julie" ran her eyes over him and his outfit. "Yes," she replied contemptuously.

The boy—for that was all he was, really—blinked. "I, er, have a message from Wei Zhou. He says he's very sorry, but he's having to work late."

"Oh. He couldn't call?" One might have guessed there'd be a mobile in the *Guci, Milano* bag—even if it had recently developed an intermittent fault.

"His meeting is continuing much longer than expected."

"When will it be finished?"

"It is not known." The boy grinned. "He says he'll ring you tomorrow."

"Oh. Well . . . thank you."

"No problem." The lad grinned again and began to walk away. Julie seemed on the point of summoning him back, but instead she just watched him go, out past the ever-jovial Colonel

and into the mass of busy Beijingers bustling up and down Qianmen West Street.

Only when he was well out of view did she produce the mobile, dial, press it to her ear, then curse as the same old recorded
message began.

"Meeting . . ." she said, with scorn in her voice, both for Wei
and herself. Then she stalked out of the restaurant and into the
twilight.

The summer city air was hot and damp; heavy with diesel
fumes, dust, and smoke. It was noisy with bike bells, car horns,
engines, and distorted Cantopop from the nearby tourist market.
In the distance, a police siren proclaimed an emergency in someone
else's life. . . . Beijing. A big, booming, contemporary Pacific Rim
capital, as remote from the exotic, sinister Chinoiserie of its
Imperial or Maoist past as "Julie" was from those peasant visitors.

"I'll get a taxi," the young woman told herself. But even the
tinny yellow "bread vans" cost ten kuai minimum: to take a taxi
when nobody was watching was an extravagance Julie knew she
couldn't afford.

The underground circle line would take her some of the way
home, but she hated the noise and the trapped feeling she got
whenever it stopped between stations. So Julie headed for the bus
stop: with any luck, one of those 800s with proper seats and air
con would come along. After about ten clammy, exhausting
minutes, a Mao-era trolleybus came hissing up, crammed with
passengers despite the late hour. Julie took one look at the human
zoo and knew she couldn't face joining them. Which left only one
option.

Actually, she began by enjoying the walk. Back up Qianmen
Main Street, around the crescent and through the cool, marble-
walled underpass onto Tiananmen Square—or at least onto the
side of Tiananmen Square, as the square itself was barricaded off
while being prepared for the celebrations on October 1. *The People's
Republic of China, 1949 to 1999!* a poster declaimed, but Julie

felt no excitement at this backward-looking anniversary: for her, the arrival of the new millennium, just a few months off now, was the big upcoming event.

By the time she reached Tiananmen Gate, the walk was beginning to seem less sensible. Her feet were starting to hurt—she would have been better off in peasant clogs—and she began to feel angry at herself for making a wrong decision. Turning onto Nanchang Street, her discomfort was increased by the bustle of the narrower pavements. All those evening people: vendors, cops, restaurant-goers, businessmen. Julie felt small, suddenly, and envious, for they all seemed to have purpose while she had none. Then she caught her toe on a raised paving stone and was down on her hands and knees.

A young man was by her side in a moment.

"Fuck off!" she hissed at him involuntarily. He merely held out a hand, and she grabbed it and helped herself back up to her feet.

"Are you okay?" he asked.

Julie, embarrassed at her anger, gave him a smile. He was young. Quite handsome, too. Long hair, which made guys look either silly or rebellious and romantic.

"Here." The young man reached into a pocket and produced a handkerchief. "It's clean," he added with a grin.

"Thanks." She brushed the horrible, defiling dirt off herself.

"Come and sit down," said the young man.

She was about to say, No, look, I'm really okay, but suddenly she felt faint, so she followed him across to a little canvas stool he'd set up in front of a shop.

"You live here?"

"I sit and watch people."

"Young female people?"

"All kinds of people."

This guy was weird. But nice. Julie sat down. A brief silence fell—between them, anyway: a street in central Beijing was not a place to seek overall silence.

"Do you ever think about life?" said the young man.

"What d'you mean?"

"Its purpose. What it's all for?"

Julie grinned to cover a sudden embarrassment. "Make money?" she suggested flippantly. "Have fun?"

"That's all?"

Julie paused. "Yes," she said finally and with much more seriousness. "I think it probably is. You don't believe all this Socialist Spiritual Civilization stuff, do you?"

"I'm not sure about the Socialist, but the Spiritual . . ."

Julie resumed her flippant tone. "Ah, you're from the Fa Lun Gong, then!" In the spring, the center of booming, contemporary Beijing had been brought to a halt by a demonstration of thousands of devotees of the new religious cult. They had filled this very street, and all the others around Zhongnanhai, the "New Forbidden City" where China's leaders lived, chanting messages of protest at modernity: at Western music, at television, at homosexuality, at drug-taking. Since July, the authorities had been clamping down on them, and America protesting the clamp-down.

The young man laughed. "I'm not. Promise. But I do share their belief that human beings are more than machines, more than animals."

Julie frowned.

"Every human being has a piece of the divine in them," the young man went on.

"You, me, that guy over there—" He pointed at a beggar going through a rubbish bin behind a shop front.

"I see very little evidence of that."

"Modern society isn't designed to keep us in contact with our true selves." He shook his head. "It's too materialistic. Buy this, buy that; look like this, look like that; don't stop, don't think . . ."

"You *are* from the Fa Lun Gong!" said Julie, adding a grin. The young man smiled back. There was an ease to his manner that was absent from Julie's.

A brief silence fell—then suddenly Julie felt a rush of nervousness. She gave another grin, the Chinese cover for so many feelings, including embarrassment, glanced rather obviously at the *Carter, Genève* watch (and felt an odd tremor of embarrassment at it, too), and said, "I must go. It's been . . . nice talking to you. And thanks for helping me up."

The young man simply kept smiling. "Please take one of these." He took a small pack off his back and dug a booklet out of it. "Have a read, when you feel like it, and come and talk again."

"Thanks," said Julie.

"My name's Yong," the young man said. "Yong, as in 'valiant.' "

Julie nodded. A Chinese syllable can have a number of meanings: even spoken with the third tone, as Valiant's name was, *yong* could have meant *eternal, incantation, a figurine, to pour, a chrysalis, enthusiastic, the city of Ningbo* . . .

"I'm Julie," she said.

Valiant looked impressed. "A Western name."

"Yeah. I chose it myself."

"Ku," said Valiant.

Julie grinned again, but this time with pleasure—there could be no higher term of approbation in late-nineties Beijing than *ku*, cool—and began to walk off, putting the booklet carefully into the *Guci, Milano* bag.

Julie lived with her aged parents in one of the capital's *hutong* alleyways. The *hutong*s were the real, old Beijing: narrow, angular back lanes where single-story courtyards hid behind tall grey brick walls and ancient wooden doors. Though cars sometimes barged down them, the *hutong*s belonged to cyclists and pedestrians: at night the old alleys were quiet apart from tinkling bike bells, the conversation of old people, a songbird in a cage, someone's TV up a bit loud, and a baby too hot to sleep.

Julie, of course, hated the *hutong*s. She wanted a proper mod-

ern flat in a proper modern high-rise. What she did like about
living at home was that Mama and Baba kept themselves to themselves. Julie could go for days in which the only time she was aware of her fast-aging parents was when she woke early and heard them shuffling about. By the time she was up, they'd be off to Houhai Lake to do those funny old tai chi exercises; when she got back from work, they'd either be immersed in that ridiculous Beijing opera on TV, asleep, or round at Professor Li's drinking tea and complaining about some aspect of the contemporary world.

The latter looked to be the case tonight. Julie kicked off those shoes—at last!—and sank down, as much as you could, onto the stiff, old-fashioned sofa. Her encounter with Valiant had calmed her, despite her sudden bout of nerves at the end, but she still had to talk to Big Sister about Wei Zhou. That bastard . . . She took out the mobile and punched in the number.

No answer.

"Fuck its mother!" said Julie. It was so nineties for a young woman to swear like that. Mama had probably never said "fuck its mother" in her life.

She threw the phone down onto the sofa, then stared round the room. The calligraphy scrolls, the heavy furniture, the photos on the dresser—Mama and Baba at some academic ceremony, grinning inanely; Rosina at her wedding to that police "dog" she'd had to accept because nobody else would marry her. Julie suddenly felt a great weight pressing down on her. Was this what life had lined up for *her*? A series of roles in a costume drama as absurd as Beijing opera, staged purely for the benefit of other people?

She certainly didn't seem to be very good at creating workable alternatives.

She frowned, and began rummaging through that ever-present source of solace, her handbag. The mirror? No, she'd be looking a state now. The novel? No, not in the mood. Her fingers found the booklet that Valiant had given her, and she pulled it out.

The Enigma of Human Suffering, it was called.

Julie found this ironic, given her current state. She began to read.

A new millennium is about to begin.

Yes! she thought at once. The young man was of her generation: he knew instinctively, as she did, that the future was what mattered. Not some stupid historical anniversary.

A new millennium is about to begin, on an abundant planet, surrounded by the fruits of a technology that has apparently been designed to fulfill every human need. Yet even in the super-rich West, people are not happy. Why?

A new millennium is about to begin, in a world that believes science can answer any questions we ask it. Yet that world is ravaged by wars and injustice, just as it always has been. Why?

Julie nodded. Actually, she did ask herself these sorts of questions sometimes, though she would never admit the fact to anyone. People might think she was stupid or, even worse, clever. She read on.

We think we understand ourselves, our society, our world, our nature. The evidence all around us shows that we don't. It shows that we are deceiving ourselves. What can we do? Very little, it seems.

But there is help available for us.

The source of this help is not new. It is a set of teachings that has been understood in the West for two thousand years, a set of teachings whose power made the West powerful and rich.

Julie nodded again. The West was a source of novelty, change, excitement, truth.

It is a simple, well-known fact that the West grew strong by following the teachings of Ye Su, first son of the Lord Ye Huo Hua. What is less well known is that Ye Huo Hua sent a second son to the world, this time to China. He has brought us a message by which we can transform ourselves, our society, and our world.

"I'd be happy if it could transform my love life!" said Julie in her flippant voice. But she read on.

Hong Xiuquan was born into a peasant family, and grew up in a rural community like hundreds of millions do today. But he was no ordinary man: by the end of his life he was an Emperor, providing *southern China with a benevolent and radical government. He abolished the cruel binding of women's feet, he returned land to those who worked it, above all he restored to China's then downtrodden people a pride in themselves. . . .*

Julie had never let on, but she'd actually rather enjoyed history at school. And particularly the Taiping Rebellion. Its leader, Hong Xiuquan, had sounded charismatic and romantic; his interest in the West had seemed forward-looking rather than reactionary— which was what the teacher had called him, as anything that wasn't Marx or Mao was "reactionary."

So Julie read the booklet to its end, then sat staring at it. She'd never had any time for religion—Mama and Baba were, of course, convinced atheists—but was this because religion was all lies, or because what she had been told about it was all lies? She'd been deceived by so many other parental and schoolroom "truths."

She pondered this question for a while, then the hurt of Wei's "meeting" came back to her. She slipped the booklet back in her bag and redialed. This time, her sister answered.

"Everything okay?" Rosina asked. Julie's older sister had chosen a name, too. A few years ahead of Julie, actually. But— typical—she'd got it all wrong, sounding more like a Cantonese than a proper Westerner.

"No."

"Oh, what's up? Tell me all about it."

Wang Anzhuang wheeled his black, three-speed Flying Pigeon bicycle into the yard of his apartment block. He was in his late forties, brown-eyed and black-haired like almost all his countrymen—though he was balding a little and wore an old cap to cycle to and from his work. He was also wearing a Western-style suit. Wang was a middle-ranking detective in the City Xing Zhen Ke, or Criminal Investigations Department, and preferred to wear a uniform to work. But suits were now being encouraged for officers on desk assignments, officially to create a "friendlier" image, but also, cynics suspected, to save money on uniform allowances.

He glanced up at the tenth floor. It was getting dark—he had just finished another excessively long day's work—but there didn't seem to be a light on in the flat. Rosina was probably watching that silly *What Is Love?* thing on TV.

"Good evening!"

The detective started at the voice, so close to him, then gathered himself and turned to face the speaker. "Mrs. Zeng! How are you?" He smiled politely, then added, "I haven't forgotten." Awhile ago, Mrs. Zeng and her husband had asked Wang and Rosina to join them at a restaurant for dinner, but he had had to back out because of a round-the-clock surveillance operation. "Things are still so busy!"

"Let's try and make it some time this millennium!" Mrs. Zeng replied good-naturedly.

Wang nodded agreement. He was not a man to turn down good food, and the Zengs had been kind in the past. His regret at having to turn down the invitation was genuine. He locked the bike in its rack and began the long climb up to the flat. There was a lift and it was reliable, but he liked to keep fit. He hoped his next job would be away from his desk.

Puffing more than he cared to admit, he reached his door. He turned the key in the new lock that had recently been fitted to all the flats in the block (concerns about crime were growing in booming, late-nineties Beijing). On entering his tiny hall, his nose twitched, not from the smells that a Westerner's would—soy sauce, garlic, mothballs, that vague drainy smell from the plumbing— but unusual smells, of cheap imported perfume and, strangest of all, wine. On entering the lounge he found two glasses and a bottle of Great Wall, three-quarters empty.

"Julie!" he said.

He crossed to the window and opened it to let the stink of his sister-in-law's perfume out, then took off his bicycle clips and sank down on his sofa, where he sat eyeing the bottle. Young *ya pi* business-types paid hundreds of yuan for Western wine, just to impress other *ya pi*. This Chinese-made stuff was more affordable, but still a waste of money.

Still, Rosina liked it occasionally, and she didn't drink it in public. Rosina had too much grace ever to do that.

Wang Anzhuang secretly, quietly, adored his wife. He knew why she had married him—to escape a shameful incident in her earlier life—but this did not seem to affect his feelings at all. Quite the contrary, he still couldn't really believe that someone as beautiful and intelligent as she had accepted the offer of a peasant's son like him. Not that he was ashamed of his background, but he'd learned how the world works. Sometimes on hot summer nights he'd lie awake and look at her, naked beside him, and want to cry with happiness.

They had no children; that was a sadness. He had a son by a disastrous first marriage, who had been taken away to Shanghai by his son's well-connected mother. He felt Zhengyi's loss keenly, albeit sporadically nowadays. About his current childlessness, he consoled himself in different ways at different times, at one time imagining things might change, at another reminding himself that at least he had a child—Rosina was the one with the real burden—and at a third by simply being grateful for the joys they did have. These joys were many: the official in charge at the Bureau of Human Happiness on the day their case had come up for consideration had been Maoist enough to add some sorrow, but had been fundamentally generous.

He stuck the cork back in the wine bottle and looked up at the clock, a fine picture of the real Great Wall in mother-of-pearl, mounted in a box of traditional Chinese rosewood. He and Rosina had bought it at Badaling on their honeymoon. The ornate hands, also of mother-of-pearl, said it was nearly nine. How long would he have to wait till the sisters returned? An hour? He crossed to the home entertainment center and selected some music from the CDs shelved neatly above it.

Music from Shandong Province.

Wang hadn't quite got used to all the buttons on the center's remote control—they'd only had the thing six months—but finally music emerged from the futuristic, pyramid-shaped speakers. A Qin zither and an Erhu violin; the music of his home province; timeless, superficially simple and actually very complex, slightly melancholy and deeply stoical. In other words, quintessentially Chinese.

To perfect the experience, Wang took out a Panda cigarette and lit it, drawing the rich, tarry smoke long and deep into his lungs.

Pleasure!

About ten minutes later, there came the sound of tramping footsteps outside, a key rattling in the lock, and a familiar voice.

"Pig! Monster! Bu shi ren!" *Bu shi ren*—inhuman—the ultimate insult.

A tearstained Julie strode into the room, threw herself down onto a chair, hurled a pillow across the room, then ran into the bedroom.

"Aiya," Wang muttered.

Rosina followed. She came up to her husband and put her arms around him. This was a Western habit—Rosina had copied it from the TV—which he had initially found embarrassing but had come to take secret pleasure in.

"What in heaven has happened?" he asked.

Rosina gave a snort of disgust. "It was horrible!" She held him even closer, then let go and crossed to the table where she popped the bottle open and poured herself a glass of Great Wall.

"Tell me the story," he said.

Rosina did so, pacing up and down the room and taking swills from the glass. "Julie phoned up, with the usual complaint: another rejection from another man. So I told her to come 'round here, which she did. We opened a bottle of wine, and she cried a bit, then she suddenly said she had to find out the truth, and that she knew where they would be. A place called Café 2000."

Wang couldn't help grimacing. Places like that were not for the likes of him or his family.

"We didn't have to eat anything," said Rosina, noticing his expression. "We just needed to walk in and see what was happening. So we headed over there and Julie talked her way in. And we found him sitting at a table surrounded by bowls of food and a bottle of Champagne; and opposite him—well, she was no more than a kid."

Wang grimaced again, this time with vicarious embarrassment.

"And that was just the start, Anzhuang. We should have left at once, of course. Julie could have called him next day and told him to go to hell. But she was so angry, she walked up to him and began shouting at him. I couldn't stop her!"

Wang's grimace grew worse. Loss of temper meant loss of face for all involved.

"And he began shouting back. He stood up and launched into a kind of speech, to the whole restaurant. 'Fellow diners, may I present "Julie" Lin . . .' He said such awful things of her: that she was silly and vain and superficial and materialistic—out loud, to a room full of people! And poor Julie just stood there, too shocked to reply. I had to drag her away in the end."

The policeman's expression was turning to one of anger—humiliation such as this could extend to family members not present—but Rosina came and put her arms around him again and laid her head gently on his shoulder. Instead of rebuking her for allowing such embarrassment to occur, as a Chinese husband should have done, he simply leaned his head against hers.

Meanwhile, from the bedroom, the sobs continued unabated.

"You'd better go and see to her," he said.

Rosina did so, leaving her husband slightly aroused by her proximity and very confused at the ways of city people. He sat down and let the Qin zither and the Erhu violin take him back to Shandong province.

2

The millennium was not being totally ignored by officialdom. Clearly both the anniversary of the People's Republic and the return of Macao to the motherland (on the nineteenth of December) mattered more, but the Beijing City Criminal Investigations Department had been issued a banner to hang in their meeting room.

MAKE A CLEAN AND BEAUTIFUL CITY FOR THE
21ST CENTURY!

The banner was suspended from two hooks in the wall above the room's podium. Many banners had hung on these hooks over the years. Some examples: "Fight corruption, waste and bureaucracy!" in 1951, "Let a hundred flowers bloom, let a hundred schools of thought contend!" in 1956, "Criticize the reactionaries Confucius and Lin Biao!" in 1973, "Support the four modernizations!" in 1985.

"Make a clean and beautiful city for the 21st century!"— 1999—was made of rather cheap cloth, yet another departmental cost-cutting exercise, and bets were being taken on whether it would last till 2000, still over four months away. Sergeant Ye was keeping the book, and a collapse in mid-November was emerging as a clear favorite. Wang Anzhuang, who could no more resist a bet than could his colleagues (or most of his billion fellow Chinese), had put ten yuan on October. To judge from the way he kept walloping the banner with his pointer while speaking, Team-leader Chen had big money on an even earlier date.

"What do we need to do to ensure that these aims are met by January 1, 2000?" Chen called out, adding another *thwack*.

Wang was one of the group of police officers seated around the podium in a semicircle. A glance at his face would reveal intense interest in Chen's words: the chance to read his mind would reveal this interest to be an illusion. He had long ago mastered the art, essential for all Party members, of feigning attention: he was in fact still pondering the business last night with his sister-in-law. He was fond of Julie, despite his disapproval of, and bafflement at, her behavior.

"Answers please, colleagues," said Chen, his voice rising to a Mao-like squeak, as it always did when he became excited by the content of his own speeches—an event that happened with some regularity. For a moment there was silence, apart from the whir of a fan and a police motorbike spluttering into the yard below the dusty window.

"I think we should take a tough line on crime," said Lu, an earnest-looking young officer with close-cropped hair and shiny boots.

Team-leader Chen nodded with approval. "I agree. Good attitude, Lu! Detective Wei, what do you think?"

A round-faced young woman sitting at the far end of the semicircle thought for a moment, then met Chen's stare and replied that she agreed with the last speaker.

Wang was amused by this. Detective Wei was one of the new "fast-track" appointees to the force, straight from college. Old hands said people like her knew only theory and were ignorant of practice—but Wei was picking up the practical techniques of Party meetings with great speed.

"Hao, hao," said Chen, nodding his head. Fine, fine. "Sergeant Fang?"

The veteran policeman to Wang's left seemed to have been asleep during Chen's talk, but sat up the moment he was addressed and began to expand on the quality of leadership in the Party and the readiness of the people to follow that leadership into the bright new future that beckoned on the horizon, provided, of course, that the four cardinal principles of (1) the socialist road, (2) the people's democratic dictatorship, (3) the leadership of the Chinese Communist Party, and (4) Marxism–Leninism–Mao Zedong thought continued to be upheld with diligence, efficiency, and patriotism. . . .

"Hao, hao," said Chen after a while. He turned away and gave the banner another wallop, making a small hole between the 2 and the 1 of the beautiful new century. Those officers with bets on early destruction nodded eagerly.

"The Party is currently canvassing views," said the team leader. "For my part, I feel that to crack down hard on vagrancy and petty crime is an excellent idea. This is not a new policy here in Beijing, and I find it amusing that other police forces in other parts of the world are moving in our direction."

Wang took this information in and pondered it. Old-style clean-up campaigns now had a new name: "zero tolerance." Whatever the name, he disliked the indiscriminate persecution of marginal people. Officially he argued—and he did believe this— that if treated well, these people made better informants. Unofficially, he felt these campaigns brought out the worst in officers with a weakness for bullying and cruelty, vices that the manly, fair-minded detective despised. Deep inside, he felt sympathy for many of these people, who, like him, had come to the capital from poor rural areas, but unlike him did not have a spell in the People's Liberation Army and a medal (Combat Hero, Second Class) to boost their careers.

"The policy has been particularly successful in New York," Team-leader Chen continued.

Wang nodded. No doubt, but would it work in a *civilized* city like Beijing?

Julie stared into the mirror, the big mirror in her bedroom, the one with old party (*not* Party!) invites and pictures of Chinese movie stars and Western supermodels around the sides. And what stared back at her was unsmiling, puffy-eyed, humiliated, and hideous.

Not to mention *silly, vain, superficial, materialistic . . .*

She found herself rerunning last night's disaster for the hundredth time, and on each rerun it seemed to hurt more. But she could no more stop recalling the incident than she could stop breathing. It was as if it were alive inside her, a monster that had been implanted there and was now gorging itself on her heart and her soul. All night she'd raged, she'd cried, she'd pummeled her pillows, she'd lain on the bed hugging Maomao till the one-eyed panda—at least something had been faithful to her throughout her life—was about to burst. . . . But all these things seemed to do was to dull her other feelings apart from the pain.

"Silly, vain, superficial, materialistic . . ." Julie said to the girl in the mirror.

This sad-looking girl could make no reply. Instead, a voice came into Julie's mind. It was male, and youthful—serious, but not lecturing.

The nearer she got to Nanchang Street, the more Julie began to wonder if Valiant would be there. Or if he would remember her; or if he would be glad to see her; or if his smile would be quite as attractive as she remembered.

"Ge men-r!" Hi! He was there; and he did remember; and he did look glad to see her. And his smile . . . "You're looking better today, Julie."

"I don't feel it."

He bade her sit down on the stool. "What's up?"

"Oh—just a relationship."

"Relationships are important."

Julie looked up at him. "Yes. You're right. They are."

Silence fell between them, but it was now a silence of understanding. "You liked the booklet?" Valiant said finally.

Julie nodded. "It was—interesting."

"Good. Lots of people find the booklet a real consolation in trouble."

Julie nodded again. "We learned about Hong Xiuquan at school."

"Ah. Then you learned a *little* about Hong Xiuquan. Did they tell you that he got all his instructions in dreams?"

"No."

"Well, he did. Everything he achieved, he did thanks to instructions given in dreams. Instructions given by God."

Julie paused. "How do you know they were from God?" she said finally.

Valiant smiled again. "Because the dreams said they were. And because they were right about everything else. Look what that man achieved!"

Julie pondered this. "He was killed in the end, wasn't he?"

Valiant laughed. "Only once his job was done. Don't forget, he was a messenger. All that stuff happened back in the last century. The real time is now: the millennium. Things are really going to change when we get to 2000 A.D."

Julie grinned. "How do you know?" she asked earnestly.

"Well, I could tell you about a man who is a living prophet, or I could give you a long theological argument about numbers and Holy Scriptures and all that. But the real truth is because I know God, and I know he doesn't lie."

"You . . . know God?" Julie's tone was one of puzzlement rather than skepticism.

"Yes!" said Valiant eagerly. "I know that right now you don't understand what I'm talking about. But you will, or rather you can, if you choose to." He reached out a hand and touched her on the arm, just briefly, but long enough to create a bond between them. "To know God is the best feeling in the world, Julie. Take it from me. I led a dissolute life in the past, which I'm ashamed of now, although it taught me a lot. My folks are quite senior in the Party; I could get anything I wanted. Alcohol, drugs, sex . . .

But you have to believe me; none of those things comes near that moment when you first know God. None." He smiled. *"That's when you know who you really are: the real you, deep inside, not all the silly, superficial stuff we have to put out into the world out there. You, a whole, real human being, for the first time in your life; you know that's what you were meant to be and what you're meant to do with the rest of your life."*

Julie nodded. In her mind, she was back by that mirror, staring at that silent, red-eyed girl. *Silly, vain, superficial, materialistic . . .*

"It sounds—amazing," she said finally.

"It *is* amazing, Julie, believe me." He paused. "Look, why don't you come and meet us?" Valiant dug into his pocket and produced a card, which he handed over.

"New Church of the Heavenly Kingdom," Julie read. Her face puckered with instinctive distaste.

"I know: *church* sounds uncool, doesn't it? But I can tell you're the kind of woman who makes her own mind up about things."

Julie grinned as the flattery went straight to her, unquestioned.

"We meet on Sundays at eleven," Valiant continued.

Unit 32, Commerce Road, Shi Jing Shan, said the card. Julie's face puckered again: Shi Jing Shan was one of the poorer parts of Beijing, a place of tower blocks and shantylike brick houses in the shadow of the giant Shougang steelworks.

"It's—a long way . . ." she said hastily, to cover her distaste. "How do people get there?"

"Most of us cycle."

Julie still had a beat-up old *Five Rams* bike, made in Guangzhou, but used it as rarely as possible. Bikes were not really the things to be seen on, unless they were bright-colored and had lots of gears and fat tires: the Five Rams was, like all bikes sold in China until recently, black and three-speed and had thin, self-effacing wheels. "And, er, what do people wear?"

"Anything simple. No one's trying to impress anyone else with looks."

"No . . . of course not . . ." There was still great hesitancy in
Julie's voice.

"I dare you to come!" said Valiant.

Julie spent much of Saturday sitting in her room, thinking, wondering, reading the rest of her romantic novel—which suddenly seemed extraordinarily shallow—and pacing about. She even went out and walked back to Nanchang Street, but Valiant hadn't been there. Saturday night, she hardly slept.

"It's ridiculous," she'd told herself. "A church!"

Then she heard Valiant's voice again. A vision of what it meant to be human . . .

Communism had promised her parents' generation a vision, one of service to a noble ideal. But it had reneged on that promise in the cynicism and viciousness of the Cultural Revolution, and now it was just a ghost, lingering on in the form of platitudes like the goody-goody Lei Feng or that picture of Mao on Tiananmen Gate. If anything promised fulfillment to Julie's generation, it was money. The religion of money had its shrines in places like Café 2000. Julie had gone there and had been humiliated, in front of money's high priests and icons, in front of Westerners and women in foreign designer dresses, in front of bottles of Champagne and menus with prices higher than what factory workers earned in months. Money had staged its one-woman Cultural Revolution, just for Julie. To tell her she wasn't good enough for it? Or the other way around?

I dare you to come, she heard Valiant say.

Yes! I'll go!

But supposing people found out? What would the girls at the office think? Julie remembered their acid comments about the "ignorant shit-shovelers" from the Fa Lun Gong.

They can think what they like! Anyway, I don't have to tell them. I don't have to tell anybody. It's an adventure, my adventure.

Going to a church, an adventure?
Julie looked in the mirror again.
I've got to do *something!*

Commerce Road, Shi Jing Shan, was a strip of cracked concrete
vanishing into the heat-haze. Along it, metal poles held up a spider's
web of electricity and telephone cables; on either side of it, poorly
built factories and warehouses stood and baked in the summer sun,
light reflecting dimly off their rusting tin roofs and broken, dusty
windows. A few of these factories had rickety chimneys from which
smoke billowed up into the clear cobalt sky, but most of them stood
silent, it being Sunday. Commerce Road itself was almost deserted:
Julie guessed people didn't come here unless they had to.

Few of the buildings had numbers, and she was beginning to
wonder if she'd find unit 32 when she saw a lone bike ahead make
a turn into a gateway. A man was standing there, too, she noticed,
and as she got closer, she recognized Valiant.

"I knew you'd come," he said.

Julie grinned and dismounted; Valiant took her bike and
wheeled it around to the back of the unit, where about fifty sim-
ilarly unfashionable machines stood in neat rows.

"Follow me," Valiant continued, heading into the building.
Julie followed, and felt a moment of panic as she entered. The
darkness was total.

"Sit wherever you like," Valiant whispered. "On this side of
the aisle, of course." And then he was gone.

Julie's panic rose . . .

. . . Then passed, as the darkness—an illusion caused by her
own eyes before they adapted to the lower light—began to recede.
She became aware of rows of benches in front of her and a kind
of gangway down the middle. She made her way to a place, sat
down, and began taking stock of this place.

Ahead of her was a high, barred window. Beneath it were

two points of light: two lamps, on a table covered with what looked like a golden cloth. She stared at the lamps for a while— their still, patient flames were very calming—then around at the other attendees. For a second she didn't notice it—many males had long hair, that was why—but then it was obvious: all the people on one side of the building were women, all the people on the other side, men. How odd. . . . But then, why not? It actually felt good and safe. Barring one exception, she'd had enough of the male sex.

More people came in—young people. Then Valiant entered with another woman, and Julie felt a rush of jealousy. Like her panic, this did not last. She told herself not to be so silly. He'd been out on Nanchang Street all week looking for losers.

"There are plenty of us about," she reminded herself, and redirected her attention to the lamps and to the dance of their smoke in the light raying down from the window. She just watched, and her thoughts became still, and then suddenly she felt a great peace welling up inside her. Was this the moment of "knowing God" that Valiant had talked about?

"May the Heavenly Kingdom of Great Peace last ten thousand years!"

The voice belonged to a man who had emerged from the shadows and was now standing in front of the table.

"May the Heavenly Kingdom of Great Peace last ten thousand years!" the audience shouted back to him.

"Dear brothers and sisters, welcome," the man continued, in a gentler, but still sonorous voice. He was portly, middle aged, and balding a bit, but his voice was strong and musical. "Welcome to those of you who are already on the path to wisdom; welcome to today's newcomers. This could be the day that will change your life forever!"

He made a sweeping gesture over the heads of his audience. "Out there, the world is going about its usual business, blindly stumbling along, telling itself in ever louder voices that its trivial actions really matter. In here, something truly important is happening. Something so important, even I have to remind myself sometimes that it is happening, and that I am so fortunate as to be born when and who I was."

"Amen!" the woman next to her exclaimed suddenly. Julie hadn't noticed her arrive: she had a pockmarked face and teeth that stuck out at all angles. Julie couldn't help an instinctive revulsion at her physical appearance.

"In four months', two weeks', and a day's time it will be the year 2000," the man continued. "The third millennium will have begun. Brothers and sisters, have *any* of those people out there really stopped to think what this really means?"

He smiled and lowered his voice. "We have, brothers and sisters. It means a totally new era. An era, we have been told, of peace and love, here in China and all over the world. Some say it will come overnight; others that it will grow slowly but with gathering force, like a river flowing to its home in the sea. I believe in the latter."

He produced a book from under his robe.

"Many old works are idolatrous, and deserve to be consigned to the dustbin of history. But I have a fondness for this one: the yijing. This ancient and wise book talks of six lines of change. The first line is the brothers and sisters at New Tianjing, who have already crossed from sin to godliness. The second line is us, here, now: we are crossing, we are changing, as I speak, as you listen. The third line . . . I see new faces among us: welcome—you are part of the third line, beginning your change, as the truth of the Lord Ye Huo Hua first enters your lives. Congratulations! This is a truly beautiful time for you. Midnight on December thirty-first will be the moment when the fourth line of change begins, the moment the cosmic balance truly shifts, the moment change begins to accelerate in a way we can hardly imagine. When the fifth and sixth lines begin, first China, then the world—how great will be the number of souls flooding back to the Heavenly City, how unstoppable that force will be!"

"Amen!" went most of the audience.

"Our Kingdom shall stand on a golden mountain!" the man continued, his voice rising in volume. *"Its palaces will be brilliant and shining! Its forests and gardens will be fragrant and flourishing, and its air will be full of harmonies far beyond the beauty of earthly music. Cleansed and purified, the chosen ones shall fast and bathe, respectful and devout in worship, dignified and serene in prayer. Praising the Lord with fervor, we shall be granted happiness, love, and joy!*

"Brothers and sisters, this is prophecy! It has been given us by the Lord Ye Huo Hua via his son, Brother Hong Xiuquan, whom he sent to us, here in China. To a simple Chinese family, to grow among them then to preach his message to China and to the world, a message that will conquer all by the simple power of its truth."

"Amen!" went the audience, as one.

"Our Kingdom shall stand on a golden mountain," the man called out again. "Brothers and sisters, that time is coming. Soon! And then . . ." He paused theatrically for a moment, then bellowed out: *"May the Heavenly Kingdom of Great Peace last ten thousand years!"*

"May the Heavenly Kingdom of Great Peace last ten thousand years!" the audience chanted back. The audience, including Julie.

On the way home, Julie wondered what she had been through. Part of her said it was all crazy. Ridiculous to have gone there, even to have thought of going there. To a church!

But the nearer home she got, the less the oddness of the occasion troubled her, and the more its passion and its communality lingered. *"Out there . . . in here . . ."* These people believed and belonged.

As she rode across the little concrete bridge between Western and Back Lakes and turned off into the *hutong* area, she told herself she'd keep an open mind about going again. See what the week brought . . .

Julie arrived at unit 32 bit earlier this time so she could sit in the darkness and watch the lamps and smell their smoke. The middle-aged man strode out and preached again, about love, this time. Not sexual love, but love within a community of seekers for truth. Julie, in the semidarkness, blushed at the thought of how she had sought love in affairs with harsh, uncaring *ya pi*. Then the meeting was over. So soon. Julie felt a pang of sadness that she wouldn't be here again for a whole week.

Blinking as she reentered the summer daylight, she crossed over to the bike rack and began unlocking the Five Rams—

"Don't hurry off!"

Julie turned and found herself facing the woman with the pockmarked face and the teeth, who was holding out a hand to her.

"My name is Tiao Laizi-r," the woman continued. She spoke her given name, which meant *bring sons*, without bitterness and with a real *lao Beijing* twang on the *r* sound. "You are enjoying our services?"

"Yes."

Bring Sons smiled, revealing those teeth in all their multi-directional awfulness. Julie felt ashamed again. *Silly, vain, superficial, materialistic . . .*

"That's good," Bring Sons went on, grinning toothily. "My father was a Communist and taught me that churches were agents of foreign imperialism. But there are no foreigners here." She sighed. "If only I could have brought him here."

Julie nodded.

"I pray for his soul, of course, but it is so much easier if you find Truth in this life."

Another nod.

"What brought you here?" Bring Sons asked.

"Curiosity," Julie replied. Then she felt more shame at this lie. "No. I was unhappy. I read one of your booklets. It—made sense."

Bring Sons smiled again. "There is much unhappiness in the
world out there. And are you finding that what you hear here
makes sense?"

"I'm not sure. I like the services. Isn't that enough?"

"It depends. You sound like an educated woman, the sort of
person who would need more than that."

Julie felt a new twinge of pain, pain at being so well understood.

"You would be welcome at our discussion group," Bring Sons
went on.

"Discussion group?"

"A few of us gather on Tuesday evenings. It's not formal.
Sometimes someone from New Tianjing comes and talks to us;
other times it's just us." Bring Sons flashed those teeth again. "Do
come, er . . ."

"Julie."

"Zhu Li?" she said, puzzled at this mannish-sounding name.

"Julie. It's . . . Western."

Julie wasn't sure how Bring Sons would react to that, but the
older woman just grinned, said, "You must be *very* educated!" then
reached into her pocket and produced a *mingpian*. A business card,
something Julie associated more with *ya pi* than the New Church
of the Heavenly Kingdom. "Here's where we meet, Julie. It's a
friendly group: we all feel we belong. Join us."

For a moment, Julie wasn't sure what to say. Then suddenly
she was.

3

"So these are our new orders," said Wang Anzhuang.

"Looks like it," replied Lu. "I thought the Party was still deliberating."

"It's had over a week," Wang commented ironically.

"That's true..." said Lu, missing the irony. He knew he'd missed something, though, so he grinned and began reading the orders out. Teams of officers were to be formed, with the express purpose of cracking down hard on minor criminals.

"Aiya," Wang muttered, his face falling as the details emerged.

Lu eventually noticed. "You're not pleased about this, Lao Wang?"

"We've better things to do."

"We have to keep crime off the streets, don't we?"

"It's better out on the street than behind closed doors. Easier to spot and easier to sort out." Wang forced a grin onto his face. "Still, orders are orders. Do we get a car for this new patrolling, or will we be taking Bus 11?"

"It doesn't say anything about buses here, Lao Wang. I think we'll be on foot. I like that. Contact with the People."

Wang sighed. Of Beijing's eight million inhabitants, 7,999,999 knew "Bus 11" was the simplest means of transport of all, one's own two legs.

"I don't think the 11 goes this way, anyhow," Lu went on. "I'll check if you like."

"No. Don't bother. How big are these patrols to be?"

"Groups of three. Who d'you think we'll get assigned to us?"

"I've no idea."

"I hope it's that new detective, Wei. She's rather a dish."

"She's also rather intelligent, Lu."

"I can put up with that," Lu replied. "I think Chairman Mao overstated the case about intellectuals."

Wang wondered which aspect of the Great Helmsman's views Lu was alluding to. His demotion of intellectuals to the ninth, lowest rank of humanity? Or his boast that while Qin Shihuang buried 460 scholars, he, Mao, had buried 46,000? He decided not to ask. Lu did have a virtue: loyalty, and Wang genuinely valued that. There was also the fact that Team-leader Chen had no intention of moving the young officer, so Wang had to get the best out of his assistant.

"I can ask for Detective Wei to be assigned to our group," he told Lu. "Of course, that's no guarantee of success."

The young man nodded eagerly, and got back to reading out the orders. "We are to patrol the area around Tiananmen Square and the entrances and exits to the Forbidden City, and pay particular attention to anyone playing tricks on tourists. . . ."

Wang's disquiet grew. He wasn't sure which aspect of this new detail depressed him most, the job or the location. Protecting tourists was not what he had joined the police for. But he knew he hadn't been able to make his way up the ladder. Not being from the capital hadn't helped, and he wasn't keen on or good at politicking: he made friends, not *guanxi*—connections; he spoke his mind too often. Without striving for such a thing—and actually rather disapproving of it—he had acquired a reputation for individualism.

Then there was Tiananmen Square. After June 1989, people in key services had had to make old-style self-criticisms and commit themselves to the rightness of the government's crackdown. Wang had been unable to do so, until . . . Well, his tardiness had left a mark.

"Tiananmen Square!" Lu reiterated slowly and with awe.

Wang grinned. He did understand this reaction, because the square was supposed to be a source of pride to China. As the center of the capital of the world's greatest nation, it should have been special. But whenever he thought about it, he still thought of gunfire and death.

"And we can get there on foot," Lu continued. "No need for a bus after all!"

The first patrol set off next morning: Wang, Lu, and the third team member, who had introduced himself as Xiao Fei. Young Fei, a term of friendliness that was belied by the man's coldness and arrogance. Wang knew him at once for what he was, and hated him on sight.

The patrol made its way up the side of the now-invisible square to the great ochre gateway at its far end. Here, the usual crowd of visitors swarmed beneath the giant portrait of the man who had buried 46,000 scholars, grinning into cameras or looking seriously in the big eyes of their children and telling them what a great man the Chairman had been. The policemen noted nothing more than a few vendors and tour touts plying their trade a little overzealously, and walked on. At the beginning of Nanchang Street, Wang noticed an ice cream vendor. He paused for a moment, then rebuked himself for pausing, and went over to speak to the man.

"Lao Zhang! Doing good business?"

The vendor nodded—summer 1999 was breaking records for temperature—and dug into his trolley. "Fancy something new?" he said, producing three lollipops. "These are English. Seven kuai—to paying customers, of course."

"Seven kuai?"

"That's right." The vendor held out an ice.

There were rules about this, but the rules didn't comprehend the importance of gifts in maintaining face for the giver as well as the recipient. Wang took his seven-yuan ice cream and began to peel off the wrapper. Lu was offered one and did the same. Wang knew Fei would decline, and did not care.

"The department is having another of its crackdowns," Wang

said, eyeing the now-naked lollipop with amazement. Seven kuai! What were they made of, gold, or something? "You've got your trading license in order, I hope, Zhang."

"Of course."

"Good. Spread the word around."

"I will do."

"Funny taste," said Lu, already several bites into his ice. "Not very sweet, are they?"

"Westerners like them," said the vendor.

That explained the price, which was nearly two hours' basic pay. And, Wang told himself, probably meant that it would lack proper taste. Western taste in food was like Western taste in everything else: bizarre and, above all, unsubtle.

He began to eat. A piece of the chocolate coating detached itself and lodged in his uniform, and he swatted it away with his hand. This was potentially undignified. The ice cream inside was quite good, however. Well, for something Western . . .

When they had finished, Wang thanked vendor Zhang and the policemen moved on.

"Who's he?" Lu asked once they were out of the vendor's earshot.

"One of my eyes and ears," Wang replied.

Lu knew to ask no more. His boss seemed to have cultivated all sorts of rather dubious people around the capital. Lu worried about this—his own friends had proper jobs and Party cards— but Wang said these "eyes and ears" were essential to him. Which was fine, but the boss seemed to *like* them, too. Sometimes Lu worried that his association with Wang Anzhuang might be damaging his promotion prospects.

"Shouldn't we be arresting people?" the young man asked, a few paces farther on. He pointed across to a character squatting on a canvas seat, watching the people passing by.

"Maybe," said Wang. "If he's up to no good, he'll be gone soon. Vendor Zhang is very well respected around here."

"Look at the length of his hair," Lu went on. "A real liumang!
I think we ought to question him, at least."

"It's not a crime to have long hair. . . ." Wang began, then reminded himself that Lu had another virtue, enthusiasm for the job. "But if you want to ask him a few questions, go ahead."

Lu walked up to the man. "What are you doing?"

"Sitting here," came the reply.

"Why?"

"It's hot."

"The People's parks provide proper shade. This street is for business."

"I like watching business."

Lu frowned, and asked for ID, which the man provided. Everyone had to carry one of the the small plastic cards. It had a photo on it, plus an official stamp and basic information—name, date of birth, address, and so forth—superimposed over an outline map of China. The map had odd, light green lines radiating out from it, patterned like a fishnet.

Lu found his attention drawn away from the picture to this pattern. It suddenly reminded him of a picture he'd seen in a magazine, of a woman wearing stockings patterned like this (and not much else). He blushed and handed the card back, taking just enough time to check the number on the bottom, the first two digits of which revealed the holder to be an official Beijing resident.

"S-selling anything?" Lu asked, regaining his composure. How right the Party was to clamp down on Taiwanese and Hong Kong pornography!

"No."

"You'd better not be."

"I thought you said this street was for business."

"Don't get smart with me!" Lu began, then noticed his superior officer signaling he should calm down. "Don't let me see you loitering here again," he said hastily, and walked off.

"Just get the information," said Wang once Lu was back. "Don't get drawn into unnecessary arguments: you can lose authority that way. But you should have checked that rucksack thing that he was carrying."

Lu winced, and Wang laid a hand on his shoulder. "We all have to learn the job, Xiao Lu."

The officers walked on. Wang glanced back at the long-haired young man, who was looking calm and unconcerned. A totally harmless character, he told himself.

Around the back of the Forbidden City was the tourist exit, with its complement of stalls. Wang looked at the stalls but didn't recognize any faces. He picked a stall at random—they all seemed to be selling exactly the same things—and told Fei to give the man a warning.

Fei began to protest. "According to procedure, if they are infringing the law—"

"Lu, then. You go and warn him. Straight and simple. Don't give any bullshit and don't take any."

The young man set off, and Wang turned to his colleague. "Xiao Fei, the first rule in procedure is that you obey your senior officer."

Xiao Fei just frowned.

"I know what you are," Wang continued. "You're from the political section. I'm not afraid of you, and if I get any insubordination, you're in trouble."

"I'm doing my job," said Fei.

"And I'm doing mine."

Silence then fell. Wang sighed, and turned his attention to the crowds. There were a few touts moving in and out of the visitors: one of them, he noticed, was targeting Chinese tourists only. The guy seemed to be handing out cards of some kind. No doubt breaking the law somewhere, but he would give the man a day: he always kept his word.

Lu returned with a book under his arm.

"Warning given, Lu?"

"Yes."

"What's the book?"

"A history of the Forbidden City."

"How much was it?"

"Er—nothing. He just gave it to me!"

"You shouldn't have accepted. That *could* be construed as bribery."

"You accepted the ice creams off—what was his name?"

"Vendor Zhang is an old contact."

Lu looked down at the ground, then looked up again and grinned. "This is a new contact!"

Xiao Fei just watched.

Julie parked the Five Rams in a rack outside the tower block. She wondered if it would still be there when she got back: parts of Fengtai were pretty rough. *In the south, there is always poverty,* as the old Beijing wisdom had it. The block had a lift, but she didn't risk it: she'd never been stuck in a lift, and didn't fancy starting now. Instead, she walked upstairs, pausing to rest only when she reached the twelfth floor and had located the flat. The view from the walkway was quite impressive, though the capital's great landmarks were all distant—a long, hard bike ride distant—and the foreground was jumbled with drab tower blocks in states similar to this one. They looked weary and weatherbeaten, tired of being lived in and walked through and not cared about.

Julie hissed a few encouraging words to herself and knocked on the door.

"Wei?" Who's there?

"Julie Lin."

Bring Sons Tiao opened the door, grinning, teeth on show. She laid a hand on Julie's shoulder. "Welcome! Come on through!"

The flat was small but bright and crowded, the way Julie (and most other Chinese) liked places to be: about ten women had crammed into a little living room and were seated on a sofabed, on cushions, or just squatting. On two chairs facing them sat two more women. One seemed young and had clearly once been beautiful, though now her face was lined in a way that spoke of hardship and suffering. It was a face Julie found fascinating. The other woman, with frizzy hair and thick-rimmed spectacles, just looked old and bitter.

"This is Julie," said Bring Sons. "Not Zhu Li, but Julie. A Western name," she added with pride.

"Hmm," said the bitter-looking woman. She took out a clipboard. "You have a Chinese name?"

"Yes. Fragrant Flower."

The woman wrote this down.

Bring Sons already had a place on the bed, and made the other occupants budge aside for the new arrival. The bitter-looking woman glanced up at a clock on the wall, forced the briefest of grins onto her face, and began to speak.

"To all newcomers, welcome. My name is Qian: an old word for modesty, a virtue we value very highly in the Church. With me is Qingai. Between us, we're going to tell you about miracles."

"Modesty" then began coughing and helped herself to some tea water from a Thermos by the side of her chair. The Thermos had a picture of a fluffy white kitten on it. Then she picked up a book. *THE FOUR GOSPELS OF BROTHER YE SU, as translated by His Holiness Hong Er, Golden Master of the New Church of the Heavenly Kingdom.* "I'll begin with a story. . . ."

Julie listened with polite interest to a tale of how a man had been brought back to life from the dead. The language was stilted and old-fashioned; the incident probably happened years ago. Probably even before communism. And she had formed an instant dislike for the teller. Julie focused her attention on Qingai instead. Her eyes seemed full of pain.

"Amazed?" said Modesty at the end. "Yes, I can see you all are. But Brother Ye Su said that we all have to be born again if we truly want to inherit the Kingdom, so maybe it is not so amazing. Qingai, tell these good people your story."

The younger woman got to her feet. "I am a whore," she began.

Julie felt a leap of excitement.

"Or rather, I used to be. I worked as a 'hostess' in a karaoke bar on Liulichang. Which means being a whore, as to make any money at all you have to sleep with the clients." The once-beautiful Qingai screwed up her face in obvious, unforced disgust.

"Even then, most of the money went away. Girls get into hostessing hoping to save to buy a flat or start a business—or just to get things for their family—but often end up with nothing. Too many people take a cut—the bar owners, the pimps, the *tongs*, the dogs—and lots of us take opium to dull our minds. But of course I still thought I was living okay. A bit of glamor, and one day I'd meet some guy who was rich and decent and who'd love me for who I really was.

"Some hope! But instead I met Valiant. You know, our young missionary. He just came up to me and started telling me about the Church, and I told him to—well, I shan't repeat what I said. But I found it hard to forget his words, and in the end I went back to talk with him. This time he persuaded me to go to one of the services."

Julie winced. A story like her own, but magnified many times over. Julie had just had a few unhappy love affairs, a few of which had ended up in bed, and she had drunk too much wine on a number of occasions. And smoked a reefer once, with the son of a Party official. This woman was a real sinner.

"Again, I resisted the idea," Qingai went on. "*Church!* But I went, and, of course, heard the Golden Master speak. He has such a beautiful voice. And then I was invited along, to a group like this, and I felt—well, I felt I belonged somewhere, for the first time since leaving Shaanxi and coming up to the city. But still I fought against God's call. For a while I led a kind of double life: six nights a week in Liulichang, one morning a week among the faithful.

"It couldn't last, of course. One evening a colleague and I were told to go to this hotel and, well, there was this *huaqiao* business-man who started beating us up. Anyway, I gathered my things the next morning and came round to the flat here. And Sister Lambent took me in and looked after me. When I could show my face in public again, I took the buses out to New Tianjing. And when I got to the door, Modesty answered it. There were no questions, just wonderful, warm acceptance."

Modesty managed a brief smile, then helped herself to more tea water from the fluffy-kitten Thermos.

"Since then, dear sisters," Qingai continued, "I have lived a decent, useful life among kind, loving people. There isn't a day when I don't thank the Lord Ye Huo Hua for rescuing me from my old life—for it was he who did it, not me." She beamed, and some of the old beauty came back. "That story Modesty read us just now: I know exactly how that man feels. I am Lazarus: I was dead in my heart, and I have been brought back to life!"

"If we truly want to inherit the Kingdom, we must all be born again," Modesty commented, to which Qingai nodded eager agreement. "Now, are there any questions?"

Silence fell, then one of the older listeners asked if people really could come back to life once they were dead.

"We believe so," Modesty replied. "We believe the body is just a vehicle for the soul. If the Lord Ye Huo Hua willed it, a soul could reenter a body, and that body would come back to life again. Why not?"

"Supposing the body has been dead for a while?" the listener retorted.

"In the Church we practice cremation after three days," Modesty replied, with ice in her voice.

"That woman is a government spy," Bring Sons hissed.

Julie felt a new tingle of excitement at that thought. Almost as much as she had felt hearing the story of—or rather the reality of—the beautiful, flawed but now-smiling Qingai. It was as if the former bar girl was waving to her across a great river of misery,

calling out that there was a way across and that once Julie got
across there was a world of joy waiting.

*If we truly want to inherit the Kingdom, we must all be born
again,* Julie said to herself.

When the session was over, Bring Sons and Julie walked downstairs together.

"Did you enjoy the evening?" Bring Sons asked.

"Oh, yes," Julie replied.

They reached ground level and the bike rack.

"Five Rams brand!" said Bring Sons. "Very smart!"

Julie grinned and began to unlock her vehicle. "Qingai was telling the truth, wasn't she?"

"Oh yes. A lot of people at New Tianjing are living reborn lives."

"What is New Tianjing?"

"Our community."

"Community?"

"Yes. The Church rents a farmstead. People can go and live there, to study and work."

"Does the government spy on them there, too?"

"I've no doubt they do. But they don't give us any trouble. We keep to the law, not like those Fa Lun Gong types. Maybe the country's leaders secretly know our truth, but are afraid to confess it. Till the millennium, anyway."

Julie doubted this but was enthralled by the notion of New Tianjing. "Can anyone go and live there?" she asked.

"Of course. If they really want to, and if they are accepted. But it's not an easy life," Bring Sons added quickly.

"No . . . Do you think I would be accepted?"

The older woman smiled. "Going to New Tianjing is a serious commitment, Julie. It's hard to back out if you decide you can't cope. The farm is in Hebei, not Beijing, so after a month you have to reregister your *hukou*. And if you leave New Tianjing, the Church will have nothing further to do with you."

Julie frowned.

"My advice is to attend more meetings, then decide," Bring Sons went on.

Julie took her bike out of the rack and watched as Bring Sons unlocked hers, an ancient-looking thing with bent handlebars, spokes missing, and no back brakes. You forgot, living in the center of the booming capital, how poor many people still were. "Have you been to New Tianjing, Bring Sons?"

"As a visitor."

"You didn't want to stay?"

"I have a husband."

"I'd never let a man come between me and what I really believed!" Julie exclaimed.

Bring Sons smiled at this comment, and a brief silence fell. In the distance, a train on the main line that arced across the south of the capital let out a long, lonesome howl on its klaxon.

"You must consider your family," said Bring Sons.

"They don't care."

"Maybe they do, but just don't show it."

"No, they don't. Not really."

"It is a decision you should not rush," said Bring Sons.

"I never rush anything," said Julie.

"Where have you been?" asked Mama when Julie got back.

"Out. With friends."

"Anyone we've met?"

"No."

Silence fell.

"There's some supper if you want it."

"Thanks." Julie looked around the flat. How obscenely big it seemed.

"We had the Lis, Mrs. Wu, and Dr. Feng round," said Mama.

"Old Uncle Feng said they're definitely going to knock the hu- tongs north of here down."

About time, too, Julie thought. She suddenly felt ill at ease in these surroundings, to a degree she never had before. She'd always felt her home to be a little unreal but had been secretly afraid of the reality beyond it. Now she had an image in her mind that there was sanctuary out there, too.

"We must do something about it!" her mother went on. "Not just for us, but for our grandchildren—if we have any. And for the city, for its history, its culture, its way of life. Beijing *is* the hutongs!"

Even the "if we have any" passed Julie by. "I'm going to bed," she said.

4

Xiao Fei did not report for patrol duty next morning.

"You've got to watch out for people like him," Wang told Lu as they set off.

"Why?"

"You didn't spot he was from the political section?"

"No ..." said Lu. Surely, though, the political section was there to help people with ideological problems. . . . But he didn't feel he could say this to the boss. They walked a little farther. "Any ideas who might be joining us, then?" he said finally.

"Not really," said Wang.

"That Detective Wei doesn't seem too busy."

"No," Wang replied absentmindedly: his thoughts were elsewhere. Fei would get some sort of revenge for Wang's reprimand, some official comment, some entry on a file, but the older man was used to this. Team-leader Chen disliked the political section's meddling in his affairs; it would come to nothing. If he thought too much about men like Fei, Wang would upset himself, not with fear but with anger at the injustice of their power—so he dismissed the fellow from his mind.

They crossed Chang'an Boulevard and came to the top of Nanchang. Vendor Zhang was in his usual place, and reported that all the other vendors had license papers ready. Wang nodded, turned down the offer of another ice, and headed up the street.

"We should have arrested that longhair," Lu said as they reached the turreted corner of the Forbidden City. "We have quotas of arrests to fulfill, Lao Wang."

"I'm not arresting innocent people," Wang replied angrily,

then added as a kind of conciliation (for Lu had been right about the quotas), "We'll check by the tourist buses."

The tout Wang had seen last time was still at work.

"Go over to that corner and cover it," he told Lu. "I'm going to have a word with him."

"Right away!" said Lu, and lolloped off. Wang strolled across to the gateway and watched from the corner of his eye as the tout leafleted a group of visitors chattering away in Cantonese. Then he turned and walked straight up to him.

A moment of fear showed in the tout's eyes, then he seemed to gain control again.

"You have a license for this work?"

"I'm not . . . selling anything," the tout replied. His nerve was holding, but the attempt at a Beijing accent wasn't.

"Let's have a look," said Wang, taking a leaflet.

HEALTH THROUGH QI CHANNELING! Master Shen Tiequan has studied many forms of traditional healing and martial arts. He spent many years traveling around China's sacred mountains and monasteries and on his journey developed his own philosophy of healing and spiritual development. QI TRANSFLUVESENCE™ uses the ancient arts of feng shui and qigong to develop a holistic system of energy direction . . .

"It's very effective," said the tout, with the most nervous of grins.

"How much does it cost?"

"The Master gives healing to the poor for nothing."

"And the rich?"

"It's by negotiation."

"How do people get to see him?"

"They make an appointment."

"Via you?"

"Er, yes."

"And pay an arrangement fee?"

"We all have to live, boss!"

"We all have to live honestly. Give me the Master's address."

"Boss..." the tout began to plead, and the policeman fixed him with such a glare that he began trembling all over, then reached into the pocket of his fake Lacoste shirt and took out a *mingpian* business card.

Wang studied this. "Jiuxian area. Very nice. May I see your ID?"

"I—I've left it at home."

"In Sichuan?"

"D'you want money?" the man said, desperation now plain in his voice.

"I want you to have proper registration. If you don't have it, I want you to go home. I don't like arresting people for minor offenses: I joined the police to fight injustice, not to check papers. But I have a job to do. Now clear off, and get yourself organized."

"Was he clean, then?" Lu asked, once the man had hurried away.

"Sort of," Wang replied. He held out the Master's card. "This looks much more interesting. A real trickster."

Like a dwindling number of the capital's suburbs, Jiuxian was a place unsure which era or even which culture it belonged to. There was a modern Jiuxian, which belonged to the Westerners who inhabited shining postmodern hotels and walled mansion enclaves with names like "Emperor's Garden." There was an ancient Jiuxian, a sprawling village of ramshackle farmsteads dating back to when this was several hours' donkey ride away from the capital's walls. Here, local families and a few incomers lived as they always had done, in cramped, noisy, smelly but never impersonal conditions. A third Jiuxian, its skies, belonged to the 1990s, as the main runway of Capital Airport was only a few li away.

Wang's unmarked Xingfu (Happiness) motorbike bumped

through the old suburb, past files of tidy schoolchildren, past workmen pedaling old black bikes, past a shabby horse pulling a cart. Fruit and vegetable vendors squatted along the roadside between piles of produce, calling out their wares and sporadically swatting at flies. One vendor in particular had a particularly fine-looking pyramid of watermelons, and Wang stopped to buy a slice. And, of course, to talk (out of uniform now, this was easy).

". . . Oh yes, Master Shen. He's just down the road there. Gets a lot of visitors. He can do wonderful things, I've heard."

"At a price?"

"Everything's at a price nowadays. But he does help the poor, too."

Wang nodded, much more impressed with this unsolicited testimonial than by that of the tout. For a moment he wondered whether he should pursue this inquiry, then reminded himself that fraud was fraud, however kind-hearted the perpetrator might be under certain circumstances. He bit into the cool, pink flesh of the melon.

"Grow them yourself?" he asked.

"Oh no," the vendor replied. "They're from the airport. Export quality."

Wang made a note to look into this another time. "Don't let the police find out," he said.

"The dogs are all too busy tidying up the city center to bother about us," the man replied with a grin.

Master Shen's "temple" was one of the old farmsteads. The Master took care not to outshine his neighbors overmuch, but the door had been recently repainted and the drumstones either side of it restored. The temple also boasted an entryphone.

A woman answered. "Who's that?"

"My name is Li," Wang replied. "I phoned earlier today."

"Ah, yes. Come in."

The entryphone buzzed; Wang pushed at the door and let

himself into a corridor with terra cotta tiles underfoot and a glazed painting of a sky-dragon along one wall. The main courtyard that lay beyond it was equally decorative—as was the lady who came out of a door and showed him to a waiting room.

"The Master will call you when he is ready," she said, pointing at a small loudspeaker above a second door. It sounded very portentous: how long did it take real Masters to be "ready"? Several lifetimes? An airplane roared overhead.

"We do ask clients to remove their footwear," the woman went on.

Puzzled, Wang did as he was asked. She placed a joss-stick in a holder and lit it.

"Do my feet smell that bad?" he asked.

"We feel this incense has a spiritually uplifting effect," the woman replied coldly. "Please feel free to read any of the brochures on the table," she added, then left.

Wang looked around the room. The walls were covered with pictures of animals in garish colors: lions, tigers, dragons, phoenixes, *qilins*. On the table were more leaflets.

QI TRANSFLUVESENCE™ can revitalize the male sex organ and increase chances of producing male offspring. It can cure addiction to alcohol, tobacco, and drugs. It can cure diseases on which Western medicine has little or no effect. . . .

The loudspeaker crackled into life. It began to play tinkly music, then a soft, prerecorded voice bade Wang enter.

He crossed to the door and did so. Beyond was another collection of visual oddities: a set of acupuncture diagrams, a statue of Buddha, a picture of a Mongol warrior on a horse, some models of warriors from Xi'an, a yin-yang symbol on a huge brass plate. But finest of all was Master Shen Tiequan himself, tall and bearded, in a pillbox hat encrusted with sequins, a blue silk robe embroidered with dragons and chrysanthemums, and black velvet shoes that curled up at the toes.

"Mr. Li," he said, in a deep voice.

"Yes," Wang replied.

"Welcome. Please sit down. You had a good journey here?"

"Yes."

"By car?"

The old salesman's ploy—find out how rich your customer is—amused the experienced detective. "Bike, actually."

Master Shen Tiequan grinned. "Much better for the health. Now, remind me of your problem."

"It's a friend. He wants to give up smoking, but can't."

"Ah yes, of course. You've brought the object I asked for?"

"Yes," said Wang, handing over a cigarette lighter. If only all crooks were this easy to catch!

The Master took the lighter, examined it, pretended not to notice its cheapness, then handed it back.

"Where does your friend live, Mr. Li?"

"In the center of town."

Master Shen shook his head. "That's a shame. You can't imagine the damage that's been done to the feng shui by all the recent building. Especially those ring roads. Old Beijing was properly laid out to allow *qi* to flow. Still—many of my clients are in the city, and the energy gets through to them in the end. We just have to work a bit harder, that's all. D'you know it's more difficult to reach certain parts of Beijing than it is to reach America?"

"Oh," said Wang. "You have a lot of clients in America?"

"A growing number, Mr. Li. You must understand that water has beneficial effects on cosmic energy. The ocean between China and the U.S.A. isn't a barrier at all, but a spiritual amplifier."

So *that* was why everything was so American-influenced these days!

Master Shen shook his head. "It's man-made barriers that cause the trouble," he continued. "If only we could return to our natural state, the way it was in the time of the Dao and Kong Fuzi." Here he gave a couple of bows, one for each sacred name. "But we cannot, of course. . . . Now, Mr. Li, I need you to assist

me. I picked up from the item you gave me that your friend is
very deficient in Tiger energy. So we must send him some."

Here Shen paused, expecting a question perhaps. "How, you
may ask, are we going to send your friend his much-needed Tiger
energy?" he said finally.

Wang just nodded. Another plane roared over.

"Do you wish me to be honest with you?" the Master asked.

"Yes."

"Totally honest?"

"Yes."

"Mr. Li, the truth is that I have no idea. But what I do know
is that these ancient systems work. In the days of Zhuang Zi and
Meng Zi" (two more bows here) "men understood these things
fully. Now, in our spiritually impoverished age, we can only guess.
But have no doubt, Mr. Li, that the power of qi is immense, and
we can transmit it by harnessing our mind energy to it. Now, I
want you to begin by forming a picture of your friend in your
mind. Just imagine him. A nice, clear picture? Good. Next, I want
you to imagine reaching out and touching him. Doing that? Excellent. Now, finally you must join with me in imagining a tiger.
Any way you like. A real tiger, a picture of a tiger, even the
character *hu*."

Wang found himself thinking back to his adolescence and the
big posters denouncing the American atom bomb as a "paper tiger."

"Concentrate, please, Mr. Li," said Master Shen. "On tigers."
He closed his eyes, then screwed his face up in concentration.
"Tiger. Tiger," he said to himself a few times. Then he shook his
head. "No. It's not flowing. Are you sure you're concentrating on
a tiger image, Mr. Li? It really is most important that you do."

This was pure showmanship, but Wang still found himself
doing as he was told. He imagined a real tiger this time, with
beautiful orange and black stripes, prowling through a bamboo
forest. Master Shen screwed-up his face again, even tighter than
before. He began to mutter "Tiger," then to say it louder and

louder, till he was shouting. "Tiger! *Tiger!*" Then: "No..." He put a hand on Wang's shoulder. "Come on, Mr. Li, we must get that qi flowing. Think Tiger, Mr. Li. For your friend's sake."

Again, the screwed-up face and the incantation. Wang wasn't sure how he could think more tigery thoughts than he had already. What about people born in the year of the Tiger? Team-leader Chen was the first one to come to mind.

"Aha!" Master Shen exclaimed suddenly. "I'm getting somewhere. A connection! To the energy source! Keep thinking the way you are, Mr. Li. Tiger! *Tiger!* Yes! It's through! Your friend... The evil power of nicotine, oh, yes—it's strong! So strong. But this Tiger energy is stronger!"

Wang duly kept on thinking of Team-leader Chen sitting at his desk reading a *neibu* Party report, and suddenly Master Shen was down on his knees, fists clenched, veins on his forehead bulging. Shen began clawing at the floor, then to make roaring noises; then he turned to his client and gave a snarl, then another roar, then he sat up on his haunches, unspread his hands, and bellowed "Heal him!" at the top of his voice. Then he flopped forward onto his face and lay motionless.

"Are you all right?" Wang asked, after a long pause.

"Yes. It's just... the Tiger energy... It's so powerful!"

"Two hundred yuan you agreed, didn't you?" said the receptionist as she showed Wang out. "We prefer cash."

He paid. Another plane flew over.

The moment he got outside, he lit a cigarette. Panda energy.

"You spent two hundred yuan on *that?*" said Team-leader Chen.

"Yes."

"Departmental money?"

"Of course."

"Why?"

"This is an obvious case of fraud. This man's conning the
public."

"And now the police department!"

"How else was I to gather information?"

Chen frowned. "Our task is to keep the streets clean, Xiao
Wang. This man is operating behind closed doors."

"Defrauding tourists."

"We don't know that yet."

"So you believe in this stuff about Tiger energy?"

"Of course not! But if people are prepared to pay for this
man's services . . ."

"He's a con man."

"Maybe. Let me know when you get proof."

"That should be available soon," Wang said with a smile.

"Hmph! You should have arrested the tout. He's the one that
people see."

Back in his office, Wang took the lighter out of its protective wrap-
ping and held it up to the light at various angles till he'd seen what
he wanted to see: a perfect print of Master Shen's thumb. He took
out his fingerprint kit and arranged it before him: brush, powder,
tape, lifting card. Then he picked up the brush and twirled it between his fingers before dipping it into the little round tub of black
carbon powder and running it along the print. Which soon stood
out even more clearly. The gentlest puff of breath to remove surplus
powder, and it was time to apply the tape.

This maneuver required the most care: get it wrong and air
pockets could form, damaging the image. He steadied himself,
then pushed the tape down.

There. Done.

Like calligraphy, which requires that you meditate on the characters for as long as you need, then act with maximum swiftness.

Finally there was the lift, which also had to be done with
speed and precision. Another breath, a pull on the tape—it came

away perfectly—then all he had to do was press the tape onto the lift card to complete the process.

He stared at the result with the pleasure he got from a work of art. Then it was time for his art to go to work.

Fingerprint records were kept by an old man named Ze, who had fought off the introduction of a computer system until a couple of years ago but was now a fierce advocate of the machines.

"A reasonable specimen," said Ze when Wang handed the lift card to him. "We should be able to get some ID, especially with this new program I've got from America."

"When by?"

"Well, the computer's down at the moment. Is it a priority case?"

Wang had to admit it wasn't.

Ze smiled. "It shouldn't be more than a week."

"A week? In the old days, everything got dealt with in twenty-four hours!"

"You cannot hold up the march of technological progress, Lao Wang, however much you might wish to," said Ze sternly.

5

The old bus bumped its way along the highway, crammed as usual with passengers. There were old women, a few still with tiny feet in little black shoes; young men in track suits; old men in—something you never saw in Beijing nowadays—Mao caps and jackets; young women in neat dresses and cheap nylons. Someone had a basket of chickens; one of the young men was shouting into a mobile phone. It was another blazing hot day. The seats were hard and sticky; the chickens smelled, the engine smelled, the passengers smelled.

Julie sat about halfway down the bus. There was a book open on her knee, but she was gazing out at the flat, shimmering Hebei plain as if hypnotized. On a piece of paper clutched in her hand were some neatly written instructions.

Modesty had been at the next Tuesday meeting, and Julie had plied her with questions. The sister had answered them all, stressing, as Bring Sons had, the importance of the decision. To enter New Tianjing was to make a commitment from which you could not back down. Julie had simply replied that she knew this, and had felt the firmness in her own voice as she spoke, and had rejoiced at this firmness.

The bus slowed down to enter a village. They passed a donkey cart—when had Julie last seen one of those?—and Julie read the instructions again.

Catch the ten o'clock bus to Pingzhou. Get off at the first stop after Wufang village. Someone will be there to meet you.

Valiant, perhaps?

She told herself she shouldn't think like this any longer. Modesty had said how men and women lived as separate lives as possible at New Tianjing. Brother Hong had taught that sexual desire was sinful. In the original Tianjing, the Heavenly Capital of his great Taiping Empire, he had enforced a strict division of the sexes.

"Think of the pain that your desires have caused you," Modesty had said, and Julie had done so. "God's love is different," Modesty had added, and Julie had felt glad.

She turned her attention to the book, a volume Modesty had lent her "for the journey."

MEDITATIONS, by His Holiness the Silver Master.

The spirit is light and the body is gross, she read. *Without the chains of physicality, the faithful spirit would soar to Heaven with the ease of a bird. Imagine the loveliness of such soaring: the soul, whole and pure, master of itself at last. And imagine the Lord Ye Huo Hua standing ready to welcome those souls, like a father waiting for his children.*

Every time she read this passage, Julie felt a wonderful excitement, like a kid being whispered secrets.

"This is Wufang," said the old man next to Julie, whom she had asked to alert her.

"Thanks."

Beyond the drab village—square concrete buildings, straight dirt-track streets—the bus jolted another kilometer or so, then halted again. Julie got to her feet, pulled her one suitcase from the rack (no need for fancy clothes any longer, though she had packed some decent underwear), and squeezed her way down the aisle. The driver looked at her with a strange expression as she got off. She heard someone mutter something about the Fa Lun Gong.

She felt sorry for their ignorance.

There was nobody waiting for her. The bus drove off, and for a second there was no traffic, leaving Julie alone with the great silence of the plain, with a cloudless blue sky and the dance of the midmorning heat on the hard, cracking earth. She felt no fear, only the beauty of the moment, which she enjoyed to the full.

Imagine the loveliness of such soaring . . .

A woman was calling from the other side of the road. Julie ran across, then stopped a yard short of the woman, suddenly unsure what to do.

"I've been sent to collect you," the woman said coldly.

"Oh. Thank you."

"Don't thank me. I do what I'm told."

"Yes . . ."

The woman picked up Julie's case, and they headed off into the fields, along a narrow bank that ran between ripening maize plants.

"It's hard work here, you know," said the woman.

"I know," Julie replied.

They walked on in silence, apart from the inevitable screech of cicadas and a rushing sound that turned out to be a river, still full and fast-flowing despite the summer, which they crossed via a wooden bridge. The sound of the water was delicious, tempting Julie to leap into its coolness. But she was sealing her soul from temptation from now on.

"What did you do?" the woman asked suddenly.

"Do?"

"Yes."

"I don't think I *did* anything. I heard a call."

"Hmph" was the woman's only reply.

Julie wasn't sure what she had been expecting New Tianjing to look like. A Hollywood castle, all towers and turrets? A Chinese monastery out of one of those Shaolin movies? What emerged from the shimmering was a set of dilapidated brick farm buildings. A tractor and a battered-looking minibus were parked in front of them. There was a simple wooden door, with a board above it. *Heaven plans an age of heroes*, the board read. Julie's escort went up to this door and knocked.

"Shei a?" Who is it?

"Sunbeam. And the new girl."

"Wait a minute."

The door opened—to reveal Qingai. Julie's spirits took wing.

"Hi! It's Fragrant Flower, isn't it?" said Qingai. "Welcome to New Tianjing." She reached out and took Julie's case, and began to usher her through the door. As she crossed the lintel, Julie squeezed her eyes shut. "When I open them again," she told herself, "I shall be in my new life."

"Don't trip!" said Qingai laughingly. She led Julie down a dogleg corridor into a courtyard, where the new arrival stood for a moment gasping with surprise.

"Like it?"

"*Like* it?" Unlike residential courtyards in Beijing, this one had not been built over to house extra people. It still had a miniature garden in the middle, trees in tubs, a small pond, and a piece of traditional-style pumice. "It's lovely!"

"Treasure the moment," said Qingai. "Imagine how I felt when I got here, fresh from a whorehouse in Xuanwu."

Julie was overcome, and reached out for Qingai, who reciprocated with a rich, warm hug, just as if they were sisters.

Sunbeam looked on with a frown.

"These are official rooms around this quadrangle," Qingai said, once the sisterly hug was over. "The Masters' offices and accommodation, the meditation chambers, their studies, and a reception room for outsiders. At the end is our meeting room. The Great Hall of Tranquility, we call it." Qingai spoke the name with a kind of joyful reverence that made Julie's spirits fly even higher.

Tranquility. That was what she was here to find.

They crossed the quadrangle and went through a small gate by the front of the Great Hall into a second quadrangle (more study and work rooms), then into a third, which had been divided in half by an ugly brick wall at least two meters high. "Sisters' accommodation is this side," Qingai explained. "Men aren't allowed on this side, and we can't go over that side. Modesty explained the rules to you, didn't she?"

Julie nodded.   61

"Good. You're in room 3. A nice group of girls. They're out finishing the new pond at the moment, but they'll be back for lunch at noon. Come and get settled in."

Qingai crossed to a door and let Julie into a dark, low room that smelled of sweat and disinfectant. There were bars on the windows, and bunk beds, double-tiered, with small numbered lockers beside them.

"It's simple, but we like it that way," said Qingai. "Luxury dulls the spirit."

Julie nodded again.

"That's your bed, there," said Qingai. Above the bunk someone had daubed characters. Her slogan, and Qingai's slogan. *If we truly want to inherit the Kingdom, we must be born again.*

"Your locker's down there. There should be a complete set of work clothes in there—if not, we'll get you fixed up." Qingai smiled at the newcomer, then laid a hand on her shoulder. "It doesn't matter what happened in your past life, Fragrant Flower, you're here with us now."

Her back ached. Her body itched where she had been sweating, though she seemed to have run out of sweat ages ago. Her boots pinched spitefully at her feet; the heat seemed to have shriveled her whole body so she felt totally desiccated, like a prune or a raisin.

Julie was blissfully happy.

She couldn't remember when she had enjoyed work so much. In her old life ... Well, that was history, the other side of that closed eye. Then, she had worked *against* others, *for* herself; now she was simply a part of a team. Then she had worked with her mind and with machines; now, she worked with her body and the land.

She looked down at her clothes, saw how dirty they were, and laughed. Mud horrified city-dwellers: it was synonymous with shit.

But this was just—mud. Earth and water, two of the five basic elements of life.

"We'll finish in five minutes," the sister in charge called out.

The tiredness that Julie had been fending off till then suddenly came at her, and the last five minutes of fieldwork seemed extraordinarily long. But then the party shouldered shovels and marched back to the new concrete outbuildings at the rear of the farmstead. In one, they stripped naked and stood under cold spouts of metallic-tasting water. Julie had hated showing her body to anyone. But here, in this new world, it didn't seem to matter.

"Kitchen duty in two bells," said the sister. Qingai had explained that time on the farmstead was ordained by the sounding of bells, the way it had been in the original Tianjing. Julie smiled at the thought of the uselessness of that ridiculous watch she had owned, and took to her bunk again to stare up at the characters on the ceiling.

If we truly want to inherit the Kingdom, we must be born again.

What did that involve? she wondered. Had she been through it already, with that blink of her eye as she crossed the threshold?

"I'll find out," she told herself. It felt good.

Wang Anzhuang and Rosina Lin—she has "Mrs. Wang" formally, but kept her family name otherwise—hardly ever went to the cinema. The last movie they had been to see had been last year, that Western thing about the ship that sank. She had dabbed her eyes at the bit where the young man froze to death; he had enjoyed the special effects, and had decided the whole thing was a rather clever image of the decline of Western society.

Now that he was on routine patrol work and thus coming home at a reasonable hour, they decided to go again. And to do it properly, not just the local Da Yuan fleapit but the big one in the Cultural Palace on Chang'an. He let her choose—another Western movie, something about people sending e-mails to each

other and falling in love—but he would be happy to sit through 63
it: she always felt very romantic after these films.

Wang was sitting on the bed slowly putting on some socks
and watching her change into a *qipao* when the phone began
ringing.

"You answer it," said Rosina.

He got up and went to the sitting room. "Wei?" He did not
answer with his usual politeness. "Oh, Wanrong . . . ! Rosina, it's
your mother."

Wang heard a curse, and then Rosina entered the room, still
half naked and totally desirable. "Hello, Mama. Are you all right?
Oh . . . Well, we could come round later. Oh, I see . . . Well, it's
happened before, hasn't it? No . . . I'll have to ask Anzhuang."

"Shit," she said, when she put the receiver down. She hardly
ever swore.

*Dear Mama and Baba, I am going away to stay with some friends.
Please do not worry about me. Love, Julie.*

Wang and Rosina sat in the little main room of the courtyard
home of Rosina's parents. Rosina was holding her mother's hand,
her father was scowling and pretending to watch TV. Wang was
reading the note again.

"It's so cold," said Mama. "Who? Where? How long for?"

Rosina winced.

"What sort of mood has she been in the last few days?" Wang
asked.

"What's that got to do with it?"

"It's often a useful question."

"Hmm. Well, she seemed better. Quite over that business with
that man in the restaurant."

"So she was planning this, then?"

Mama looked puzzled. "I've no idea."

"She didn't have some kind of resolution with the restaurant
man?"

"No. Impossible. You don't know how upset she was."

"People can do strange things."

Mama shook her head. "Not that strange."

"Mind if I look round her room?"

"No."

"Enough other males have," muttered her father.

"Baba!" Rosina protested.

"Nothing's been taken down, moved, anything like that?"

"Not since she left, no."

The little room was unusually tidy. Blotches on the walls showed that posters *had* recently been taken down. By Julie, Wang assumed. Why? To take them with her? Under the bed were some cardboard boxes and that "Italian" handbag of hers. Julie had been attached to that bag. She wouldn't leave that and take the posters, surely.

He sat down on the bed and tried to work out the *exact* logical implications of this.

"You're sitting on her diary," said Rosina.

"Oh," said Wang. He took the book out from under him and opened it. "The most recent pages have been torn out. Is there anything in the rubbish bin?"

"We emptied it yesterday," Mama called through. "That's the day the refuse men come."

"I'll take it in to work," said Wang, "and put it through the ESDA."

"What's that?"

"It puts an electrostatic charge on a piece of paper, which you then cover with tiny beads dipped in ink. These get attracted to any points where the paper has been pressed on. The mark is very clear," he added to Rosina, who was looking skeptical. "Usually, anyway."

The 337 bus to Shi Jing Shan was crowded with steelworkers on their way to the night shift at Shougang. Wang and Rosina stood swinging from the overhead handles in the bus aisle, affecting boredom and listening to the conversations all around them.

"These fucking environmentalists would close us down tomorrow if they had their way," one passenger was complaining. "Stuff our jobs, stuff our families: we make too much smoke for their soft little noses and that's that."

His colleagues agreed, and one of them hawked up a great gob of phlegm and spat it out of the bus window.

After the bus ride, they had a walk, from the last-but-one stop to Commerce Road, past an old-fashioned *danwei* factory-cum-accommodation unit behind its high concrete walls and a disused canal full of garbage and brackish water, momentarily beautiful in the setting sun. The units began at 106, counting down.

The evening was still hot—would this summer ever cool down?—and the couple walked slowly along the cracked road, glancing occasionally into the small factory units. Rosina wondered how many of them, if any, had air conditioning, and thought of people having to work there to survive. Then the interior of Café 2000 came into her mind, and that old adage of Meng Zi: "Those who work with their minds shall have comfort, those who work with their hands must endure."

"Here we are," Wang said finally. With what felt to Rosina to be a most cursory glance, he dug into his pocket, produced a set of picks, and began working away at the padlocked front gate of a unit. Rosina looked nervously around her: a cyclist pedaled by and didn't even glance at them. The lock clicked open, and they entered the yard.

Unit 32 was tall and square. It had only a few, high windows and big, bolted front doors, clearly for the loading and unloading of goods. Wang took one look at these and nodded his head to indicate they should go around the back. There, they found a simple door, which yielded easily to his picks.

Rosina gasped the moment she entered: the smell of incense was overpowering. Her husband began flashing a torch about, revealing a cavernous interior with something—boxes, it looked like—covered in sacking at one end. They walked over, he ordinarily, she on tiptoe, and she held the torch as he lifted the sacking and undid one of the boxes.

No surprise. Thin slivers of very cheap wood with paste on the end: incense sticks, in bundles of, well, it looked like a hundred. He dug into the box—was there anything else there?—but just produced more sticks.

They resealed the box and put back the sacking. The torch traveled on, revealing a number of wooden benches stacked up against one wall and, more promising, two interior doors. He crossed to the left-hand one of these and set to work on its lock. Rosina watched and suddenly felt real fear—that the door would open and there behind it, the smell of death masked by the incense, would be Julie's body.

Clack, went the lock.

The door opened, and there behind it . . .

. . . was an office. It had three uncomfortable-looking foldaway chairs and a metal desk with an old-fashioned Bakelite phone, some pens, and a vacuum flask on it. A bare lightbulb hung down from the ceiling.

Wang crossed to the desk and, using a handkerchief to avoid leaving prints, opened its drawers. They were empty.

"Nothing in them at all?" Rosina asked.

"No."

"That's odd, isn't it?"

"A little bit—though the security here has been poor so far, so I guess they put stuff in a safe somewhere."

Rosina's heart sunk. "A big safe?"

"No. About the size of—well, I bet you it's behind that." Wang pointed to a calendar hanging from the wall. He crossed to it and moved it aside with a flourish. Behind it was wall.

"I think we'd better try the other room," he said.

This room was much better secured. He tried several picks, shaking his head as he retracted each one. "Let's try the riffle," he muttered. He produced a pick with a strange snakelike end.

The riffle didn't work. He was down to his last-but-one pick when there was a *click* and the door swung open to reveal a store-room.

Rosina sighed. She was pleased her worst fears were not being realized, but her *second*-worst fears were that they'd find nothing here, no clues, no leads, nothing remotely relevant. She suddenly recalled her little sister as a child, on a day when a dog had come up to her and started barking, and she, Rosina, had come and chased the creature away. Little Xianghua had been so grateful.

"I've always done what I could to look after her...." Rosina told herself.

"Come and look at this!"

There was puzzlement more than excitement in her husband's voice, but it was enough to jolt her out of her thoughts and back into the moment. He was holding out a printed sheet.

"Prayer of a Thousand Characters," he said, reading the title, then handing it over to Rosina, who read the text to herself. Wang was already down on his knees, not praying but attacking the padlock of a chest with the picks. This opened easily. Inside the chest was a beautiful golden cloth, which he held up and sniffed.

"No mothballs. They use it regularly." He handed it to Rosina, who unfolded it as far as she could.

"It's big," said Wang. "About the size of that table at the far end. Let's see what's in here."

A second chest opened to reveal brass oil lamps and several copies of a book: THE FOUR GOSPELS OF BROTHER YE SU, *as translated by His Holiness Hong Er, Golden Master of the New Church of the Heavenly Kingdom.*

The two intruders looked at each other in puzzlement.

6

"Bureau of Religious Affairs." A woman answered the phone.

"Good morning. I want some information about cults."

"In which country? America?"

"China."

"Can I have your name please?" she added, with a new aggressiveness.

"Wang Anzhuang."

"Work unit?"

"Beijing Criminal Investigations Department."

"Ah." The voice softened a fraction. "I'll see what I can do. Please hold." The voice was replaced by jangly, synthesized music. Wang had at least been hoping for Buddhist chanting.

"Mr. Wang!" The voice was male, unctuous and insincere. "How can we help?"

"I'm trying to find out about an organization called the New Church of the Heavenly Kingdom."

"Ah," said the man with what sounded like relief. "New Church of the Heavenly Kingdom . . ." Silence followed.

"Do you know anything about them?"

"I'm sure we do. This is, of course, an official inquiry you are making?"

"Not at the moment."

"Ah. The subject of religious organizations is a sensitive one."

Wang sighed. The Religious Affairs Bureau had completely failed to monitor the Fa Lun Gong: he had been hoping that might make the bureau more cooperative rather than less. In his heart he knew that government departments didn't operate like this.

"Can you tell me anything about these people?" he said, unable to keep the resignation out of his voice.

"Not over the phone."

"Supposing I came 'round to the bureau?"

"We don't encourage unofficial inquiries."

"Can you confirm that this organization even exists?"

"If you would like to make an official inquiry, it will be dealt with in the usual manner."

Wang was about to slam the phone down but desisted. "Look, there's a family in our block—they've been good Party members all their lives—their daughter has disappeared, and I have reason to suspect she has joined this group."

"If you were running a *formal* missing persons investigation . . ." was all that the official managed in reply.

"Well, right now I'm not."

"In which case, may I suggest that the parents contact us direct."

"What would you do?"

"Whatever was necessary."

"Necessary for what?"

"The law to be upheld. How old is this girl?"

"Twenty-two."

"Aiya! Then there's nothing we, or anyone else, can do. Freedom of religion is guaranteed under the constitution. . . ."

"I thought your job was to check that freedom was not abused," Wang snapped back. Anger. Loss of face. The phone got slammed down after all.

Once he had calmed down with some *qigong* breaths, he found himself staring at the wall opposite (where there hung a Zen-style calligraphy scroll—his own work—of the characters *zheng yi*, justice). He wondered if he was as obstructive to the public as the Religious Affairs Bureau had been to him. When there were no special campaigns running, the banner that hung in the meetings room read *Serve the people!* There was probably a similar banner in the Religious Affairs Bureau, too, and in every other government department, with an official sitting beneath it being as smug and unhelpful as that bastard had been.

"There must be other sources of information," he told himself—though as he contemplated the scroll, he couldn't think of any.

Or could he?

"Wei? Oh, Lao Wang, how are you?"

The man who answered the call was an old friend, Detective Chai. Chai had been shot in the back by a drug gang in the late 1980s and was confined to a wheelchair—a fact that had earned him the unoriginal but affectionately meant nickname "Wheels." His confinement had also made him study and master computers, particularly the art of being a *hei ke*—black guest—in other people's files and systems.

"I'm fine. I have a favor to ask."

"Is it important?" Wheels's normal reply to his friend's requests for favors was to complain jokingly that Wang only spoke to him when he wanted information—not true, as the two men shared a passion for food. But today Wheels's voice was hesitant and humorless.

"Yes," Wang replied, taken aback by this. "Well, quite important."

"I'm busy at the moment."

"It's another chance to show off your computer skills!"

"I'm very busy," Chai repeated with a strange lack of enthusiasm.

"Is anything up, old colleague?"

"No. It's just—you know how it goes."

In Chai's work, in the departmental files, things went at an enviably even pace.

"Yes . . . Well, never mind." He made a few polite inquiries about Chai's family, then put the phone down, puzzled but unable to do more right now. Back to staring at the wall.

An official investigation. No, there was no way he could launch one. Julie's life was not one he wanted blazed around the department. When he had married, it had been against the advice of both Team-leader Chen and Chen's boss, Secretary Wei: "Marry into an unsound family and your career will suffer," he had been told.

But was he just to let this business drop?

The phone was ringing.

"It's Ze here, from technical. About the print you gave me."

"Yes?"

"We've got ID."

"Well done," Wang said idly. Then suddenly enthusiasm entered his voice. "I'll be down at once!"

Wang parked the Happiness in the same place as before and made his way to Master Shen's temple. He rang the entryphone.

"Mr. Li?" said the receptionist. "I'm afraid that, if you don't have an appointment..."

"It's very urgent," Wang cut in. As this didn't get the desired response, he added, "There could be a lot of money involved."

"How much?"

"Ten thousand yuan?"

"Hold on." The entryphone went silent: soon after, the receptionist appeared at the temple door, as immaculately dressed as ever. "The Master normally does his meditation at this hour," she said.

"But for ten thousand yuan..."

She made no reply to this, but took the new arrival through to the waiting room and lit another joss-stick.

"Your shoes..."

He thought of asking how many wan a deal had to be worth to keep shoes on, but desisted and removed them.

"What kind of business did you have in mind?" she asked.

"Private."

She frowned but left. He began to read about his previous
lives and their karmic consequences, then the loudspeaker over the
door came to life again.

The Master was hatless and shoeless and in a simple white
robe.

"My meditation clothes," he explained. "I meditate daily on
the Daoist notion of wu wei, nonmovement. Nonmovement of the
body, of the mind, of the soul."

"Sounds fascinating," said Wang. "Where did you learn it?"

"In Tibet. I was taken to a monastery north of Xigaze by two
monks of the *gelug-pa* sect. We practiced meditation for sixteen
hours a day."

"When was this?"

The Master looked affronted. "Does that matter?"

"It might."

"Well, let me see. It was in 1984."

"Ah yes. That would have been about the time you started
selling those fake tiger penis pills." "Mr. Li" reached into his
pocket and pulled out a police ID.

Master Shen Tiequan showed fear for an instant before gathering his composure. "What I'm doing now is not illegal."

"I'm sure we can find something."

Shen said nothing for a moment, then sighed. "How much
d'you want?"

"Offering bribes to an official of the Public Security Bureau *is*
a major offense."

The fear returned to Shen's face.

"Actually, I need your help," Wang continued.

"I knew it!" Shen said, his face now flooding with relief. "It
was *you* that was smoking! If you really want to kick the habit,
you must tell me how you started. In fact, you must tell me as
much about yourself as you can. Telling your story is a crucial
part of the cure, possibly the—"

"I need information."

Fear again. "About whom?"

"Ever heard of the New Church of the Heavenly Kingdom?"

And back to relief. "Heavenly Kingdom? That was in the last century, wasn't it? What was the guy's name? Hong something?"

"Hong Xiuquan. I'm talking about a modern organization. A religious cult."

The Master furrowed his brow. "New Church of the Heavenly Kingdom. It doesn't mean anything to me. It's a Christian organization, I assume?"

"Why do you assume that?"

"*Church.*" Shen shook his head. "I'm afraid I don't have much to do with Christianity—or any of the organized religions. My clients are looking for a new way, a spiritual path that is untainted by age-old structures of power and obedience. Why do you want to know about these people?"

"That's my business."

Master Shen thought for a moment, then broke into a smile. "Son or daughter?" he said.

"What do you mean?"

"Is it your son or your daughter who's joined this organization?"

"Neither!" Wang snapped. Then his anger left him. "Sister-in-law."

Shen nodded. "I'll ask around. I can't guarantee success, but I promise to try."

Wang wondered quite how much this man's promise was worth and for a moment contemplated adding a deadline and threat to his request. But somehow that didn't feel the right thing to do. "Weapons of war are best kept hidden," he said to himself, quoting Lao Tzu, and held out a hand to formalize the agreement.

As the work party marched home past the whispering maize plants, Julie no longer felt exhausted. They had fasted today, and worked, too: she was far beyond exhaustion, in a state she imagined possessed sleepwalkers. What she wanted to do above all else was lie down, but she did not—she was not sure what was driving her on, but something was, and she let it.

And that something did get her home, to the farmstead, to the showers, to her bunk, where she would have half an hour before the prayer meeting (no dinner tonight, either). She lay down, stared at the ceiling, and tried to fend off sleep.

"Come on, Fragrant Flower!"

"Oh . . . Is it time already?"

"Yes," the voice continued, a little surprised she should need to ask.

Julie jumped down off the bunk and followed a group of women across to the Great Hall of Tranquility. There was a "Gathering" here every evening, with prayers and preaching, usually from the Master's deputy—the man who had written that lovely piece about flying. But tonight was to be special, Julie had been told. She made her way to the front of the audience—she liked to be near the Masters—and sat down. She closed her eyes and imagined herself on the bus coming here, reading that inspirational prose:

The faithful spirit would soar to heaven with the ease of a bird. Imagine the loveliness of such soaring . . .

"The Lord Ye Huo Hua loves you!" Julie recognized the voice as the Silver Master's.

"Amen!" she shouted back automatically.

"The Lord Ye Huo Hua loves us so much that he has sacrificed his sons for our enlightenment," the Master continued. "For us, brothers and sisters, for all of us in this room. He gave his first son Ye Su for us; he gave his second son, our beloved Brother Hong Xiuquan, for us. This is how he shows his love. Feel that love, brothers and sisters, feel that love!"

Julie tried to do so.

"Let us meditate on that love, brothers and sisters."

Julie nodded. Think of that love . . .

"Let us be silent, brothers and sisters, and direct all our thoughts toward the Lord Ye Huo Hua."

Silent, thought Julie. She felt her body loosening and her mind, which had been drifting, suddenly focusing—and then a great rush of feeling, of wonderful, all-embracing feeling, that Julie suddenly knew she'd craved since, oh, she couldn't remember how far back.

The moment you first know God, Valiant had talked about.

"Fragrant Flower," said a voice. The Silver Master's. Talking to her! "What are you feeling?"

"Love, Master," she said softly.

"Tell everyone. Tell all your brothers and sisters."

"Love," Julie said again, louder.

"Stand up and tell us, Fragrant Flower!"

Julie did so.

"Louder," said the Master.

"Love!"

"So are you ready to make the journey?"

Julie didn't know what the Master meant, but she didn't need to know. "Yes!"

"What is at the end of your journey, Fragrant Flower?"

"My soul, free of all burdens. Soaring with the ease of a bird . . ."

"Yes, you *are* ready. The love of the Lord Ye Huo Hua is waiting for you. But first you must begin truly to free yourself from sin."

Julie stood still suddenly. "Sin? I thought . . . Now that I'm here . . ."

"Sin is what stands between us and the Lord Ye Huo Hua's love. Fragrant Flower, do you hate sin?"

"Yes. Of course."

"Have you had sin in your heart?"

"Y-yes."

"Tell your brothers and sisters."

Julie didn't know what to say. But she spoke, anyway. Slowly at first, then faster and faster, till the words were cascading out—words that told how she had been covetous, how she had been

vain, how she had been deceitful, how she had been lustful, and
silly and vain and superficial and materialistic . . .

"Sisters, I am evil!" she shouted out at the end. She began shaking. The people near her, who had seen this happen before, moved away. They did so just in time: suddenly Julie was on the floor, thumping at the matting and yelling at the top of her voice.

"The Lord Ye Huo Hua loves you," the Master told her calmly.

"I don't deserve that love!"

"He loves us all!"

"I'm a sinner!"

"He loves every person in this room."

"Not me! I am too wicked!"

"Sisters, take Fragrant Flower in your arms and show the love you have for her."

"I don't deserve it!"

The people began to close in, and Julie began to hurl obscenities at them.

"Love is all-powerful!" said the Master. "Brothers and sisters, show your love."

Hands began to touch Julie, and she began batting them away. But the crowd just got closer and closer. "We love you!" they were chanting. *"We love you!"*

"Daughters of bitches!" Julie screamed back.

"We love you!"

"Fuck your mothers! Fuck those old whores who gave birth to pigs like you!"

"WE LOVE YOU!"

Then hands were all over Julie. She suddenly froze, paralyzed with terror. Then she felt herself lifted, and swayed in the air, gently, ever so gently.

"If we truly want to inherit the Kingdom, we must be born again," said the Master.

"Born again," the people around Julie murmured.

And the fear was gone.

Replaced by . . .

There were no words for it.

"The Lord Ye Huo Hua loves you," said the Master.

The hands lowered Julie to the ground, where she began to do what newborns usually do. Cry.

7

The call came through next morning.

"I've found out a little about your Church," said Master Shen.

"Excellent," said Wang. He glanced around the office. "I'll come to your house. Midday?"

"Not midday. I'm seeing a client. The wife of a very important Hong Kong businessman. One-thirty?"

"Better make it after work. Six."

"Half-past? There's a Party Secretary coming to see me at five-thirty."

This time Master Shen was wearing a T-shirt, shorts, and a pair of Nike trainers. Real ones, they looked like.

"The New Church of the Heavenly Kingdom was founded by a man called Hong Er," he told Wang. "Sometime earlier this decade. I don't have up-to-date information, but he seems to think he's some kind of divine messenger, inspired by Hong Xiuquan, the leader of the Taiping Rebellion."

"Aiya! I suppose he wants to cause another uprising."

"From what I've heard they express no political ambitions at all."

"Just as well for them."

"Hong Er appears to be quite a serious and devout man."

"You mean he actually believes what he says?"

"It's the best way to convince people," Shen said with a smile. "Or to fool them."

Shen nodded seriously. "According to my information, the

Golden Master—that's what he calls himself—is completely sincere."

"Then he must be mad!"

The Master shook his head. "There are no reports of erratic behavior on his part. The story is that Hong Er started having dreams about a man trying to give him messages, then he read about the Taipings and decided Hong Xiuquan was that man. It's the name, partially, of course."

Wang recalled the name on the spine of the book. Hong Er, Second Hong. "Any confirmation as to whether my sister-in-law is there?"

"No. It's very possible, though. The Church takes in a lot of disaffected young people."

Wang was about to protest, but the words died on his lips.

"There are a lot of confused people around nowadays," Shen went on. "What are we supposed to believe in? The Motherland? Karl Marx? Technology? The size of your bank balance? The size of your dick?"

Wang grimaced, not at the crudity but at the implicit criticism of the Party whose rule he was supposed to uphold. He seemed to spend half his life criticizing it from inside and the other half defending it against critical outsiders. "Does the Church have a headquarters?" he asked.

"I believe so, but I don't know where."

He felt a moment of superiority, before Shen went on, "They hold meetings in Shi Jing Shan, I know that much. Eleven o'clock on Sundays."

"Ah." Silence fell. "Any other information?"

"Not yet. I shall keep looking."

"Good."

Silence again.

"In the meantime . . ." Master Shen began. Wang knew what was coming. "This business with my colleague at the Forbidden City."

"He's an illegal resident."

"He's a bright boy from a poor backwater. And he's honest. He's not going around picking people's pockets on buses or selling 'black' cigarettes. He deserves a chance to make it in the big city."

"There's a crackdown. If you care that much about him, buy him a ticket back to Sichuan."

Shen frowned but seemed to accept the comment.

Wang turned for the door. As he did so, a particularly strong whiff of incense hit him. As, moments later, did a thought.

"I like the smell of the incense you use here. Where d'you get it from?"

"My assistant buys it," Shen replied. "In Beijing somewhere." The Master paused, then bent down, opened his drawer again, and produced a packet of joss-sticks. "Here, have some. A token of continuing goodwill between the People and their police force."

"Thank you," said Wang. There was a note of coldness in his voice, but another side of him found he liked dealing with Shen. They were, after all, both connoisseurs of deceit in their own ways.

At the top of Tiananmen Square, a group of tourists in raincoats looked up at Tiananmen Gate. The line of red flags along the parapet hung sodden in the drenching rain: the hot spell had finally broken, for a day, at least. Wang and Rosina pedaled slowly past, the tires of their bikes hissing in the wet, and turned left into Chang'an Boulevard. During the working week Chang'an was clogged with traffic; like the square it was also undergoing massive rebuilding work. But on a rainy Sunday . . .

He disliked going down this wide tree-lined avenue, as it took him past Muxudi, where he had witnessed one of the worst incidents of June 1989. But it was the quickest way to where they wanted to be, and he didn't like to think of himself as a man who let emotion get in the way of effectiveness.

They reached Commerce Road ahead of their planned schedule. On their previous visit, he had noted a new, as yet unoccupied factory almost opposite unit 32: it was still unoccupied today, so they parked around back and let themselves in. There was even the shell of an upper-floor office where the couple could dry out from the rain. Rosina had brought a flask of coffee, some steamed bread, chicken legs, and a plastic tray of *dofu*—the plan had been to save these till lunch, but the damp had seeped under her coat and she felt she needed some food inside her now. He took first shift at the window.

The first vehicle to arrive was a minibus. About ten people got out, all shrouded in plastic raincoats. Wang handed the glasses to Rosina, who scanned the party and shook her head. Then people began to arrive, on foot, a couple of cars, mainly by bike.

"There're loads of them!" she exclaimed.

"Including Julie?"

"I can't recognize anyone in those coats and hats."

"You'd recognize her, I'm sure."

"Maybe. Aiya! This damn rain!"

At about ten to eleven, the arrivals ceased. A man came out from the building and turned on a pump, which began to chug noisily, neatly covering any sounds from within the building. Rosina let out a sigh.

"We *are* looking in the right place, aren't we, Anzhuang?"

On Monday morning, the patrol groups gathered as usual in the meeting room for their briefing.

"Zero tolerance!" Team-leader Chen said with unashamed relish. "That's what we have been told to show to street criminals of any kind." He whacked the banner with his stick. A new gash appeared, between the characters for *beautiful* and *city*. "I don't think some of us realize how large the problem of our migrant population is. Recent figures estimate that there will be over two million out-of-towners in the capital by next year. Many of these are here illegally, and many of them are involved in petty crime. I want ten arrests by this evening per group. And that includes you, Xiao Wang."

"We have the situation under control." The reply was com- pletely calm.

"I hope so."

"How seriously does he mean that?" Detective Wei asked Wang as they were leaving the briefing room.

"He'd like it. But he'll live if he doesn't get what he wants. And so will we. This isn't nineteen fifty-seven."

"Nineteen fifty-seven?"

He was about to give a history lesson about Mao's Anti-rightist Movement, when thousands of innocent people had been sent off to labor camps to fill quotas of political criminals, when he noticed Xiao Fei standing nearby, unashamedly listening to them.

"Many years ago the Party made mistakes," he said. "Of course, these have long since been rectified."

It was a rare quiet moment at the nurse's station in Capital Hospital. There was a new girl on the ward, Yuchang, and this was the first time Rosina had had any chance to talk to her in any other way apart from giving out orders.

"Getting on okay?" she said.

Yuchang smiled. "I think so, sister. It's all a bit much sometimes."

Rosina felt a stab of guilt: she'd not been the best of bosses in the last few days. "You'll get used to it. You're doing well. I remember my first ward. . . . Still, at least we didn't have this damn thing to deal with!" She nodded in the direction of the computer that had recently been installed.

Yuchang's smile turned into a laugh. "Ai, that's easy."

"Maybe it is for you," Rosina replied. "Computers are the big difference between your generation and mine. I just don't understand them."

"I'll teach you. What d'you want to know?"

"I don't know. Anything. Everything. How the damned thing works. How to stop it sitting there and gawping at me."

"D'you want to make a database? Enter Chinese characters?"

"I've got pen and paper for that!"

"What about the Internet?"

Rosina shook her head with great resolve.

"The Net's ku," Yuchang replied. "If you want information on anything, it'll be there!"

"Anything?" said Rosina, her interest suddenly aroused.

"Yes. The government tries to restrict access. But if you know where to look ..."

"I though it was all pornography and stuff for terrorists."

"That's just propaganda," Yuchang said dismissively. "Those sites exist, but they're not why the authorities don't like the Net. The government wants to control what people read."

No, *that* was the difference between Rosina's generation and Yuchang's. Rosina wouldn't be happy even thinking those things, let alone saying them.

"We can't get the Internet on this machine anyway, can we?" she said hastily.

"Not yet. But we could go to a café."

"A café?" This conversation seemed to have gone completely crazy—what had eating to do with computers?—and then a patient at the far end of the room began sounding his buzzer. Not just a push, either, but a series of irate stabs. He was a former political commissar and had been admitted with acute constipation. This morning he had been recovering fast.

"If he wants the lavatory again, I'll throttle him," said Rosina.

"Lavatory!" shouted the man.

"So we're going to an Internet café ..." said Rosina, as the two nurses stood in the queue for the 105 bus.

"That's right. We go and use the computers, and we can eat and drink while you're doing it. And meet other Netheads, too, if we want to."

"Netheads?"

"Freaks. People like us."

Rosina winced. "And how much is it going to cost? I insist on paying for both of us."

Yuchang grinned. "The café owner is, er, a friend. He'll look after us."

The wrong bus stopped, disgorged passengers, refilled to the bursting point, and set off again.

Rosina wasn't sure she was doing the right thing. In order to see if there was any information on the "Net" about the New Church of the Heavenly Kingdom, she might have to tell her story to Yuchang. And this story was *not* for outside consumption: shame is something you keep inside families. But this was such an opportunity!

The next bus was a 105. The two nurses battled up the steps, looked in vain for seats, grabbed hold of the rail, and handed their two-jiao notes to the people next to them—the money would be passed down the bus, and two tickets would eventually be passed back.

"It's not far," said Yuchang. "I do this journey a lot."

Rosina grunted as a woman barged past her. Aiya, buses seemed to be getting fuller and fuller . . . All these people coming to Beijing from outside, the papers kept telling her.

Walking into the Y2K Internet Café was the nearest Rosina had come to time travel. One moment she was on the familiar uneven concrete slabs of a Beijing pavement, walking past street vendors and cheap noodle restaurants and sweating in the summer heat; the next—the twenty-first century had arrived. Fierce air conditioning. Western music, very modern and very loud. The future was bright: chrome gleamed everywhere. Powerful lights shone into her eyes. And, of course, there were the computers, rows of them, all occupied, some by foreigners, others by Chinese, none by people over about twenty.

"Yuchang!" A man in a suit, a blue shirt, and bulbous white tie raised his dark glasses and put an arm around the new arrival.

"Tuo, this is a colleague from work," said Yuchang.

"Ah." Tuo looked at Rosina conspiratorially. "I hear it's tough there. The ward sister is a real cow!"

Yuchang blushed.

"I've been under a lot of stress in the last few days," said Rosina.

Tuo simply laughed a laugh as loud as his tie. "So you've come to try the machines, have you?" He lowered his voice. "We're a bit busy at the moment. Those people at the bar are all waiting to get on."

"We can wait," said Rosina, who was fast becoming intrigued by this place.

Tuo shook his head and whispered, "While they wait, sister, they spend money. Number seventeen will be available shortly."

Rosina didn't like jumping the queue with such ease, but suppressed these feelings—or, rather, allowed them to be steamrolled by what was now full-fledged excitement.

"Drinks in the meantime, ladies?" their host continued back at normal volume. "A cocktail, a coffee?"

Rosina looked at the list of cocktails, few of which she'd heard of, all of which seemed to contain alcohol. She didn't approve of women drinking in public, except at banquets (and then only in moderation). "Coffee, please," she said.

"I'll have my usual," said the quiet new girl on the ward, and Tuo trotted off and began filling a large glass with various shots of alcohol.

"Welcome to the twenty-first century!" Rosina said to herself.

A few minutes later, Tuo showed the new arrivals to a machine, muttering to the people waiting at the bar about "prior reservations." The nurses sat down on hard, tubular steel chairs, and Yuchang began whirling the mouse. (Rosina knew enough terminology to get that right: the mouse was the thing you held

in your hand and jiggled around while the computer did nothing.)
For Yuchang, of course, an array of boxes and pictures came up on the screen instantly, with Western-style writing.

"What d'you want to find?" she asked.

Rosina took a deep breath. "Anything about the New Church of the Heavenly Kingdom."

Yuchang showed no reaction: she was far too interested in the machine. "Okay. We'll try *Heavenly Kingdom* first." *Tianguo:* she typed the word in Pinyin into the machine and clicked. For a moment the screen became inactive.

"What's it doing?" Rosina asked.

"Searching the Net."

"What, the whole thing?"

"Of course."

"Oh," said Rosina. She sat back in her seat and contemplated her coffee: perhaps if they came back tomorrow . . .

"Here we are," said Yuchang. "*Tianguo*. Sixty-four matches." She began running through a list of sites. "I didn't know you were interested in history, Sister Lin."

"It's a modern organization we're looking for," Rosina replied.

"Oh."

Next 20 matches.

"These all seem to be about some historical thing in the last century," Yuchang said. "Two centuries ago, it'll be soon."

"I'm talking about a modern religious group. A cult. Like the Fa Lun Gong," Rosina added with sudden shame in her voice.

Still no reaction. "Let's try a different engine, then."

Yuchang tried again, several times, but all she seemed able to find was stuff about the original Taipings.

"Have you tried entering the Chinese characters?" Rosina suggested.

With a touch of disdain, Yuchang summoned up some software for entering Chinese characters, then ran another search. It yielded no more about the New Church than the Western searches.

"Never mind," said Rosina. "It was worth a try." She suddenly felt overcome with despair. Julie had disappeared, and there was nothing she could do about it.

"Want to look for something else?"

"Not really."

Silence fell. "Why did you want to know about the New Church of the Heavenly Kingdom?" Yuchang asked.

"Just interest," Rosina said, then felt guilty at the lie.

"We could find out about the Fa Lun Gong, if you like. I know the government has tried to shut some of the sites down, but there are ways around."

"No," Rosina replied wearily. "It's the New Church in particular I'm interested in."

And suddenly she had to tell Yuchang the story.

Yuchang was on nights after that—Rosina was senior enough to work almost all day shifts—so the two women weren't due to coincide at work for a while. But a couple days later, Rosina arrived at work to find Yuchang waiting for her at the hospital entrance.

"I've found someone you must meet," said the young nurse.

"Who?" Rosina replied. It had been a hot, sweaty bus ride, and her thoughts were still ungathered.

"A woman who used to be in the New Church of the Heavenly Kingdom."

Rosina's mind focused at once.

"I thought about the story you told me," Yuchang went on. "I got on the Net and did a proper search, sent some e-mails, that sort of thing. Someone told me to contact this woman, and I did. Miss Hu, her name is. She sounded a bit strange on the phone, but I think she's genuine, and she said she'd be happy to meet you."

"That's wonderful!" Rosina managed. "When could we . . . ?"

"She said she was busy tonight. She's a Party member now, and there's a meeting she has to attend. Thursday's fine, though."

"Great. Where?"

"The café?"

"Fine."

"The café, then. Ku!"

"Ku," Rosina replied.

The Y2K was even busier than before. "Just go upstairs," Tuo told Rosina, Yuchang, and the third woman who joined them at the bar. "You know where to go," he added to Yuchang, who led them up into a kind of office where they sat down on sofas and, for a moment, stared at each other.

"This is Miss Hu," said Yuchang.

"Pleased to meet you," said Rosina. "Very pleased."

Miss Hu was apparently Yuchang's age, but wore the drab clothes of a woman twice that. She exuded a strange mixture of nerves and control, as if the two were battling for supremacy. She had hair on her upper lip, which Rosina found distracting, and she did not smile.

"It's . . . kind of you to come and talk to me," said Rosina.

"That's okay, Mrs. Wang. It is my duty to talk to people in your position. I wish there were more I could do." She managed a grin. "What would you like to know?"

"Well—how can I check if my sister really has joined the Church?" Rosina then relayed the tale of the diary, the ESDA, the trips to Shi Jing Shan.

"Sundays at 32 Commerce—yes, she's found the Church."

"Where is she, then?"

"Most likely at a place called New Tianjing. That's about a hundred kilometers east of here."

"In Hebei?" Rosina exclaimed.

Miss Hu nodded.

"Outside the capital!" Rosina went on. She'd left Beijing on a handful of occasions in her life. The thought of leaving to live appalled her. "Is she a prisoner?"

"No. She's free to leave whenever she likes. But not many people do."

"Because they've been brainwashed?"

"That's an emotive term I like to avoid, Mrs. Wang."

"What *has* happened to her, then?"

"She's decided to live in New Tianjing. She's legally an adult, your friend told me."

Rosina shook her head in disbelief. "And what are they doing to her?"

"She will be living a communal life, working hard, but probably quite enjoying it, as she'll be told it's good for her. And she'll be getting doses of Master Hong Er's religion thrown at her—but if she's gone there voluntarily, she won't mind that, either."

"Religion . . ." said Rosina.

"What you need is patience, Mrs. Wang. Forcing people to leave rarely works: the best solution is disillusionment, and that takes time."

"And during that time?"

"You keep the door open. You communicate positive messages. Not 'I told you so' or anything like that. You tell them that you love them, and that if they want to come home they will be made welcome. No lectures, just affection."

Rosina nodded. "Right. But—how do we do this? What's the name of the place again?"

"I'll give you an address."

"Thank you," said Rosina, with great emotion in her voice.

Miss Hu wrote some words down on a scrap of paper. She had neat calligraphy, precise but not beautiful: the best calligraphy is full of character. But to Rosina, it was of great beauty. A place to find her little sister. "Can we visit New Tianjing?"

Miss Hu shook her head. "It's not encouraged. But I can get a message through. There's—a network."

"Please do. Can you tell her . . . well, what you said. About coming back and not getting lectured."

"I shall."

Silence fell, apart from traffic noise in the street outside and the boom of bass from downstairs. Rosina was imagining Julie's life.

"When you said 'work hard'—what did you mean exactly?"

"They do farm work or make incense sticks," Miss Hu said, rubbing her hands together to demonstrate the latter activity.

Rosina thought of the boxes of sticks piled high in unit 32. "For sweatshop pay?"

"She will have no expenses there."

Rosina shook her head. "Aiya! Aren't the authorities doing anything about this?"

"Not much. I believe that the Bureau of Religious Affairs does maintain a watch on the Church, but their resources have become very stretched since this, er, other business."

"They ought to do something! Even the Fa Lun Gong don't take people away from their homes."

"Nobody's been taken anywhere," Miss Hu reiterated. "And there are political aspects to the matter, too. Religious freedom is an important issue in the West."

"Who cares about the West?" Rosina snapped. She was surprised to hear herself say that. She'd always been a fan of things Western, but the recent NATO bombing of China's embassy in Belgrade had dented this enthusiasm. And if the West started meddling in her family . . .

"Good relations with the West are still important for China's long-term prosperity," said Miss Hu calmly. "It is also the case that the New Church lays great stress on obeying the law. They teach that to all their members—some of whom have, let's say, less than perfect past histories."

Rosina winced.

"And in their own way, Mrs. Wang, they are very patriotic. The figure they revere most, Hong Xiuquan, was Chinese, after all."

"Revere?"

"They believe him to have been the Second Messiah, the second son of the Christian god."

"Ai, she's even stupider than I thought!" exclaimed Rosina.

"Have you always been that critical of her?"

"I don't see that's any of your business!" Rosina exclaimed, then went bright red and grinned. "And you say there's nothing we can do, except to stay in touch and not be superior?"

"That's right," Miss Hu replied. At which point she did almost smile.

8

Wang Anzhuang opened the throttle on the motorbike to full. He rarely got the thing out into the countryside, rarely got a chance to get some real speed up, and was determined to make the most of this one. As the needle passed 100 kph, he thought of his boyhood in Shandong province and his first rides on a push-bike. Faster and faster he'd freewheel, down the track toward— well, the track toward everywhere, really, as there was only one proper road out of Nanping village. Then he'd toil up to the old Buddhist pagoda, which in those days still had its complement of statues. Young Wang would sit and stare at these, wondering who they were and what they really meant. "Feudal relics," his father had told him when he'd asked later. "A reminder not to forget the old ways," his grandmother had added, when out of earshot of the rest of her family.

One hundred twenty kph. Coming to the capital, he thought he'd left all that stuff behind him. Now Rosina had met this woman who had told her all about the New Church. The woman had also said that Rosina had no chance of getting to see Julie. Wang had pointed out that, as an official of the Public Security Bureau, they had to let *him* in, and Rosina had grudgingly agreed to let him go alone to this New Tianjing place.

"I'll be tactful," he had promised.

The needle passed 130 kph. This was the life!

He pulled up outside the front door of the farmstead, kicked down the Xingfu's stand, and swung himself onto solid ground. For a moment he felt unsteady, then he wiped his brow and walked across to the doors. Heaven planned an age of heroes, apparently.

He knocked. Silence, apart from cicadas and a ringing noise in his ears from the roar of the bike. And was that singing in the far distance?

"Whose there?"

"My name is Wang."

"What d'you want?"

"To talk to whoever is in charge."

"Go away!"

Wang remembered his promise to his wife and said quietly, "I'm from the police."

"Ai! You have a warrant?"

"I'd—like to talk."

"You have a warrant?"

"No, but I can get one very easily. Talking now would save trouble later."

"Hng! Wait, please."

"Okay."

Footsteps, then silence. Or near silence. Yes, that *was* singing. Not a tune Wang recognized. Or, from what he could hear, one he particularly wanted to be able to recognize.

More footsteps.

"Hello." A woman with frizzy hair and thick glasses appeared at the door. "Can I help? We don't often get visits from the People's Police."

"I'm looking for a young woman."

"Name of . . . ?"

"Lin Xianghua. Otherwise known as Julie."

The woman showed a flicker of recognition.

"Her family wants to know she's all right," Wang added.

"If she's here, she's fine. People come here of their own free will and leave of their own free will."

"Can I come in, or are we going to have to go through all

this business with warrants?" said the Beijing detective, producing his ID.

The woman studied it carefully. "I—I can ask if this person is currently resident," she said finally.

"I would like to speak to whoever is in charge here. That would be the easiest thing for all of us."

She scowled. "I'll see what I can do." The door slammed shut.

He returned to the bike, which he sat on sidesaddle while he enjoyed a Panda cigarette. He let his awareness of the quiet and solitude of this place fill him. He had gotten so used to city life: how would it feel to have to live in the country again? He'd go crazy, probably.

The door was open again, and the woman was beckoning to him. . . .

"You must understand that we have rules here," she explained as she let him in and led the way down an entry corridor. "Rules that are agreed to by everybody who enters the premises. Males and females keep apart, except when, er, administrative duties make contact necessary. If you see a female inmate, you are to avert your eyes."

"Hao." Okay.

"And visitors are asked to stay in designated areas."

"Reminds me of a Party HQ," said Wang. The woman didn't find this amusing. They entered a quadrangle—attractive, nice traditional-style pond in the middle—and crossed to a room where he was asked to wait.

New Tianjing made a lot less effort to sell itself to visitors than Master Shen Tiequan's temple. There were no pamphlets in the room, just a book entitled *Life and Mission of Brother Hong Xiuquan* and a picture on one wall of the famous rebel in his tunic and turban. *Come to me all of you who are burdened down, and I will give you rest*, read a slogan daubed on another wall.

Wang sat down on the least uncomfortable-looking of the room's chairs and breathed in a lungful of incense. His nostrils puckered, and his hand reached for the Pandas. No, maybe better not to. . . . He reached for the book instead and began to read, but the style was turgid. In the end, his attention drifted to the slogan.

Come to me all of you who are burdened down . . .

His peasant, Party-faithful father would have approved totally. Was this not a basic principle of communism? Wang, too, liked the phrase. Its author must have been Chinese, he felt: you still saw them in country districts—*ku li*, human pack animals who struggled to early graves under the weight of the loads they carried. Before Liberation, millions of people had lived and died like this. Modern youngsters seemed to have forgotten this fact.

Like Julie. A pure distillation of the 1990s, she had appeared to think only of the acquisition of material goods, and tough luck on anyone who didn't have the ability to acquire them. And as for anyone "burdened down" . . .

The thought occurred to him that maybe this wasn't such a bad place. The authorities clearly tolerated it, and if it really believed what it proclaimed, it might do Julie some good.

"Officer!" A man had entered the room. He was stoutish, middle aged, and balding, but made up for his uncharismatic appearance with a fine, sonorous voice. "My name is Hong Er. I am the Master here. Please follow me."

The Master led the way back across the quadrangle and into an office hardly less austere than the waiting room. There were hard wooden seats and a plain metal desk that had nothing on it, and the floor was bare apart from a rug in the center; the walls were lined with books on Western and Chinese religion, plus a number of volumes on the Taiping Rebellion. Two pictures hung opposite the desk, one of Hong Xiuquan again, the other of a bearded Westerner. A window gave out over maize fields that rolled away toward the distant outline of the northern hills.

"I'm looking for a missing person," Wang began. "Lin Xianghua, otherwise known as Julie Lin."

The Master nodded. "It is usual for official requests to go via the Religious Affairs Bureau."

"Ah. My superiors did not inform me of this. Whom should I contact in particular?"

The Master hesitated. "Anyone . . . I have a number here for their office."

Wang took the card with the number on and put it in his jacket pocket. Silence fell. "If that's all . . ." said the Master.

"However, I haven't taken the usual route," Wang put in quickly. "I'm here. And I want you to confirm to me now that Lin Xianghua is currently resident at this address."

The Master seemed to pause for ages before replying that, yes, he could.

Wang gave a sigh of relief. "And might I see her?"

"That would be . . . difficult."

"Why?"

"Because of rules. The only males she is allowed to converse with are senior Church members."

"I'm a relative. I've come a long way. And I don't wish to cause trouble, but if necessary . . ."

He didn't need to finish the sentence, as the Master was frowning and clearly understood its import well enough. "She may not wish to talk with you."

"I'd like her to be given that choice." Wang fixed the Master with a determined stare. After a brief attempt at staring back, the Master reached for the bell and gave it a shake. It had a nice deep tone, a bit like its owner's voice. It seemed to ring for a long time, till the Master put it back down on the table, and the cicadas took over.

"We are patriotic and law-abiding here . . ."

"I've not come to question that."

Silence fell again. The Master gave another ring. "Oh, where the hell is Wu?" he said suddenly, and got to his feet and crossed to the door.

He was out long only long enough for Wang to learn that all the drawers in the Master's desk were locked, then a young man came in and asked him to return to the waiting room.

"I wondered if you'd come chasing after me" was Julie's opening comment. She looked fit enough, though the baggy cotton trousers and jacket—clothes that reminded the forty-something policeman of the Cultural Revolution—didn't suit her. "Everybody's worried about me, I suppose . . ." Julie sat down in the room's other chair and looked the visitor in the eye. "They shouldn't. I'm fine."

He met her stare. Her eyes, the first place to look for drug abuse, looked fine.

"I chose to come here," Julie continued. "And if I decide to leave, I'll leave. It's as simple as that."

"Is it?"

"Yes."

"What about your family?"

Julie looked on the point of saying something, then desisted. "Look, I'm happy. Tell them that. *Julie is happy. Really happy!* If they love me, they should be pleased."

"They miss you."

"I miss them. But I—I belong here. I didn't belong in Beijing. It was driving me crazy. Here, I'm sane; I'm me." She grinned. "Tell them that, Lao Wang. Please."

"Okay." He glanced up at that quote again, and found relief in it. "Can you be contacted here?"

"You got here, didn't you?"

"Not easily."

"It's only a few hours on the buses."

"Do you have access to a phone?"

"There are no telephones here."

He hadn't seen any lines running to the building, and there had been no set in the study. "Can you get letters? Will you write to us?"

"When I'm ready." Julie smiled. "Look, it's difficult to explain. After all those years of pollution by the world, you need time to

purify yourself, and that means contact only with other believers.
I'm only talking to you now because the Master told me to."

The visitor winced.

"I'm sorry if that hurts," Julie went on, "but it's true. Now I have dinner duty in ten minutes." She looked at the policeman with a sudden sadness in her eyes. "If only you could experience it, Lao Wang, then you'd understand."

"Experience what?"

"Being born again."

On his way back to Beijing, Wang called at the local police station to inquire whether the residents of the farmstead were properly registered. The officer in charge of *hukou* made a big fuss—a middle-ranking detective from Beijing! Even if he was only City, not National . . . Over a mug of tea and a bowl of melon seeds specially fetched from the local shop, he assured the visitor that they were.

"But they lose their city ID!" Wang said.

"That's their choice. They have a month to decide, then we cancel the passes and issue local ones."

"And what happens to the cancelled passes?"

"We send them back to Beijing. You can check the procedures if you like."

"I'm sure that won't be necessary."

The local officer grinned. "It beats me why anyone wants to leave the city and live out here, but they do. And they don't give us any trouble, so that's fine."

"They really don't give trouble?"

"No."

"And they're not being brainwashed or used as cheap labor?"

"That's more a matter for the Religious Affairs Bureau than us, but in my opinion, they're just working the land. Nothing wrong in that."

"No . . . Well, thanks for your time."

As he left the building and breathed in the fresh air of Hebei province, Wang pondered what the officer had said. His own family had worked the land of a similar rural area for countless generations, and he was proud of them. If Julie chose to follow that life—why not?

He wasn't going to say that to Rosina, though.

Wang arrived at work next morning in a thoughtful mood. Rosina had been relieved to hear that Julie was alive and well but had been disappointed by her negative reaction to returning.

"She's a silly little girl" had been her only comment to the latter, after which she had refused to discuss the matter any more. Till they were in bed, that was, when she had burst into tears. After which they had made love, which had only made him feel sadder that there wasn't more he could do.

And now, on his desk was a note from Team-leader Chen, which usually meant trouble. He gave the desk a quick, superstitious tidy, then headed down the corridor to his boss's office.

"Ah, Wang Anzhuang. Sit down."

He grinned: the rather formal use of his full name did not bode well. Chen waited until he got as comfortable as he could on the low wooden seat kept especially for junior visitors, then spoke. "I have had some complaints filed about you."

"Oh. Who from?"

"An officer by the name of Fei."

Wang just puckered his face in a gesture of distaste.

"Apparently you've been accepting bribes off street vendors," Chen went on. "Is this true?"

"A man gave me an ice cream."

"That's against regulations."

"An ice cream!"

Chen repeated that it was against regulations.

"It was in the course of a discussion."

"Hmm," said Chen. "There's more. Yesterday afternoon you abandoned your official duty to go off somewhere on an official motorbike."

"Who told you that?"

"Never mind. Do you deny it?"

"No."

"Where did you go?"

"I don't make a habit of wasting police time," Wang replied. Chen would either seize on this or take the hint that further questions along this line would be embarrassing and make them both lose face. He waited to see what would happen. The latter, surely. . . .

"I know that's true, Xiao Wang. So I'm not going to take any action this time. But you must consider this an informal reprimand."

"Yes, chief."

"No more gifts, and no more mystery errands on police vehicles on police time. Clear?"

"Yes . . ."

"Good." Team-leader Chen gave one of his range of grins, the one that said, It's time for you to leave.

Once he had left and was making his way down the long whitewashed corridor from Chen's office, Wang wondered what that had all really been about. Fei's complaint was ridiculous, and both men knew that. And as for the bike—the Xingfu was signed in and out all the time. Officers were trusted not to use it for personal business.

So behind its façade, this complaint was all about his destination.

He reached his own door and gave a sigh as he entered. If someone senior were protecting the New Church of the Heavenly Kingdom, he would *never* get Julie out.

Why would they be doing that? Wang Anzhuang's detective instinct asked.

Don't ask, his Chinese official's instinct replied.

Interlude

At Autumn Moon Festival, Wang's older brother Anming came up from Shandong province to visit. Anming claimed to have given up alcohol, though Rosina found a bottle of cheap Er Guo Tou liqueur in his luggage. And he came alone, despite Rosina's attempts at matchmaking when she and Wang had visited Nanping village. "Too many memories, for both of us," was his explanation of this.

The subject was clearly a sensitive one for both Wang and Rosina: when discussing it in Anming's absence, Wang lapsed into a harsh frame of mind, saying that the woman had been right to reject Anming if he still drank. Rosina had replied that the story was the other way around; Anming drank because he had no love in his life.

Wang had not argued the point, as he knew he was appearing disloyal in criticizing his older brother, even if it was to the woman he loved.

They celebrated the festival day with Rosina's parents. In the afternoon they all went for a boat trip on Beihai Lake; all except for Rosina, who, being a nonswimmer, preferred a seat on dry land. The boats were made of fiberglass and looked like swans. Passengers—or rather Anzhuang, as Mama and Baba were too old and Anming ran out of puff almost at once—provided power by pedaling with their feet. Their swan had a natural veer to the left (a relic of the Cultural Revolution?). Rosina watched the ridiculous plastic bird circling around the center of the lake and suddenly felt sad.

In the evening they all climbed to the pagoda in Jingshan Park, the highest point of the capital. They found a place to sit on the pagoda steps, ate mooncakes, and watched a huge round moon climb out of the city smoke and pour liquid silver over the roofs of the Forbidden City. It should have been gorgeous.

Mama was the one who actually spoiled the occasion. "If only Fragrant Flower were here . . ."

"She didn't come last year," Rosina pointed out. "She said she preferred McDonald's to mooncakes and was going to a party." She bit into another cake, in search of the pleasure that the rich dry bean paste inside usually provided, but didn't find enough distraction from the melancholy that seemed to have overtaken the day. Autumn festival could be a bit like that: your thoughts turned to loss and the past rather than the future, even when a new millennium was about to appear. And when the family is divided . . .

"Why don't we sing some songs?" Baba said suddenly. Nobody wanted to join in.

And soon after that, it was October 1, and the time of the great celebrations for the fiftieth anniversary of the People's Republic. Wang and Rosina celebrated by working: he on crowd control, she drafted onto Accident and Emergency. Neither got to see the military march-past—the biggest formal show the People's Republic had put on since 1984—or the float with the great picture of Mao, which had caused so much comment. And neither really cared: she thinking the whole thing with all its marching and flag-waving was really for men (and dumb ones at that), and he, who had done military service and seen friends die in squalor and pain, feeling it was just plain vulgar.

"If it lessens the arrogance of the West, it has some value, I suppose" was his only comment on the proceedings.

Then the weather turned. The bright Beijing autumn suddenly became cold, and wind came howling in from the north, reminding the capital's inhabitants of their proximity to the wastes of Heilongjiang and Siberia. Padded jackets and fur hats came out of storage; days suddenly seemed short and the green, expansive city, entrapping and dark. Capital Hospital began to fill with sufferers from pneumonia and influenza.

Suddenly, the second millennium was hurtling toward its close.

9

Wang and Rosina were sitting at home. It was his turn to cook, and he was standing over their two-ring stove listening for the oil in the wok to start popping, a sign that it was the right heat. Too hot and you burned things, too cold and the ingredients became mushy: the job of the oil was to seal in the taste, not to infiltrate it.

A gust of wind rattled the windows. "I bet they don't have proper heating up at that New Tianjing place," said Rosina, who was sitting in the dining room, reading a magazine.

"No . . ." he replied. They'd been over this before, so many times.

"Wheels Chai—is he ill or something?"

"He's lost all his confidence. He won't do any work for me. He pretends he's busy, but he's really scared of failing."

"And you can't persuade him?"

"I don't see how he could do much, anyway."

"No . . . What about that old man?"

"Da?"

"What could he do? The entire Politburo couldn't change Julie's mind."

Another gust of wind rattled outside. It was a sound Rosina usually found comforting: they were inside. "Xianghua's a city girl, not a peasant's daughter," she said suddenly.

Wang was annoyed by this comment, but let it pass. He finished dicing the shallots and opened the Haier fridge to get some rice wine.

"Sorry," said Rosina.

He walked past the Haier and into the dining room. She

looked up at him and held out a hand, which he took and held. They then just stood there, frozen in helplessness—until popping noises started coming from the kitchen.

A hundred kilometers away, Julie was still, too. Lying on her bunk, staring up at the slogan above her head.

If we truly want to inherit the Kingdom, we must be born again.

Around her, the girls were talking. She heard their words but felt no need to join their conversation: not an unusual experience for her.

People seemed to like her, on the surface. When she joined discussions, her views were treated with respect. Nobody made fun of her voice, which was, she realized, middle class—some of the girls twanged like springs with their Beijing accents. Her need, something she had only discovered since coming here, for tranquility and solitude was respected.

Qingai she saw only occasionally. Julie sometimes felt afraid of her feelings for her—were they totally natural? It was maybe just as well that the older woman didn't do much fieldwork and never took a shift in the stick factory.

Maybe my true relationship is with Brother Hong, she thought to herself. She consoled herself with that, closed her eyes, and imagined the great rebel Emperor on a horse, charging into battle. Then she felt an itch of sexual pleasure, and chased the image from her mind. Perhaps it was Brother Ye Su she was supposed to love? But he was Western, and one of the things she had learned here was that the West had been in a spiral of decadence since 1836. (Which was a significant number, because that was 164 years short of the millennium, and sixty-four was an evil number, as Tianjing had fallen to the demons in 1864, and was also the square of eight, which was a lucky number to the heathen and thus an unlucky one for a true believer. . . .)

So maybe her soul belonged to the Lord Ye Huo Hua himself.

There could be no other. That felt right. The thought came into her mind that she needed to give herself to the Lord somehow. That, again, felt sexual, but maybe there was a way of giving that was nonsexual, sinless . . .

Outside, a bell sounded. Four times, which meant bedtime and lights out. And whispered conversations for some of the girls, but just sleep for Julie. Which was fine. She pulled the blankets over herself and lay still. Sleep came quickly.

Running feet.

Shouts.

Someone in tears.

Julie thought it was all a dream at first, but she was awake now, and the commotion was still going on.

"What is it?" one of the girls was asking.

"The Master!"

Half an hour later, they were all in the Great Hall of Tranquility. The Silver Master was addressing them. His face was stained with tears, and he looked to be fighting back more as he spoke.

"We will carry on. We must carry on!" "The Church has suffered loss before, and marched on . . ." "So near to the millennium, the Lord Ye Huo Hua must have had a reason to call our beloved Master home!"

To this last comment Julie began nodding her head. A reason. There had to have been a reason.

It was a week later that Rosina got the call. Anzhuang was working late, and she was watching TV: they were showing *Legend of Tianyun Mountain* again, which always made her reach for the handkerchief, even though it was old stuff. It had just got to the bit where young Geologist Luo is called into Cadre Wu's office at the start of the Cultural Revolution. Rosina nearly didn't bother to answer the phone.

"Wei?" she said, when she finally did. The answer you gave to officials, not to friends.

"Mrs. Wang, er, it's Miss Hu here."

She knew at once that something was wrong. "What's up?"

"I've heard this report from New Tianjing. Is your husband there?"

"What's it got to do with him?" Rosina said angrily.

"It's more his line of business."

"What, there's been a robbery or something?"

"No. Worse."

"Is Julie okay?"

"Yes. But the Master . . . Could we all meet?"

Wang nearly missed the rendezvous, the place looked so dowdy from outside. Inside, it was all chrome and computers, loads of them, manned by foreigners and dubious-looking Chinese youngsters. To cap it all, the place reverberated to the worst music he had ever heard in his life. Most Western stuff was bad, but this plumbed new depths.

His wife and a nervous-looking woman were sitting at the bar. He went up to them.

"I'm very glad to see you," said the woman.

Rosina introduced her as Miss Hu.

"Thank you for reporting the crime, Miss Hu," he said.

Miss Hu grinned. "I don't *know* that there's been a crime."

"But this man is definitely dead?"

"My informant is usually reliable."

"I'd better go and see for myself."

"Can I come, too?" Rosina put in.

He winced. "It might be difficult. . . . At this stage . . ."

She let him flounder for a bit, then nodded her head. "I understand," she said. Which she did. Sort of.

It was midafternoon by the time Wang got clearance to go to, and actually rode out to, New Tianjing. When he knocked on the big front door, a different woman opened it.

"I suppose you want to talk to the Master," she said.

"Yes," he replied, hiding his puzzlement. According to Miss Hu . . . The woman led the way to the waiting room.

"I'll fetch him," she said with a coldness to match the new, autumn weather. "Please wait here."

He stared around the room: no change, except the smell of incense was stronger than ever. He reread the slogan on the wall and thought of his home back in Shandong. Then the woman reappeared.

"The Master is finishing a meditation. He will be ready to talk with you in twenty minutes."

The Master received Wang in his study. He was, of course, a new Master—how quickly and seamlessly this man seemed to have replaced his predecessor! He was taller and thinner than Hong Er, and had an intense expression that made the visitor a little in awe. Wang was expecting some fearful profundity from him but his opening words were: "May I offer you some tea?"

Getting a positive reply, the Master rang the bell: it gave a tinny, unconvincing ring. The same young man as before came in and took the order for refreshment. The lad was unable to hide his fear at the sight of the policeman, who in turn was perfectly able to hide his having noticed this fear.

"You've been expecting me?" Wang asked the Master, once the youngster had gone.

"Straight after the death, yes. But as time went by we assumed you weren't interested. It was a natural death, after all."

"Yes . . . So how long ago did Hong Er die?"

"Eight days."

"Eight days! Where's the body now?"

"We've cremated it."

"Aiya!"

"That's our custom."

"But the law states—"

"We believe that the body is a vehicle for the soul. When the soul has left, the body has no value. Except, of course, to fertilize the land of the godly. Our beloved Golden Master was cremated five days ago and his ashes scattered across the fields. It was a most moving ceremony." The new Master paused. "Cremation is, I believe, the method of disposal recommended by the Communist Party."

Wang looked out of the window—any evidence would be scattered over that wide, autumn-bare expanse of land—then turned his attention back to the Master. "You're prepared to sign a form identifying the deceased, I take it."

"Of course."

"You and one other person."

"That won't be a problem."

A brief silence fell. "So, tell me what happened."

The Master looked puzzled. "You've not received the report?"

"Of course," Wang lied at once. "But I always like to hear things firsthand."

The Master seemed to accept this. "He was in his meditation room. Young Wu found him lying on the floor, facedown. He had been summoned home by the Lord Ye Huo Hua."

There are plenty of euphemisms in Chinese to avoid the brutal simplicity of *si le*, dead, but this was the first time Wang had heard this one.

"What time was this?"

"Early morning. About five."

"Had he been in there all night?"

"I don't know."

"Did Wu come and tell you the moment he found the body?"

"I assume so. Who else would he tell?"

"I don't know."

"He would tell me. I was Hong Er's designated successor. By the authority of the Lord Ye Huo Hua," the Master added.

This was also a new slant on things: interviewees from the streets of Beijing didn't usually tell you they had been allocated their status by a divine being. Undeterred, Wang took the Master through his story, noting it down as he did so—how the Master had been awoken by a distraught Wu; how he had gone to the cell and found the old Master's body; how they had taken it to the old Master's study and lain it out there; how the news had been broken to the community; how a vigil had been organized for the next evening where the community members filed past him; how a huge fire had been built and the old Master had been cremated and his ashes scattered across the land. A wind had blown some of this divine ash onto the fields of the neighboring farm, which had upset everyone until the Master had realized this was a symbol of the old Master's teachings spreading out into the world.

The Master smiled, recalling his own quickness of mind.

Wang then asked about the routine in the community. The Master seemed well prepared for this question.

"We rise at the first bell, which is sounded at five-thirty. Prayers and meditation are at six. That lasts an hour. Then we have breakfast. Then there's study, followed by work."

"Work?"

"In the fields or making incense sticks. We work till lunchtime, after which we take a short rest, then it's back to work. Early evening we have a little free time, then we eat our evening meal. Finally there's a Gathering, then we go to bed."

"Gathering?"

"At the end of the day, we gather to share our thoughts and feelings."

"What time is the Gathering?" he asked.

"It depends on the time of year. Right now, it's at eight."

There had been no electricity in Nanping village when Wang was a boy, so everyone's life had followed a cycle determined by the day's available light—the way it had for thousands of years. Even in clock-crazy Beijing, he still found himself lying awake on early summer mornings and having to be dragged out of sleep to go to work in winter.

"And the Master's day was the same?"

"No. He spent a lot of time in study and meditation."

"Where?"

"Study, he did in here," said his successor, gesturing around at the shelves full of books. "Meditation . . . Ah, that was in the cell where he died."

"So he could spend days unobserved?"

"Not days. He valued his connection with his people very highly."

"Okay. But he could have had visitors that no one else knew about. . . ."

"It's not likely. There're only the front and back doors, and they are either locked or attended at all times."

"Who has keys?"

"Sister Modesty."

Wang noted the name. "Was the Golden Master at the Gathering the night before he died?"

"No."

"So when did you last see him alive?"

"Midafternoon. I wanted to talk about a new arrival. A young man who had run away from home and who was having problems settling in. It was a matter he had raised with me, and I had been thinking about it and had come up with some ideas."

"What mood was he in?"

"He seemed fine. He was engrossed in some scholarly work. He felt that a core part of his duties was to counteract the negative images of our forerunners the Taipings in so much academic writing."

"They did rebel against the government of the day. . . ."

"So did the Communist Party," the Master countered at once, backing his words with a faint grin that Wang found oddly unnerving. "We are not interested in politics. We would not be that foolish."

"No. . . . Did the Golden Master have enemies?"

"Oh no! He was a gentle man. Very spiritual."

"But you must need to have some kind of discipline here. All these young people . . . Supposing someone steps out of line?"

"If anyone misbehaves, they are criticized by their fellows. Sometimes we have to make them criticize themselves, too—sit them down in a room and close the door on them. It usually works."

"Usually? Have you ever had to expel people?"

"Not expel, no. Sometimes people are told they would be better off elsewhere, but nobody gets thrown out. That is not in the spirit of Brother Ye Su. I trust you read the words written up in our reception chamber."

"Yes," Wang replied. His writing hand was beginning to ache: Lu (and now Wei) kept nagging him to buy some kind of portable tape recorder, but he liked to make notes of gestures, expressions, and so on. And he didn't trust gadgets, anyway. To give himself a break, he got to his feet and walked over to the window. Outside were neat rows of crops—maize, a bare field, a section with rows of polythene raised on hoops to protect whatever was growing underneath from the increasingly inclement weather.

"This land," he observed. "Do you own it?"

"No. We have temporary right of use—just like any other cooperative."

"You are officially a cooperative?"

"We *are* a cooperative." The Master gave another of his half grins. "In many ways, we are the true Communists. Unlike much of modern China, which seems to have been consumed with material greed. I am old enough to remember that slogan, *'devoted to others, without a single selfish thought.'* "

Wang remembered it, too. The slogan had been a favorite of his father's. "How long do you have right of use?"

"Sixty years. I believe that is standard."

"Yes..." The Beijing detective glanced down at the window latch and gave a sudden start. "And what do you grow here?" he asked quickly: a pointless question, but the first one he could think of.

"What you see. The usual local crops: maize, sorghum, wheat. Plus a few ingredients for our sticks."

"And, er, do you keep animals?"

"No. We don't believe in exploiting our fellow creatures."

"No..." Wang turned away from the window. There were clear scratch marks on the latch: somebody had broken in here. Recently, too. He wanted to keep up the questions, unwilling to let the Master know he had noticed—but at that moment he was rescued by the door's opening. The young man entered with a mug of green tea, which he deposited on the table.

"Thank you, Wu," said the Master.

"Is that the lad who found the body?"

"Yes..." The Master was hesitant suddenly.

Wang turned to the youth. "Tell me what happened."

The young man grinned. "I wanted to use the room myself. For a meditation. I opened the door, and..." He fell silent.

Wang just looked at him. Let the silence work.

"He was dead," Wu went on finally. "Lying there. I thought he was asleep at first, but—I don't know. He seemed so still. Then I realized he wasn't breathing."

"Was the body cold?"

"No."

"Did you notice any marks or unusual skin color?"

"Ai...I don't remember. I was upset."

"But you noticed the body temperature."

"I...touched him," Wu said slowly and with sudden embarrassment.

"Where?"

"On his face. To see if there was breath coming from his nose or his mouth."

Wang let another silence fall, then asked: "What time was this?"

"Before the first bell."

"Right. I'd like you to take me across to the place and describe what you saw in greater detail."

"Must I?"

"You must understand how much we loved our Golden Master," the new Master's replacement put in.

"It would help with my investigation," said Wang.

"In that case—come on, Wu. We must be cooperative."

The "meditation room" was a room no bigger than a cupboard.

"Describe the exact position in which you found the body."

Young Wu did so. Wang made more notes, then took a close look at the floor and walls of the cell—there were a couple of marks that at least matched the young man's story, but hardly proved it. Then he opened and closed the door a few times, checking the flow of air when the door was shut. There should have been enough air, he reflected. On an impulse he looked to see if anyone had taped over the main air source, but saw no trace of that.

"You can go now," he said. Neither Wu nor the Master seemed in a great hurry to leave, but finally they did, leaving Wang looking into the tiny room and shaking his head.

It was a bright moon that night, and still. And therefore cold. But the experienced detective had come prepared, with a jacket full of duck feathers and a Soviet-style fur hat with flaps that tied down over his ears. He'd noted a clump of trees not too far from the farmstead and he hid himself there, watching, listening, and waiting.

First there was singing, lots of it, then a long, ranting speech by the new Master, of which he only picked up the odd word: "soul," "soaring," "demons," "Hong Xiuquan," "millennium" . . . This, he assumed, was the daily Gathering. The longer it lasted, the more dislike he felt for the process. He thought of Julie listening to this, then of his own generation, which had gone through similar experiences of being hectored and bullied in the name of ideals.

When the ranting stopped, he breathed a sigh of relief. Some chanting about the Heavenly Kingdom lasting ten thousand years followed, then a mumbled prayer, then shuffling feet and slamming doors. Soon after that, New Tianjing was enveloped in silence.

He waited a little longer, then got to his feet and padded over to the compound wall. Freezing ground crunched beneath his feet.

The window into the Master's office was the third one along. He walked up to it and shone his torch, first at the ground beneath it—a number of prints, but none of them very clear—then at the lock, where more scratches confirmed a break-in. Not by a professional criminal, but definitely by someone very determined. In search of what? He stood staring in through the window, pondering. He produced a plastic bag from his pocket and swept the contents of the window's small sill into it, then took out a pocket knife that he slid between the upper and lower frames.

Wang was inside the study in under a minute.

He crossed to the desk and began checking the contents of its three drawers. The top one opened easily and contained pages of handwritten notes on religious and historical texts: the note-taker had been serious about his reading. The most recent appeared to be on an article in a scholarly periodical about Taiping inscriptions. All the notes were in the same spidery characters.

In the second drawer, he found some bills and receipts. Several were signed Hong Er, in the same writing as the notes. None made any reference to incense sticks. There was no trace of proper accounts and no money or bank statements.

The third drawer was more resistant to his attempts to pick its lock, which naturally made him more determined than ever to get inside—so determined that he didn't notice the sound of feet in the corridor outside until it was almost too late.

Just in time he froze, then crouched down behind the desk, congratulating himself on having remembered to shut the window behind him. The footsteps grew louder, reached the door of the office—and passed on.

When they had died away, Wang resumed his work, alert this time. The bottom drawer finally succumbed to the riffle and creaked open. It was empty, apart from a piece of blank paper. He lowered his face to the drawer and sniffed it. At last, a smell different from the incense that seemed to fill every corner of New Tianjing.

For a second, he couldn't place it—then he could. The bottle Rosina had found in Anming's suitcase. Er Guo Tou liqueur.

So was the Golden Master of the New Church of the Heavenly Kingdom a secret drinker?

He squatted by the desk and pondered this. Then he closed the drawer, locked it, stood up, and ran his torch over the desktop, taking up the bell and examining it carefully in the sharp, directional light. The crack was obvious. Had the bell been used as a weapon? It hardly seemed big enough. Had it just been dropped? Had it fallen to the floor in some kind of struggle?

He ran his torch around the room walls, but nothing seemed willing to provide an answer. Outside, the moon went behind a cloud.

Enough questions for one evening. It was time to head home.

10

"Come in."

Team-leader Chen had a large office, with a proper window that looked out over Qianmen East Street, a carpet, and an electric blower-heater to supplement HQ's own erratic heating system.

"I was right," said Wang. "It's a suspicious death."

"Weather getting a bit rough for street patrols, eh?"

"It could be serious, Lao Chen."

"For society, or for you?"

"A murder may have been committed." Already a voice in Wang's head was telling him there was no point in doing this. Someone senior had scared Chen into keeping him away from the cult; the toadying team-leader would no sooner allow him to return to New Tianjing than make a joke about the Party or forget to read the *People's Daily* on his chauffeur-driven way to work in the morning.

"Tell me the facts," said Chen.

Wang did so. Confusion about the cause of death. An apparent "report" that had not been passed on to the police. A body quickly disposed of, maybe innocently, maybe not. The attempted break-in; the fear in the eyes of the young man who had found the body; missing money, or at least missing accounts. Even that broken bell. . . .

Chen listened, wearing his usual superior expression. Wang knew what was coming next: a speech on the new clean-up, the importance of carrying out Party policy and the nonimportance of pursuing personal aims and intuitions.

The old bureaucrat looked out of his window. A number 54 bus went splashing past.

"Well, Xiao Wang, you'd better look into it. Take Detective Wei, and Lu, of course, and get me a progress report at the end of the week."

They even got a Beijing Jeep.

At the farmstead, the investigation team was greeted with puzzlement but politeness. Wang requested the use of the waiting room as an incident room, and the request was granted without fuss. Extra desks were moved in; he let his subordinates squabble over who was going to have the smallest one and thus show magnanimity (Lu) or independence (Wei).

Wang had his orders ready. "Wei, I want you to prepare a list of residents, then for you and Lu to fingerprint everyone over the next few days. I shall take prints from the Master's study and the place where the body was found. Then we'll interview—not everybody, that would take forever. But the top people and a sample of others. I want you both to sit in on the interviews. I need six eyes and six ears!" He clapped his hands. "Let's get to work."

Sister Modesty sat and glared at the three police officers, in between curt answers to questions establishing her identity and about her movements and experiences during the days up to, and just after, the Golden Master's death. Trying to move conversation on, Wang asked her how she came to join the Church.

"I don't see what that has got to do with the Master's death," she snapped back.

"Probably nothing. I'm just curious."

"Hng! I joined because the Lord Ye Huo Hua told me to."

"How did he do that?"

"You wouldn't understand."

"Try me," said Wang, but Modesty just shook her head disdainfully.

He moved on to another topic. "You're a 'Sister' here. What does that mean?"

"We're all sisters. Sisters and brothers."

"Not everyone seems to be called Sister, though."

"We're older. We have served the Lord Ye Huo Hua longer, and maybe seen more of life than some of the young people who come here."

"Did you knew the dead man well?"

"I knew his work. I heard his message. I had no need to know him personally. That's not the point."

"What is the point?"

"To live life according to the teachings of Brother Hong and Brother Ye Su."

"Yes . . . Do you have special duties here?"

"A few. Everyone has to do all tasks, however."

"Even the Masters?"

"The Lord Ye Huo Hua has spoken to them. You don't expect them to dig ditches or clean toilets, do you?"

"It's part of my job not to expect things," Wang replied, a little anger in his voice now. "When I came here last, you opened the door to me. Is that one of your duties?"

"Yes."

"Do you have keys to other doors, too?"

"Yes," said Modesty.

"To all of them?"

"Someone has to."

"And what about drawer and safe keys?"

"Safe? What safe?"

"You mean there isn't one here?"

"Why should there be? We don't carry money. Possessions are spiritual weights, dragging down the soul. Since coming here, I'm glad to say I haven't once soiled my hands or mind with money."

"Somebody must."

"Not me."

Modesty answered more questions with the same terseness. She confirmed the identity of the body, which she had seen at the vigil. She described the cremation—the intensity of the heat, the horrible smell when the coffin had finally caught fire—and for a moment allowed an emotion out: grief. Then, cold again, she asked if the police had any more questions. Wang was relieved to be able to answer "No."

"She's hiding something," said Wei once Modesty had gone. "I'm sure of it."

"I agree," Wang replied. "But what? A relevant fact, or just that she regards people like us as oppressors?"

"Why should she do that?" Lu asked.

"History."

Lu frowned. He hadn't been very good at history at school. "I reckon she locked the Master in his meditation room," he said after a pause.

"Motive?" Wei put in instantly.

"I—I don't know," the young man stammered. "Perhaps that's what she's hiding."

"A motive may emerge," said Wang. "But it's extremely unlikely that being locked in would be a cause of death on its own: he'd shout, and in a quiet place like this people would hear."

"So he was drugged, then locked in?" said Lu.

"Drugged with what?" said Wei. "How?"

"That's the sort of thing we're here to find out, Xiao Wei. Lu, fetch the next interviewee."

Young Wu was as frightened of the police as he had been before. Wang affected not to notice this and calmly took his name, then got him to repeat the story of his finding the body. There were no serious discrepancies with the first telling.

"You seem to have something of a privileged position here," Wang said at the end.

"What d'you mean?"

"You're close to the Masters, running errands for them, that sort of thing."

"Yes. They trust me. I can type, and used to copy out the old Master's manuscripts. . . ." There was a look of great sadness in the young man's eyes as he said the word *Master*. "He sent his pieces all over the world," he went on, after a heavy-hearted pause. "About the Taipings, and how misjudged they were."

"Did you keep accounts, too?"

The young man shook his head.

"Do you know who did keep them?"

"I'm not sure anyone did. The Master always said that the Lord Ye Huo Hua would provide what we needed."

"Yes . . . Tell me about the Master's state of mind. Did you notice any differences in the period before he died?"

"Not really."

"Had he been complaining of any aches and pains?"

"No."

"Had he heard from anyone recently that he hadn't heard from in a long time?"

"No."

The quivering seemed to be getting worse, and suddenly Wu buried his face in his hands and began crying.

Wang did nothing, just watched. When he had finished, the young man looked up and apologized. "Everybody loved him."

"So why do you think he was killed?"

"He wasn't killed, he was called away. He was too good for this world."

Silence fell. The young man sniffled.

"You can go," said Wang.

"Why did you let him off so easily?" Wei asked once Wu had gone.

"I don't know," Wang replied, then added, "He seemed to be telling the truth."

"What, that Hong Er was *called away*?"

"I think he really believes that."

Wei frowned. "I think they had a homosexual relationship."

Lu looked a little uneasy at the mention of a subject he found distasteful; Wang smiled at the bright young detective and said to her: "That's an interesting thought, Xiao Wei. How would you follow that up?"

"Look for any pornographic materials? Confront him? The medical section could carry out an examination of his anus."

Lu fidgeted on his seat.

"Good ideas, Xiao Wei. But we don't want to alienate people more than necessary at this stage."

Because it was right, or because of Julie?

"Lu: fetch the next interviewee."

They spoke to the Master again, whose story was, like Wu's, clear and unchanged, and to a sample of ordinary Church members. Few of the latter looked the police officers in the eyes; most of them answered with simple *yes*es or *no*s; none of them had anything really new to say. Only one young woman whispered something about the hand of Yan Luo in the matter, then took the statement back at once. When pressed for an explanation, she just said that the Master had been such a perfect guide: why take the perfect shepherd away from his flock, so near the millennium? When asked for an explanation of what was special about the millennium, she had launched into a long, rambling piece about the number 2000.

"We'd better talk to this Yan Luo guy," Lu had said at the end of that interview. Detective Wei had seemed greatly to enjoy pointing out that Yan Luo was king of the demons in ancient mythology.

In the afternoon, Wang left his team instructions to get on with the fingerprinting and called in at the local police station again. The same officer who had been in charge of the *hukou* registration on his first visit was today manning the front desk. The officer was surprised to hear of the death and quite saddened.

"He did good up there on that farm," the officer commented. "We never had any trouble from them at all. Except this one lad, who went a bit crazy, but he left."

"What happened?"

"Oh, just one evening someone came running over and said a young man was threatening people with a pitchfork. We went there and calmed him down. Nobody wanted to take it any further, and I believe he left soon after."

"D'you know his name?"

The officer shook his head.

"Do you have an incident report?"

"I imagine so . . ."

"Find it for me."

The officer grinned.

"In the meantime," Wang continued, "tell me: do they buy and sell things?"

"I think so," the officer replied. "I've seen stuff being delivered there."

"So where does the money come from?"

"I think they sell produce. They make incense sticks, I believe."

"Correct . . . And there aren't any disputes with anyone in the area—about water rights, or boundaries, or goods supplied, anything like that?"

The officer shook his head again. "No. They always pay any bills promptly and in full. About the only people around here who do. Of course, the local Party head disapproves of them on ideological grounds, but they have official clearance from Beijing, so she can't do much."

"Clearance from whom in Beijing?"

"The Religious Affairs Bureau."

"Ah . . . You weren't informed by them of the death, I take it?"

"No."

"Doesn't that strike you as odd?"

"No. The Bureau keep themselves to themselves. They *should* have contacted us, of course—but I'm not surprised they didn't. I imagine they're under pressure at the moment, with this Fa Lun Gong business."

"I imagine they are.... Contact me when you find that report," said Wang, handing him a card. "And if you hear anything; any rumors, anything like that."

The officer promised to do so.

At the end of the day, the investigation team drove back to Beijing in a reflective mood. Lu and Wei had a brief conversation about reading—no, the young graduate didn't like *gongfu* stories but did like books by foreign authors—then silence fell. The boss was glad: it gave him time to think, to try to pull strands of meaning and emotion out of the day's events.

That evening, Wang took Rosina to Shopping World at Xidan. Places like this hadn't existed in Beijing ten years ago. Great complexes with floors and floors of consumer goods, most of them (especially the clothes) *ming pai*: foreign label. Escalators wafted you up and down; assistants in neat dark suits or high-heeled shoes and shoulder pads watched you from behind computerized tills, trying to work out if you were really there to spend or—as were 99 percent of the visitors—just to gaze. Rosina enjoyed wandering around, getting ideas for clothes that she might then make herself.

While she was doing this, he made his way to the counter that sold incense sticks. There were a number of brands, some Chinese, some foreign.

"How much are these?" he said, holding up a packet of Chinese-made ones.

The young woman behind the counter looked up from a magazine and said, "Three."

"Three jiao?"

She eyed him as if he were an imbecile. "Three *kuai*."

"Aiya!" Even despite the recent pay raise for all public officials, this represented the better part of an hour's basic pay. He'd rather have half of one of those Western ice creams. "That's a lot of money for a packet of sticks."

"Go to another shop if you can't afford our prices."

He ignored this and took out a pack of foreign sticks. "And these?"

"Five."

He emptied the packet into his hand. Ten pieces of cheap wood, with paste of some kind wrapped round the top—just like the ones he'd seen boxes and boxes of in unit 32.

"Are you actually going to buy anything?" the assistant asked after a pause.

"Not from you," Wang replied, and walked off contemplating the economics of the joss-stick business.

11

Wang wasn't sure who to talk to first. In the end, chance decided. He called for the Master, but instead Sister Modesty appeared and told him that the Master was meditating and mustn't
be disturbed.

"Maybe you can help," he replied, adapting his plan at once.

She forced a smile onto her face and stammered a positive
reply.

"I want to have a look at the storerooms," he continued. "You
have the keys, don't you?"

"Yes."

"Will you come with me and open them?"

"If you wish it." Wang was a little surprised by Modesty's
change of attitude. She was still finding it hard to cooperate, but
was clearly now trying so to do. Why?

The two of them walked to the stores around the outside of
the farmstead, as Modesty didn't want to walk through the man's
section and didn't want a policeman walking through the women's
section. When they reached the outbuildings, she fiddled slowly
with her huge bunch of keys before finally unlocking the door.
Wang observed this ritual with interest—keys might be important
in the story—then entered the shed.

The place was dark inside and had no lighting of its own.
The small torch Wang always carried in his uniform belt illumi-
nated a collection of items: digging tools, a row of sacks, a roll of
polythene and some metal hoops, a shelf full of jars, and, in one
corner, some barrels. He crossed to one of the latter and sniffed
the air around it, wrinkling his nose with distaste.

"What's in this?"

"Weed killer," Modesty replied calmly.

"Where did it come from?"

"A local farmer."

"Name of . . . ?"

"I don't know. The Master dealt with him."

"With no assistance?"

"He protected us from the world. Many of us have been cruelly treated by it."

"I understand that," said Wang. If he could get a proper conversation going with this new, friendlier Modesty, he might learn a lot. "Who among you handled the weed killer?"

"Anyone leading a work party. That would be myself, Sister Verity, Qingai, Brother Reliant."

"And nobody else? Who brought it to the shed?"

"It was delivered."

Wang paused. He didn't want to ask *too* many overt questions about the weed killer. "Tell me more about your incense sticks," he said instead. "What happens to them when they leave New Tianjing?"

"I don't know."

"What form do they leave in?"

"Bundles."

"How many in a bundle?"

"I don't know. Ask Sister Virtue, she's in charge of the workshop."

"Do you receive money for them?"

"Yes," said the Sister, with a trace of shame.

"Do you know how much?"

"No."

"Not even approximately?"

"I think it's about a yuan a bundle."

"One yuan?"

"Yes. It doesn't sound much, but it mounts up."

"I'm sure." Wang tried to recall how many bundles there had been in the box he'd opened at unit 32. A lot, certainly. And there

had been columns and columns of boxes. . . . "Tell me how the
stick-making began."

"The Lord Ye Huo Hua told us to start making them."

"How?"

"Through the Golden Master's dreams. The Lord Ye Huo Hua always spoke to us that way." Modesty then looked at him and gave a sigh. "Ai, I can see you don't believe me."

"It doesn't matter what I believe. I use the yijing sometimes: many people would consider that irrational. Tell me more."

She seemed amused by this revelation. "We were told that we needed to trade with the world, and that to do so we were to make incense sticks. It was hard at first, but after a few months of stick-making, we were able to start buying in tools and building materials."

"And the minibus?"

"That was a gift."

"Do you know who from?"

"I believe a businessman who took an interest in our work donated it."

"About the time you started making the sticks?"

Modesty paused, then said, "The Lord Ye Huo Hua provides for his own. Not with wealth, but with what is necessary."

"To each according to his need."

"Exactly!"

Wang examined a few more items—other, smaller barrels reeked of incense—then asked, "Does anyone keep accounts here?"

"Accounts? Of people's deeds?"

"Of money."

The Sister shook her head. "This is a spiritual place. We've had enough of the world, where money matters so much that every fen piece has to be accounted for. Many of us have been hurt by money and its lure. You may think we're naïve about it, but I think we are very wise."

"Maybe you are." Wang found he liked the new-look Sister

Modesty, though he was wise enough not to let himself be swayed by this liking. She might be attracted to him sexually—he was not without vanity—but maybe she wanted to influence him in some way. . . .

"I'd like to look in the other outbuildings, but I don't wish to detain you," he said. "May I borrow your keys for half an hour?"

"Of course," she said, handing them over. "I'll be in my room when you wish to return them."

When Modesty had gone, Wang spent a few minutes looking around the other outbuildings, which were all kept locked, and which all contained various implements that would also make excellent murder weapons, then went back to the main courtyards. He walked through the men's section to the Great Hall. At the corner of this was a locked door: he tried some keys, but none worked. Then, aware of time, he went on to the Master's study. As he had hoped, the room was empty. He let himself in and knelt down by the desk, trying various keys in the third drawer.

To his annoyance, none of them fitted.

"Lavatory!"

The former political commissar was back in again. Rosina cursed and sent one of the other nurses to sort the old sod out. Then she got back to filling in the patient admission records, by hand.

Yuchang came over and asked if she wanted a drink of tea.

"That's kind," said Rosina, and gave a sigh.

"Still worried about your sister?"

"Yes. There's been a suspicious death at that place where she's staying."

"Aiya!"

"Well, people say it was an accident, but I'm not sure. My husband's investigating it."

"So he's back there? That's good, isn't it?"

"Yes." Rosina grimaced. "In a way. But it doesn't help get

Julie back. He's just doing fingerprints and stuff like that. I feel
so helpless!"

Yuchang nodded, unsure what to say. Then she had an idea.
"Have another talk with Miss Hu."

"What good will that do?"

"Maybe she'll know something the police could use. If not—
well, at least it's doing something. It can't do any harm," Yuchang
added.

What Rosina really wanted to do was forget all about New
Tianjing and pretend her kid sister was fine.

"Good idea," she said.

The interviews and the fingerprinting took till lunch on the second
day. The team all took a break at midday: mandatory in summer,
when it gets so hot you have to take a *xiuxi* (siesta); pleasant in
winter, to rest the mind. Wang sat and scribbled on a piece of
paper—links, clues, ideas. Detective Wei read a magazine: *Police
Monthly*. Lu suddenly produced a copy of *Crime and Punishment*
and opened it. Wang assumed the young man had mistaken it for
a cops-and-robbers novel.

Outside, a bell sounded.

Wang glanced at his watch, returned to his paper to make a
last few notes, then spoke, with new determination in his voice.
"Lu, I want you to go back to Beijing and investigate a warehouse in Shi Jing Shan. Find out how often they receive deliveries
and how often goods are collected from their premises. Just ask
around, don't confront them directly."

Lu looked up from his book—he'd gotten to page four—and
grinned eagerly.

"Wei, I want you to drag the new pond they've been building
here."

The fast-track trainee seemed equally pleased.

"Lu, I'll run you down to the railway station. Let's get moving."

On the way back from the station, Wang revisited the local police. The officer on duty—the same man—looked even more embarrassed than ever not to have the incident form to hand and went off to have another search for it. While he was away, the visitor manned the desk. At one point a farmer came in, complaining about a missing goat. Wang took the opportunity of asking him about the people at New Tianjing.

"They're all crazy" came the reply. "The shouting that goes on there in the evenings!"

"Have you made an official complaint?"

The farmer shook his grizzled, bald head. "What's the point? We told Secretary Ma when they first came here, but then big shots from Beijing came and told us they were fine and we should leave them alone."

"Which big shots from Beijing?"

"I don't know. Officials. Party men."

"Did they just come here once?"

"No. I've seen them here a few times. But I mind my own affairs." The farmer stared at Wang for a while, trying, perhaps, to place him. "You don't think they've stolen the goat, do you?"

"No, but—"

"City folk think they have a right to do anything. They've probably taken it to the city and sold it to foreigners for more money than I'll make in a year!" He frowned. "Of course, that's the way it is now. Foreign money rules everything."

Wang nodded. His thoughts went briefly to that building full of joss-sticks. Three jiao each, they could fetch. And there were tens of thousands of them!

Having finally extracted a promise that the new desk officer would report the crime to the "proper policeman," the farmer left. Soon after, the "proper policeman" reappeared with a frown on his face.

"Files do go missing sometimes, boss. They turn up in the end, though."

Wang nodded. He knew the first part of this statement to be true. The question was *why* they went missing.

"Keep looking. In the meantime, I want a list of all people who have registered at New Tianjing, then left."

The officer's face fell.

"Oh, and I've an incident to report," Wang added, in an attempt to add a touch of levity. "The disappearance of a goat."

It didn't do much good.

He was back in time for the pond-drag to begin. They began at the north end of the pond, raking piles of muck from the bottom and rummaging through it by hand—a job for which Detective Wei volunteered. "I don't mind getting my hands dirty," she said eagerly.

More scrapes. Finally the rake felt to them as if it had connected with something and dragged an object into view: a long, round-topped plastic tube with battery acid oozing out of the base.

"Sexual aid," said Detective Wei, putting it in a plastic evidence bag. "Pretty necessary around here, I'd imagine."

Wang nodded. As Wei began the next drag, he reflected on the similarity of this place to old, revolutionary China, with its sexual repressiveness and sloganeering. But another side of him still valued the content of those slogans.

They carried on working but found little else.

"What were you were looking for?" Wei asked as they walked back to the farmstead.

"I'm not sure. A bloodstained murder weapon? A bag full of clothes covered in blood or vomit? Or a key—but that was always a long shot."

"A key?"

Wang told Wei about the Er Guo Tou in the third drawer.

"The old hypocrite!" exclaimed Wei.

I am a master of disguise! Lu said to himself.

He wouldn't say this to anyone else: it would be boastful, and also they might disagree. But deep down inside, he knew this to be the case.

He wondered which of his many disguises to assume. The bicycle repairman had worked well in the past, but didn't seem appropriate here. Maybe some kind of official from the transport department. Or a reporter, that was a good one. He'd seen several movies where policemen had posed as reporters and got spectacular results.

In the end, however, he decided on a student—of urban studies. (He'd read somewhere recently that they did a course on that at Beida.) What did urban studies students look like? Untidy, probably. Smoking drugs? Possibly, but not necessarily. But they would have a foreign book in their pocket.

At last—a use for the accursed thing!

I'm doing a survey on lorry traffic on this road....

The line worked well with people Lu met on Commerce Road. Most complained about there being too many lorries, or the smell of the exhaust, or the rudeness of the drivers, who all seemed to believe the rule of the road was the same as that of the jungle.

"Any particular lorries?"

At this point, the ruse stopped working. "No" was the usual answer. Or a complaint about the coal lorries from unit 47. Nobody mentioned unit 32.

The boss had said to avoid direct dealings with that unit, but as the afternoon wore on, Lu decided that there was no other way of finding out about their lorry. He walked up to the gateway of the unit, then a spasm of doubt hit him.

Obey orders in all your actions! His grandparents had been told that on the Long March; his parents had been told that in the 1960s and 1970s.

Lu began to walk away, then stopped. He stood in the middle of the road, paralyzed by indecision—then was aware that a lorry was hooting at him.

"Sorry," he said meekly, and stepped aside.

That seemed to crush his resolve. The young policeman began to trudge back to where he had left his bike, at the bottom of the road. He gave a sigh, and turned to give one last glance at unit 32.

The lorry was parked in its yard.

Lu had read about people stowing aboard lorries and suffocating, but that was in containers. This was an old Jiefang (Liberation) truck, with a tarpaulin on the back, slung over iron hoops. It would be easy to climb on. Just make sure nobody was looking. . . .

The sound system of the Y2K Internet Café burst into life.

"Aiya! What's that racket?" said Rosina.

"Prodigy," Yuchang replied. "They're very popular with young people in England."

"Oh," said Rosina.

"It's not my type of music, either," said the third member of the party. "I like Western music, but classical, especially the works of W. A. Mozart."

"Who are they?" said Yuchang.

Tuo appeared and poured them all drinks, and Rosina told Miss Hu about her worries. She in turn listened thoughtfully, then spoke. "I've been talking to other survivors about the death. They don't reckon the Golden Master was murdered, because people saw the body, and there weren't any wounds on it."

"The whole body?" Rosina asked. "Naked?"

Miss Hu blushed slightly. "No, just, well, the head and arms. Like Chairman Mao in his mausoleum. They also said he looked very peaceful."

"That just means he wasn't bashed over the head," said Rosina.

"Yeah—he could have been shot in the stomach, or through the heart, or poisoned," Yuchang put in gleefully. "All sorts of things!"

And I'd thought, What a nice, quiet girl, Rosina told herself. To Miss Hu, she said, "So you think there's no danger to my sister? It sounds such an enclosed world: imagine the damage a maniac could do in there!"

Miss Hu shook her head. "New Tianjing is absurdly enclosed: you are never alone. But that would make it almost impossible for a crazy person to stay there long without being unmasked." She took a sip of her orange juice. "I have a theory, but it's only a theory—"

"Tell us!" Rosina cut in.

Miss Hu gave her downy upper lip the faintest of licks, to ensure no orange juice was daring to lurk there. "I shall, Mrs. Wang. Most of us survivors are sensible, balanced people. Some even get to join the Party. But a few . . . the Church claims it never throws anyone out, but some people do leave and feel bitter about it afterward. My belief is that one of them killed the Master, as a kind of revenge." Miss Hu held out a hand and laid it on Rosina's shoulder. "It's the Church's leaders who have to worry."

"Serves them right," Rosina muttered.

Prodigy was replaced on the sound system by something gentler: Rosina's mood seemed to match this. If the killer was outside, and had a clear hit list of Church leaders, Julie was safe. It might even hasten the breakup of the whole accursed organization.

"There are really people out there who'd kill the leaders?" she asked, just to make sure.

"There are people who have threatened to." Another near smile. "Crazy Cheng used to spend all his time doing that."

"Who's Crazy Cheng?"

"A boy who joined the church awhile back. He was always unbalanced, and he had to leave after a while. Our group got a series of letters from him a year or so ago threatening to do all kinds of horrible things to the Masters."

"Like what?" said Yuchang.

"One of them said he'd cut the Golden Master to pieces with a machete and crucify the Silver Master like the Romans did to Brother Ye Su."

"Weird!" exclaimed Yuchang.

"But that's just the leaders?" Rosina put in. "No threats to anyone else?"

"No," said Miss Hu.

Rosina looked relieved, then felt a pang of guilt. "I think my husband ought to know about this man," she said. "Do you have any of these letters?"

Miss Hu shook her head.

"Do you know where he lives?" said Rosina.

"I can try to find out," said Miss Hu. Then the sound system made another attempt to deafen them.

"Ku," said Yuchang. "Left field."

"I must go," said Miss Hu. "I'll see what I can do about Crazy Cheng."

"I wonder what he's like," Yuchang said enthusiastically, once Miss Hu had left.

"Who?"

"Crazy Cheng. I've never met a real madman."

"Are you down to do a psychiatric placement?"

"Not yet."

Rosina shook her head. "Madness isn't romantic, it's sad." And generally harmless, she thought, mindful of how much time crazy people spent filling their heads with violence that usually didn't get translated into reality. But not always.

They'd been on this road for over an hour now. A straight, busy-sounding highway. The light was beginning to fade and the cold to envelop Lu. The young man suddenly wondered what would happen if they were heading north, to Russia perhaps. He'd heard that Chinese goods were smuggled across the border one way and immigrant Russian workers the other. (Serve them right: Russia should never have argued with China back in the days of Khrushchev). He'd have to get off. The alternative was to freeze to death.

Then the lorry began to slow. Another traffic jam? Then it made a violent swing, jolted over bumpy ground, and came to a halt.

For several minutes, Lu did nothing. Then he raised the tarpaulin a crack and glanced out into a parking area full of similar vehicles. Perhaps he should get out here: he'd be able to tell his boss which way the Jiefang was headed, anyway. He needed the toilet, too. He began working at the tarpaulin bindings and soon had enough room to crawl out. He crossed to the park wall and relieved himself against it, then turned to seek a telephone. And saw a man getting into the cab of the lorry.

Lu ran toward the vehicle, then stopped—supposing he was spotted?—then simply stood there, not knowing what to do.

The lorry's engine spluttered into life; Lu cursed and waited for it to move off.

But it didn't.

"He's letting it warm up," Lu told himself.

A minute later, he was safely was back on board; soon after that, the vehicle pulled out onto the highway again and continued its journey into the night.

12

It was early morning before the lorry came to a proper halt. Lu smelled first industrial pollution, then a new, fresher smell, of the sea. He prised open the tarpaulin and stared out with bleary eyes. Yes, they were on a wharf. Two men were arguing. One was the driver; the other had a clipboard in his hand. Behind them was a big ship being loaded up. The *Yangzi,* it was called.

If he could just get out unobserved, take a leak again, brush some of the creases out of his clothes, then he could get his dignity back and, with it, his power. If . . .

The driver and the man with the clipboard disappeared from view. Now was his chance! Lu yanked the tarpaulin back, scrambled out through the hole, and tumbled onto the concrete. For a moment he lay motionless. Had anyone seen?

Then he was up on his feet, walking calmly around the back of the lorry. Into the warehouse, where a forklift was lifting crates.

"Can I help?" said a voice by Lu's ear.

Lu drew himself up to his full height.

"I'm looking for Mr. Chen." The boss always said, "If in doubt, ask for Mr. Chen."

"That's me."

The boss didn't say what you did if this happened.

"Ah. Well, I need to know—where's the lavatory?"

"Around the corner."

"Right. Don't go away."

Lu raced off.

The moment he was gone, the man called Chen took a mobile phone out of his pocket and dialed a number. ". . . And you haven't let anyone in? Better get the docks police over here, then."

There was another man in the gents. Lu didn't like starting conversations in toilets—he'd read that sexual deviants did this. But this person could be a source of information.

"Got to load all that lot onto the *Yangzi* today?" he asked as he unbuttoned his fly. No, this wasn't right.

"Yup."

But duty called. "All those boxes?"

"Yup. Why d'you want to know?"

"Can't tell you."

"Hmph."

The good Communist always puts Party before self. "When does the ship sail?"

"Why the hell are you asking all these questions?"

"Police," Lu blurted out, suddenly terrified the guy really did think he was, well, one of those people you read about.

"Hmph," said the man. He finished pissing, then walked out—without washing his hands: hadn't he heard of the Four Hygienes? Lu dutifully immersed his hands in ice-cold water, opened the door of the toilet—and saw a police car drive up to the front of the warehouse. What a piece of luck!

He began walking toward the car, then caught a snatch of dialogue. ". . . He knew my name. He's up to no good. . . ."

Lu smiled and reached for his police ID.

It wasn't there.

He scrabbled through his other pockets, just in case he had put it back in the wrong one, but no . . . so it must have fallen out somewhere. Where? In the lorry? Or when he had jumped out? Aiya!

He had to get out of there, fast.

There was a wall ahead of him—fifteen feet high, with glass along the top. Across from that was another barrier—the water, black and smelly. So should he make a simple run down the quay? But which way was the gate, and would he be able to talk his way out through the gate, anyway?

Then a lorry appeared, moving with extraordinary slowness. So slow that Lu wondered if it would reach him in time. But it did, a few seconds before the docks police came running around the corner and into the toilet—by which time Lu lay among a new set of cargo, in the back of a new lorry.

He held his breath, waiting for his pursuers to follow.

And waited.

And waited.

"Where's Lu this morning?" said Team-leader Chen.

"I don't know."

"He hasn't phoned in sick?"

"No."

"He's never sick, anyway," said Chen. "And I've called his home and got no answer. Wang, go by way of Lu's flat and see if he's there."

This was quite a detour, but Wang wouldn't think of questioning his superior directly, and couldn't think of an indirect way quickly enough. Instead, he grinned, then muttered a curse to himself, not at the inconvenience but at what he would have to do if the young man wasn't at home. Raid unit 32? If Lu had stumbled onto something serious, he needed to act quickly. But to overreact would damage the investigation. . . .

Check the flat first, he told himself.

Lu lived with his parents in a modern apartment block in the north of the city, near Andingmen. Both parents came from excellent Revolutionary backgrounds: three out of his four grandparents had been on the Long March. Wang felt a little in awe of this, a fact that annoyed him—he'd achieved enough in his life not to have to be in awe of anybody.

The block had a *fuwuyuan*—a concierge—who gave Wang and Wei superior looks as they entered her office.

"I'm looking for Lu Weihong," Wang told her, producing his police ID.

"Flat 305," the concierge replied. "The lift's just around the corner."

The lift was in order. It had a carpet. It made virtually no noise as it whisked them up to the third floor. They made their way along a litter-free corridor to 305, where Wang paused to dismiss another pang of social unease before rapping on the door.

No reply.

"Did you see him last night?" Wang asked the *fuwuyuan* when he got back to ground level.

"No."

"Nice flat," said Wei as Wang turned out onto the outer ring road.

"It's okay," Wang replied, trying not to feel jealous.

"Pity he's so thick," Wei added, as the Beijing appended itself to the inevitable traffic queue. "What are you going to do about him?"

"Wait till lunchtime. He's very conscientious—normally."

So why no contact?

When the team reached New Tianjing, Detective Wei got straight on with typing up reports, while Wang simply sat at his desk and began fiddling with a pen, wheeling it round and round over the back of his hands like a propeller. . . . What had happened to Lu?

A few minutes of this was quite enough: he got up from his seat and strode across the quadrangle out to the front of the farmstead, from which point he made his way around the side of the building to the window of the Golden Master's study.

This window, Wang felt sure, held a key to the mystery. Who had been climbing in here? Why? He looked down at the ground—the prints were no clearer by day than under the beam of his torch—and tried to summon up the scene in his mind.

Nothing.

He tried again.

"Mr. Wang!"

Wang gave a start, then turned to the speaker. "Hello, Sister."

"Looking for clues?" asked Modesty.

"Yes."

A brief silence fell.

"Found anything?"

"No."

Modesty shook her head. "The Master was called away: whatever angel summoned him would leave no earthly traces." She grinned at him. "But you must find that out for yourself. I came to see if you wanted some refreshment. Tea?"

"That's very kind," Wang replied. His concentration broken, and his curiosity about Modesty rekindled, he followed her back to another room in the front quad, with chairs, a desk, and the inevitable pictures of Brother Hong and Brother Ye Su. Here the sister put green leaves in two mugs, added water from a plastic flask with a picture of a kitten on it, then handed one to her visitor.

"The Master looked at great peace in his coffin," she said.

"Expressions can be changed."

"But there's nobody who would want to kill such a gentle man," the sister went on.

"Maybe. As you say, we will find out." Wang smiled and took a sip of the tea. Ai! Too hot. He blew across the surface, then asked Modesty, "How long have you been a member of the Church?"

"Many years."

"Has the New Church of the Heavenly Kingdom been in existence for long, then?"

"No. Only since 1995. But I've always been a believer. My family were Christians. During the Cultural Revolution they had to make all sorts of self-criticisms and so on, but we were lucky: many people in our village were believers, so we weren't picked on. After 1976, I refused to join the Three Self churches, because

I felt they were too close to the authorities. I just prayed and read my Bible on my own. Then I joined a house group—you know, meeting at a flat and having services. Then I found out about Hong Er, and I knew at once I had to be here."

"How did you know?"

"I believe the Lord Ye Huo Hua told me."

Wang tried to look as neutral as possible. Not with much success, as Modesty continued: "I can see you're skeptical. But I believe in divine intervention. The Lord Ye Huo Hua is watching over us. He will intervene if a true believer needs help."

"Intervene? How?"

Modesty smiled. "Through thought. And, at crucial times in history, through messiahs."

Wang was about to say something, but Modesty, clearly enthusiastic now, carried on.

"History demonstrates I'm right. Look at the West. It was only under the religion of Brother Ye Su that the West established its dominance. And exactly at the time when true religion began to decline there, the Lord Ye Huo Hua sent Brother Hong to China. Do you know the year when Hong Xiuquan was handed the word of the Lord by a Western missionary?"

"No."

"Eighteen thirty-six. And do you know the year that Charles Darwin went to the Galapagos Islands and invented the so-called theory of evolution that purports to 'prove' that God did not create man?"

"No. But I can guess."

"I don't know the exact month or day, but I'm willing to wager they are the same, too. I believe that seconds after those sinful ideas first came to that foreign devil, the Lord Ye Huo Hua sent his dream to Brother Hong." Modesty grinned, then paused. "Well, maybe not seconds, as Brother Hong mightn't have been asleep at the exact moment the foreigner had his thought. But the night after . . ."

Wang took a sip of tea. Modesty was beginning to sound like

the Marxist Education Officer in the army unit he had served in as a young man, who had tried to show that scientific Marxist–Leninist–Mao Zedong thought could prove anything. One day the guy had tried to predict the weather using the method. "It must be sunny tomorrow!" he had insisted. The next day it had poured with rain, and the officer had simply said that showed that he needed to study more.

"The Lord Ye Huo Hua sends prophets and Masters to us, as well," Modesty continued. "He sent many to the Middle East before Brother Ye Su, and to China he even sent his second son to prophesy."

"Prophesy what?"

"The new millennium." Modesty's eyes began to shine. "If only you could have heard the old Master speak!"

"Was he better than the new one?"

"They are both divinely inspired," Modesty said, suddenly cautious. "But the old Master had such humanity . . ." She grinned. "And you still think someone killed him . . . Do you know who?"

"No."

Modesty nodded.

Wang wondered why she was so keen to know. Natural curiosity? Or something more?

Lunchtime came with appalling slowness. On the dot of twelve, Wang phoned Team-leader Chen. No, there had been no news from, or of, Lu.

"We'll have to go after him," he said.

"How?" Wei asked.

"Go down to unit 32; ask questions; use force if necessary. We may need firearms: I'll get Chen to sort that out." He spoke these words without enthusiasm: he disliked acting this aggressively, like a hero in some cheap movie. It raised stakes so much; people got hurt; information within reach got driven underground. But there was no alternative.

"If only I knew what his plan of action had been . . ." he muttered as he and Wei crossed to the Jeep.

This time they took the inner ring road. The jam there was even worse than the one they had encountered on the outer ring road in the morning. And when they reached the office, Team-leader Chen insisted on summoning a complete Armed Response Unit, then began complaining about the cost.

"We must stand by our men under all circumstances!" said Chen. "The unit will be here in half an hour. Four of the finest young men in the force, with the latest weapons and technology, worth . . . aiya, I daren't think what this will do to the departmental budget! But we must stand by our comrade. Shoulder to shoulder, united against a common foe!"

It crossed Wang's mind to wonder if his boss would stand shoulder to shoulder, united against a common foe, with the offspring of less-influential parents, but he said nothing. Instead he simply followed the team-leader down to the front yard where the ARU was going to arrive.

Chen seemed now to be enjoying the drama of the situation. "Decisiveness!" he muttered.

Then nothing happened for a while. It was a bright day, but the sun was low and weak, and CID HQ only provided partial shelter from the sharp northeasterly wind. Wang was beginning to feel cold—and annoyed at himself for noticing such a trivial thing—when he heard the sound of a siren; moments later, a black unmarked van pulled up at the gate, and hooted once. The barrier began to rise.

"Fine, fighting men . . ." Chen muttered.

Wang nodded: he admired these guys, too, knowing that they must feel fear every time they were called into action. Having served in China's brief 1979 war with Vietnam, he understood fear and its power to corrode the personality. He also understood the exhilaration of overcoming that power. But to do battle with it day after day . . .

These thoughts were suddenly interrupted by another sound.
His mobile phone.

"Can't you shut that up?" said Chen.

"I'd better answer it."

"Hello," said a female voice. "This is ship-to-shore communication. Are you Wang Anzhuang of the Beijing Criminal Investigations Department?"

"Yes."

"Go ahead please," she said, before her voice was replaced by another.

"Lao Wang!"

"Lu! Where the hell are you?"

"On a boat."

"Where?"

"On the sea."

"Where are you *going*?"

"Venezuela."

The van drew up in front of them.

"Venezuela?"

"It's a long story, Lao Wang. But I've got the information about those incense sticks. They're on another boat, the *Yangzi*, that's probably leaving Tianjin today. I don't know where for."

"Ah. . . . Well done. . . ."

"Can you get me off this tub? Nobody speaks Mandarin."

"We can try. . . ."

"All I've got's this book to read, and it's—"

"How do I contact you?" Wang cut in. He began writing down a number.

"What's going on?" Chen asked.

The van door opened, and a man in black clothes got out. "Team-leader Chen Runfa?"

"Yes," said Chen.

The man gave Chen a snappy military salute and announced himself as Sergeant Fu.

"We'll do our best," Wang said into the phone.

"Who is that?" Chen cut in.

"Lu," said Wang.

"Lu? *Lu?* Ai! Give me that!" He snatched the phone. "Lu, where the fuck are you? What...? Where...? *Ai-yaa!*"

For a moment, Chen looked totally flabbergasted. He glanced up at the armed policeman, then down at the phone, almost as if Lu were inside the little plastic case, then back up at the sergeant. A look of fear and helplessness came over him.

Team-leader Chen Runfa was just about to lose more face than he'd ever lost before.

He began to stammer: "I ... er ... There's been ..."

Wang glanced down at his watch. "Fourteen and a half minutes," he said to the sergeant. "That's quick. Well done. We'll be passing the results of this test on to our superiors, as ordered. Stand easy."

Once Chen had calmed down, Wang put a call through to the port authorities in Tianjin, who confirmed that the *Yangzi* had left that morning for San Francisco.

"How do you plan to follow this lead?" Chen asked him as the team sat in Wang's office afterward.

"Interpol?"

"The cost!" the team-leader exclaimed, then began shaking his head.

Wang watched. Suddenly, he had an idea. "I need authorization to make some international calls!"

"Some? How many?"

"It shouldn't take many. I'll need an English speaker to help me—to start with, anyway."

"English? Aiya, why can't they learn Mandarin? More people speak it than any other language on earth. Why all this craze for English? Detective Wei, do you speak English?"

"Not properly."

"Fine. We have to pay for these English speakers, you know, Xiao Wang."

"Surely money mustn't be allowed to stand in the way of the pursuit of justice," Detective Wei put in, adding her most attractive smile.

"Well, no. Of course not. But budgets are important, you know. When you reach a more senior position, you'll . . ." Then Chen's voice faded, and a smile stole over his face. "Your idealism does you credit, Detective Wei. Xiao Wang, organize an interpreter and make those calls. I have an important task to carry out."

Nobody asked, but Chen had to tell them. "Someone must go and tell Lu's family that he's going to be away for a while, but that we're doing everything we can to get him back. That's a job for his team-leader!"

The interpreter came to the office at half-past five on the dot, and sat fiddling with a pencil till it was time for him to make the calls. He made three: during the third, he handed the receiver to Wang and told him, "That's your man."

13

Sergeant George P. Lim had grown fatter since his trip to China. Too much desk work. His wife had lost some of her looks, but not many—some women in Chinatown began to look so dowdy after forty: their hair frizzed out all over the place and they began to dress in cheap, dull clothes and, apparently, lost interest in sex. The kids, naturally, had changed the most, especially Bella, who seemed to have no interest in Chinese culture at all, except for "Shaolin raps," which George didn't count as Chinese or culture.

When Wu-tang Clan was thudding down from upstairs, George would often look up at the Tang dynasty horse that had pride of place on his mantelpiece, think of his journey to China, and regret not having gone back there. He'd think of the fellow cop he had met there. What was the guy's name again? Anzhuang, that was it. *Calm and robust,* the name meant. He'd sometimes think of calling, but Anzhuang hadn't left a number. The guy probably didn't have a telephone!

Then one morning, George arrived at the station and had just sat down with his second cup of coffee when the phone rang. It was someone with one of the worst English accents he'd ever heard telling him he had a call from Beijing. Then on the other end, Anzhuang. Speaking Mandarin, of course. George P. Lim had been going to Mandarin classes for years—ironic: the guy teaching it was a WASP, half the students were American-born Chinese. Time, at last, to use it.

"Don't tell me you're finally coming over to the States, Anzhuang?"

"Er, no. I'm phoning up to ask for some help."

"Ah." Since his visit to the Middle Kingdom, Lim hadn't been involved in any liaison work with the Chinese police. Even so, he knew there were always political problems involved. Sometimes cooperation with America's fast-reforming Pacific Rim trading partner was encouraged, other times any dealings with those cruel, perfidious Communists were out of the question. Right now . . . George thought things were in a "perfidious Communists" phase, thanks to this business with the Fa Lun Gong, but he wasn't sure. Another round of trade negotiations were never far away.

"What's the problem?" he asked.

Wang Anzhuang told him.

George had a good relationship with the San Francisco Port Authority, and had little trouble establishing when the *Yangzi* was due to arrive, what cargoes were on board, and which shipping agent was responsible for the cargoes. The shipping agent, when contacted, was equally cooperative: the incense sticks were going to Flying Spirit Products Inc. in Monterey. A call to the DEA revealed that they had made occasional routine checks of these incense shipments and never found them to contain anything other than what was claimed.

The agent had given George both Flying Spirit's number and the name of its owner. He was on the point of calling this man when he remembered a previous trip to that part of the state and decided a visit in person might be more effective. He had a few days' leave coming up.

The little California resort of Monterey hadn't changed at all since George's last visit. Lazy, quiet streets; the sparkle of the Pacific in the distance; the occasional bark of sea otters. He left Amy and the kids at the aquarium in Cannery Row—the only time he was interested in fish was when they were on a plate—and walked to the address of Flying Spirit Products, which turned out to be a shop in the old part of town, among white-boarded bungalows.

Clearly a good business.

An assistant showed him through to an office, where a long-haired man in a checked shirt was operating a computer.

The man got to his feet and introduced himself. "Jeff Tolman. And you must be George Lim."

He produced his ID, and Tolman looked at it carefully. "Call my office to confirm if you like," George added.

"That shouldn't be necessary," said Tolman. "I ran a check on you after you phoned. Sit down. Get comfortable. Now, what was it you wanted to talk about?"

"The incense sticks you get from mainland China."

"What do you want to know about them?"

"Can we begin with the name of your supplier?"

"That's important business information, Sergeant."

"It could be important police information," George replied. This time he produced his badge. "I've worn this for twenty-two years, Mr. Tolman. It means I'm not for sale to the highest bidder, or to any bidder. Nothing we say is going anywhere it doesn't have to."

Tolman frowned for a moment, then scratched his head. George assumed him to be assessing whether those words had been sincere or not.

"Okay," Tolman said finally. "He's called Wei Ming."

George couldn't help breaking out into a broad grin on hearing this. "How long have you been doing business with Wei Ming?"

"A couple of years."

"And how did you first hear about him?"

"Through a Chinese up in Frisco we do a bit of business with."

"Name of?"

"Kwan. Joe Kwan."

George nodded. "Did Kwan contact you or you contact him?"

"He contacted me."

"And you've never met Wei Ming?"

Tolman seemed surprised. "No."

"Or spoken to him?"

"No. I've never needed to. Any problems, I'd talk with Kwan. But there haven't been problems. The stuff is good; it comes on time."

"And how does Wei Ming get paid?"

"The money goes into a bank."

"In China?"

"Yes."

"Into an anonymous account?"

"Hey, what the hell's this all about? If you know it all already—"

"D'you know what *Wei Ming* means?"

"No."

"It means *no name*."

"Oh," said Tolman.

"Now, if you could try to remember the details of that bank."

Tolman looked doubtful again, and George told him a recent story about a China-based businessman who had run up substantial lines of credit over a period of time, then disappeared. He only embroidered it a little.

"It's the Commercial, Industrial, and Agricultural Bank," Tolman said finally. "In some place beginning with an *x*. CIA bank: I like that!"

The businessman began clicking the mouse and details appeared on the computer screen. "How the hell do you pronounce that?"

"Shee-ah-men," said George, noting as he did so the number of the account.

"Why do they spell it with an *x*, then?" said Tolman.

"No idea. To get their own back on the West probably," George replied with a laugh.

Tolman wasn't amused. After a pause he said, "D'you think Joe is in on this, too?"

"I've no idea. What do you think?"

"No, but . . ." Tolman's voice was hesitant now. "If you find anything out . . ."

"Our job is to protect the citizens," said George. "I'll do my best."

"Thanks," said Tolman, with real warmth. "I'd appreciate that."

Getting information out of people *and* leaving them feeling grateful to you—now, that's the way to do it!

George Lim knew most of the bad guys in Chinatown, and Joe Kwan was not one of them. When he got back from his break, he found out where Kwan lived—in a house similar to his own, a few streets away.

So close, in fact, that he walked over that evening. Walking— he did so little of that! Once you get past forty you get stuck behind a desk. He wondered if that was true in China, too.

The street was just like his: small, weatherboarded houses with nicely kept front gardens and compact, practical 1994 or 1995 automobiles sitting outside. Criminals either made a lot more money than this or a lot less.

Kwan was surprised to find a cop on his porch, and more surprised that the cop wanted to talk about his business affairs— but not horrified, especially when the cop said it was a routine matter and told him a story about a China-based businessman who had run up substantial lines of credit over a period of time then disappeared. He sat Sergeant Lim down in the front room and fixed him a pot of proper Chinese green tea.

"You speak Mandarin?" George asked him, once they were comfortable.

"Yidianr."

"Enough to know what *wei ming* means?"

"Yes, but the guy who put me in touch is someone I trust."

"Name of?"

"Chang. Chang Hu."

George produced an envelope from his briefcase—had he joined the force to end up carrying a briefcase around?—and took some photos from it.

"Are any of these Chang Hu?"

Kwan looked at them carefully, shaking his head and showing no signs of recognition, not even at the one of the Golden Master that Anzhuang had faxed him.

"Sounds like your guy is straight," George said at the end.

Kwan nodded nervously. "Will you tell me if you do find anything out?" he said.

"Our job is to protect the citizen," said George.

Early next morning, he called Anzhuang and told him all he had discovered. The names, the bank details, the price paid for the sticks . . . Anzhuang seemed very grateful.

"You know, that invitation to come visit us still stands," George told him.

"Yes. I appreciate it. Maybe some time in the future. You know what it's like with work!" Wang did not mention the real reason for his not going to the States, not political but financial: he could no more afford a holiday in the U.S.A. than he could buy a trip to the moon. "You should come back to China," he added instead. "I'd like you to meet Rosina."

"I'd like that, too." George began thinking of China again. The children *should* see their homeland. Then a phone on his desk began ringing. "That sounds like trouble," he said. "Zai jian."

Zai jian meant "good-bye" but was literally "See you again."

"The CIA bank?" said the Public Security official at Xiamen to whom Wang's call was routed.

"That's right."

"We don't have much information about it."

"Why not?"

"It has not proven necessary in the past."

"You can't even check the details of a particular account there?"

"That would be inconvenient."

"How inconvenient?"

"Extremely."

"I see," said Wang, and put the phone down.

Wheels Chai looked glum when asked to run a check via his computer.

"Bank security was always reasonable, but it's gotten better over the last couple of years," said the veteran policeman. "There are these things called firewalls."

Chai launched into a long description of these, of which Wang understood little. What he *did* understand with sad clarity was that, a year ago, Chai would have seen their complexity as an irresistible challenge.

"You're still the best we've got," he said at the end of the description.

"Am I?" Chai replied moodily. "Things move so fast in the IT world. Ask some teenage black visitor to do your search." Black visitor—*hei ke*—hacker.

Wang scowled. "So there are kids who can do trickier things now. They don't have your police skills!"

"They can walk," said Chai.

"Lao Chai, that's not the kind of talk I want to hear from you. Ever. Understand?"

Chai managed a smile. "I wish I could get into that bank for you, Xiao Wang, but I can't."

"Ai, it's not that important anyway," Wang lied.

Back in his office, he toyed with the idea of contacting Norton Ho, the young *hei ke* he'd met on his Red Mandarin investigation. But to do that would be to show disloyalty to a friend.

Colonel Da still had his office on the fifth floor of the department, though he came in less and less often. Team-leader Chen had been heard to complain of the waste of space this represented, space that could better be employed by men like, well, him, for example. But Chen never made these complaints official, and neither did anyone else.

It was true that Lao Da was an old man now. He always arrived in a car and always battled his way up the entrance stairs on a stick, never accepting assistance. His journey down the corridor to the lifts was a similar struggle—he'd given up the stairs years ago—and once ensconced in his room, all he seemed to do was read reports and drink prime-quality tea. Wang had known the Colonel for fifteen years, and the old man had watched over his career, giving advice and protection. In return for this, Da got . . . what? An audience for his stories? A surrogate son, maybe: little was known about Da's own family, except that his oldest son had not survived the Cultural Revolution and that his daughter now lived in the West.

Yet in other ways the relationship between the two was still superficial. Da belonged to a generation that had learned to conceal, not just because it conferred advantage but because it could save your life. In this way, Da was heir to a tradition as old as China itself, a tradition of living in the shadow of absolute power. Chairman Mao, the man Da had both loved and feared, had learned his imperious deviousness from age-old Chinese classics, from *The Romance of the Three Kingdoms* and *The General Mirror of Government*.

"Can't your friend Chai find this out for you?" the old man said, once the important matters like t—he tea the visitor was to

accept had been dealt with, and once Wang had explained the
situation.

"He's having a few problems at the moment."

Da nodded. "Oh. That's bad. Personal?"

You see, that was it. Wang trusted Da—almost. But not enough to tell him all about Chai. "I'm not sure," he replied.

The colonel took a sip of *wu long*. "What about that young lad you worked with in Xianggang?"

And *that* was it, too. He hadn't told Da about Norton, yet the old man knew.

"If you want to look after people, you have to keep an eye on them," Da went on, noticing Wang's reaction.

The younger man grinned acknowledgment of this fact.

"I'm sure that lad could do this for you," Da went on. "He's spoken of very highly, I believe."

"If Chai found out, we'd lose face with one another."

"Sometimes you have to lose face with individuals to do what is right for the general good," said Da.

Wang frowned. His father, back in Shandong province, had said things like that. His wife, when they argued about politics, said people who said things like that were bad, that it was those kinds of sentiments that had visited the tragedies of the Great Leap Forward and the Cultural Revolution on China. As so often, he felt himself stranded between two worlds, between Mao and modernity.

"Not if those individuals are old colleagues," he said carefully.

Da seemed pleased with this answer. "I'll see what I can do."

The veteran Communist took the paper with the bank details and put them in a tray. "It may take a little time," said Da.

Wang sat at his desk, drawing a diagram. At the center, the dead man; radiating out from him like wheel spokes, links of motive, means, or opportunity to other people. Then, most interesting of all, links *among* these others.

The Religious Affairs Bureau featured in several places on the diagram. He had little appetite for further dealings with these people: he knew how difficult it would be, and how unlikely it was that anything would be revealed. But someone there was clearly protecting the New Church, and he was pretty sure they were doing it because they were profiteering on those incense sticks.

This was a crime in itself, in his eyes. And if the bureau was acting illegally, then it was possible that the Golden Master had needed to be silenced.

He *had* to find out more!

He took a taxi to the bureau. The Happiness was booked out, and the only alternatives were "Bus 11" or the Flying Pigeon. Besides, he wanted time in the back of a car. Time to think. He got plenty of that, thanks to another Beijing traffic jam.

Despite his mode of arrival, the woman at the bureau reception still gave him a superior look.

"I need to talk to someone," he said.

"What about?"

"A small religious group, called the New Church of the Heavenly Kingdom."

"I don't know anything about them."

"Who does?"

"I don't know."

"Can you find out for me, please?" Wang was aware of the sudden weariness that had entered his voice. It was pointless coming here. That Great Wall of official unhelpfulness would be thrown up, even to him, an officer of the Public Security Bureau. Once he would have felt rage at this; now he felt a kind of boredom. Any residual anger was directed at himself, for being so naïve as to come here.

The woman seemed to sense his mood, maybe even to feel some sympathy. Perhaps she was new to the job. "Is this a small group, like a house church?" she asked.

"Yes."

"Well, Deputy Director Guan is probably the man to speak to, but he's out of the office today."

The boredom was gone instantly. "Guan?"

"Yes."

"Can I see him tomorrow, then? It is of, er, some importance."

"Thursday?"

Wang mustered all the calm he could. "Thursday. Yes, that's fine."

14

Deputy Director Guan of the Religious Affairs Bureau was middle aged, slightly overweight, and sweating. From fear, or just general poor condition?

"Take a seat," he told Wang. "How can I help?"

"I'm trying to find out about the New Church of the Heavenly Kingdom."

"Ah. In our dealings with People's Police we normally like to—"

"There is a personal aspect to this. I'd appreciate it if we could get around the formalities."

"Personal?"

"Yes." Wang told him about Julie.

This seemed to relax the deputy. "The New Church of the Heavenly Kingdom is a small group of Christian believers," he began. "They are based at a village about a hundred kilometers from here, but also hold regular meetings in the capital. . . ."

He proceeded to tell Wang a few things about the Church that he, Wang, already knew, then sat back with a satisfied expression.

"So you keep them under surveillance, Director?"

"Of course. But the New Church of the Heavenly Kingdom keeps to the law, expresses no political ambitions, and rehabilitates a number of young people who—if I may say so—would otherwise be giving you trouble. They have a healthily patriotic flavor to their belief system. We don't consider them a danger at all."

"Their leader has recently been murdered."

Something flickered in Guan's eyes, but his voice stayed calm. "Their leader has recently died."

"In suspicious circumstances."

"We're not aware of any suspicion. You are the first member of the People's Police to have contacted us about the death."

"Isn't it your job to inform us?"

"Only if we consider the death suspicious." Guan, aware no doubt of the circularity of his argument, shook his head. "The man died. What's suspicious about that?"

"There are procedures to go through."

"To do with family? He had no family as far as we know."

"Supposing he had an infectious disease?"

Guan did look contrite here and grinned. "Yes, well, the trouble was that the body was cremated before we could get a doctor to view it."

"Doesn't that sound suspicious to you?"

"No. That's their belief: after three days, the soul takes its final leave of the body, which is then useless. So the body is burned. Cremation is the method of body disposal recommended by the Party."

Wang recalled having heard these words before. "So you don't think that my sister-in-law is in any kind of danger there?"

Guan relaxed still further. "No."

Silence fell. "Do you have any files on the Church?"

"Yes."

"I should like to see them."

"It might be difficult to organize that straightaway."

Wang had been expecting that, whether Deputy Director Guan was guilty of any crimes or not. The Great Wall again. He thought of Colonel Da and those bank details. If the account could be traced to Guan . . . But now he had to be polite and show no suspicion.

"That's fine," he said.

Guan grinned. "I'll get a courier to send them round to your office."

Silence settled again.

"How did you get to hear of the death?" Guan asked.

"A friend told me. They know about my sister-in-law and thought I'd be interested."

Guan nodded. Wang guessed he wouldn't dare ask more.

"I hope there's not going to be a fuss made about this," the deputy director said instead, after another long pause. "After all this business with the Fa Lun Gong . . . I blame the West. They bomb our embassy, then complain when we try to keep order in our own streets."

Wang simply nodded assent.

The files arrived next morning in a tatty cardboard box marked *New Church of the Heavenly Kingdom*. Wang went through them carefully and found nothing to do with financial dealings there. Just agents' reports, internal memoranda, a plan of the New Tianjing farmstead, and a copy of a book about the Taiping Rebellion. He took a photocopy of the plan, then began with the first report.

Rosina sat and stared at the piece of paper in front of her. An address, in Miss Hu's perfectly formed characters.

"Tell Anzhuang," she said to herself. But the longer she gazed at the paper, the less she wanted to do that.

She thought of Yuchang and her juvenile view of the mentally ill. In many ways Rosina had come to like her young colleague, but when Yuchang had gone on about meeting a madman in the same tone of voice that you used about going to the zoo . . . The trouble was, that attitude was still common. Among her husband's colleagues, for example.

If she put Anzhuang onto "Crazy" Cheng, and the young man turned out to be an innocent simpleton, then all kinds of terrible things could happen, and she, Rosina, would feel responsible. She knew Anzhuang wouldn't mistreat the boy but had no trust at all in that oaf Lu or that fascist Chen. And she hadn't met that Wei woman, but she sounded ambitious, the kind who wouldn't let scruples get in the way of advancement.

Then suddenly Rosina knew what to do.

"I'll go myself! I know how to deal with these people. And I can read them. I'll know almost at once if he's a threat to anyone."

She felt better at once.

"He may have recovered, too. Maybe he'll be able to tell me some more about this bloody cult."

The thought did cross her mind that Cheng might be dangerous. But in fifteen years of nursing, Rosina had come across some pretty disturbed people and had treated them with professionalism, with kindness, and, most important of all, in safety.

She checked the address and got up to get her city map.

Rosina was used to the center of Beijing, where buildings were either high rise or (as in the old *hutong*s) single story. Estate 14 was just a jumble of buildings, most three or four stories high, all rectangular, looking permanently unfinished, with concrete beams sticking out of the sides and low-quality, unfaced brickwork.

She was glad she had treated herself to one of the little yellow taxi-vans that the City Corporation was trying to phase out. The driver began telling her how he had come from Liaoning province to find work as a skilled mechanic and had ended up driving this vehicle.

"... It's still better than back there," he said over the whine of the underpowered little engine. "There's so little work, and it's getting worse as they close down all the loss-making factories. Every time I go back another place has shut."

She made a sympathetic comment back, then lapsed into silence. The driver responded by putting on a tape of Western rock. She was amused by the music; it contrasted with the pendant hanging from the rearview mirror, with the pandalike face of Chairman Mao on it—a statement of fashion, not of political allegiance—and the slogan painted on the dashboard in front of her: "When you take a guest somewhere, do it with a piece of your heart," a slogan usually attributed to Confucius.

Rosina tried to imagine Confucius, Mao, and a rock musician actually sitting in this cramped little vehicle together. *Only in Beijing!* she said to herself.

It was only when the van reached the actual address that she suddenly, out of nowhere, felt afraid. Maybe the driver sensed this, as he asked, "D'you want me to wait?" adding that he wouldn't get a fare back from here, anyway.

"That would be kind. I'd like that very much."

"Hao." Okay.

She thought of Yuchang, forgave the young woman her ignorance in a moment, and wished she had come with her on this mission.

But Yuchang hadn't. Rosina was alone.

So she left the taxi, and its music and Mao and Confucius, and crossed to block 86. The stairwell stank of urine; half the lights were out; two thirds of the way up she passed a gangly teenager who stared at her with ill-concealed suspicion.

Flat 372.

She knocked at the door. No reply. Somewhere else, a door slammed and someone let out a stream of oaths. *Cao* this, *jiba* that . . . Language in a busy hospital wasn't always quite what Rosina had been taught in the Young Pioneers, but there was a viciousness behind this cursing voice, a viciousness directed almost as strongly at the speaker himself as at the person on the receiving end. She glanced down gratefully at the little yellow square of the taxi roof.

"Yeah?" A young woman had opened the door.

"Er, I'm looking for Cheng Leiming," said Rosina.

The young woman scowled. "Don't know that name," she said, then broke into a big broad smile. "Want to come in?"

"Oh. Yes . . . thank you."

The woman showed her into a room with a tatty sofa, an ancient Panda black-and-white TV on a wooden box, and a cassette player sitting in a corner, with a cassette of Dou Wei's angry rock beside it. And nothing else, apart from some papers strewn over the floor.

"Yeah, it's a mess," said the woman, grinning with embarrassment. "I try to keep it tidy, but the guys just screw it up again."

"Guys?"

"Xu and Huang. We share this place. Xu might know—what was the guy's name you were looking for?"

Rosina repeated the name, which brought on more headshaking from the woman.

"Sit down, anyway," she added. "Tea?"

Rosina accepted. The sofa was as comfortless as it was unsightly.

"It's nice to see a new face," the woman went on. "It gets so boring here during the day. The guys are out at work. I lost my job awhile back; I've no money to go out. All this talk about economic progress—I wish I could see some of it. Tell me about this Cheng."

Rosina knew she shouldn't, but she found herself telling the whole story—from Julie's disappearance to the murder of the Golden Master.

The young woman sat and listened, nodding from time to time. "Xu mentioned a guy here who went crazy," she said at the end of her guest's narrative. "He went off to a farm in the end."

"A farm?"

"Not the one your Julie's gone to. His family found him a place where someone would look after him and he could do a bit of work. It's a really sad story. Xu's always rude about the crazy guy, as if it was his fault somehow. That's not fair. It's not crazy people's fault they're crazy."

"I'd be very grateful if you could tell me the address."

The woman looked at Rosina with a sudden new look: suspicion. "You're not from the authorities, are you?"

"I've not been lying to you," Rosina said firmly, and her hostess's old look returned.

"Good. I just needed to be sure. I don't want the dogs coming after the poor guy and locking him up just because he's crazy. They do that, you know. *Keep the city clean!* They're bastards. They ought to try living on no money for a while instead of lining their pockets."

Rosina simply nodded.

"I'll ask Xu when he gets back," the woman continued as they began to drink the tea. "Have you got an address?"

"Best to contact me at work," Rosina said instinctively, and wrote it down.

"I've always fancied nursing," said the woman. "Helping people, that's what we're supposed to do with our lives, isn't it? Not go around bashing them up for being poor or mad, like the dogs do."

Rosina nodded again, and began telling the woman about training programs the hospital ran. When she finished her tea, she said thank you and, mindful of the taxi waiting below, that she had to go.

A letter, in neat, correct characters, arrived on the ward two days later.

Dear Mrs. Wang, it read, *It took a bit of persuading to get Xu to tell me where Cheng had gone, but I finally managed. I hope you will do something to help him.* It was signed *Zhang Hui.*

Rosina thought of this woman, and the strange edge-of-society life she led, and wondered if she had had to suffer anything to get this information. She turned the paper over and read the name and address.

Then she consulted her work schedule, took out a pen, and began to write a letter.

A few days later, Rosina and Yuchang rode a suburban train out of the capital. The view through the grimy window was of concrete blocks and dilapidated factories, busy streets and busy people. So much life, going on all around the small capital-center world that Rosina knew and took for granted. After a while, small plots of tilled land began to appear; these grew bigger and the housing compounds smaller, until Rosina reckoned they were in the countryside. The station at which they had to alight was certainly rural enough, with grass growing out of the platform and not a taxi in sight.

For a moment Rosina was at a loss what to do, but then a railway official appeared on the platform. She showed him the address, and the official shook his head—much too far to walk!—then produced a mobile phone and dialed a number. A minute or so later, a lad appeared on a motorbike.

"It's my son's lunch break," the official explained. "He'll take you for five kuai."

Rosina and Yuchang looked at each other for a moment, then Rosina said yes. The lad looked harmless enough, and the bike looked capable of making the journey.

After the first bend, Rosina regretted her decision, but by the end of the trip she'd gotten into the rhythm of swaying with the bike and was enjoying the experience. Perhaps Anzhuang would take her out for a ride sometime.

"I'll pick you up and get you back for the 14:27, if you like," said the young man.

"Yes please," said Yuchang.

"Don't you have to be back at work?" Rosina put in.

"That's, er, flexible," said the young man.

They agreed on the price, and the bike roared off. The two visitors walked in a new, welcome silence up the long, rutted drive of the farm, to an old-fashioned doorway. Rosina knocked, and a man opened the door.

"Who you?" The man had a slight stoop and spoke in a

slurred voice: Yuchang simply looked pained, and the man led them into a courtyard and up to another door, where he bashed his fist against the door, then stood grinning till the door opened. A chubby, round-faced woman greeted them.

"Rosina Lin?"

"That's me."

"Come in. I'm sorry we couldn't send anyone to the station to meet you."

"That's okay." Rosina introduced Yuchang, and the woman led them across to a desk.

"So you want to talk to Xiao Cheng?"

"Yes."

"About this religious group he joined?"

"That's right."

The woman looked Rosina in the eyes. "I can't guarantee you'll get a lot out of him," she said. "But if you do, I'd be interested to find out what happened there."

"He doesn't talk to you about it?"

"No."

"That's odd. He used to be obsessed with the Church."

"He's not a great talker. It's the pills."

"Ah . . . What do you use?"

"My husband buys them. But we can't do without them. Once we ran out and he went crazy."

"When was that?"

"Don't know. Six months ago?"

"And the rest of the time he's on medication?"

"Of course. I suppose you think we're all crooks, trying to make money out of people's illnesses. But the state won't look after them. Families can't. They don't belong to a proper work unit. Who else will care for them? We do our best."

Rosina couldn't disagree. "So he works for his keep?"

"Yes. We get money from the family for the pills, of course. It's a fair deal. You can see we're not rich," the woman added.

Rosina looked around the simple whitewashed room and nodded. Of course, the luxury could be hidden around the corner....

"Let's go and see him," she said.

"Okay. He'll be out at the piggery. He's very good with them," the woman added. "It's people he's not so fond of."

They went out and crossed a yard to a side door. Beyond this, they could hear—and smell—the piggery. Squeals, grunts, and a revolting odor of feces and rotting food. Across another yard and they were there. Brick walls, enclosing little squares of mud, in each of which stood two or three pigs. In one of them, a young man in a torn, mud-caked Mao suit was shoveling shit into a bucket. He moved with a strange robotic motion.

Rosina knew the story at once: "the pills" were heavy tranquilizers. Chlorpromazine, probably: it was widely available now, cheaply if quality control had been evaded somewhere. She doubted Cheng was being correctly monitored for side effects.

But many worse fates could have befallen him.

"Hey! Xiao Cheng!"

He didn't even look up, and the woman had to lead the arrivals around to the side of the pen and shout again. This time, Cheng looked up, with empty eyes. "Yeah . . ."

"There's two ladies to talk to you."

"Ladies . . ." Cheng began nodding his head with a regular, mindless motion.

"They want to talk about the Church."

"Church . . ." said Cheng, then began to recite, in time with his nods, *"Our Kingdom shall stand on a golden mountain. Its palaces will be brilliant and shining. Its forests and gardens will be . . . will be . . . Our Kingdom shall stand on a golden mountain. It palaces will be brilliant and shining. Our kingdom shall stand on a golden mountain. Its palaces will be brilliant and shining. . . ."*

"It's okay," Rosina said suddenly.

"Wait," said the woman. "He might say more."

"No. He won't."

The woman looked at Rosina with evident disappointment. "You've come all the way just to hear this?"

"Our Kingdom shall stand on a golden mountain. Its palaces will be brilliant and shining . . ."

"No, but . . . He never leaves here, does he?"

The woman just laughed.

"I'm sorry," Rosina went on. "We've wasted your time."

The woman looked upset for a moment, but the moment passed. "I wasn't doing anything else, anyway. I was hoping you might be able to help him in some way, seeing as you're from Beijing. But you can't, can you?"

"No," said Rosina. They began trudging back across the yard, the squeals of the pigs slowly diminishing in volume.

"Can I offer you some rice before you go?" the woman asked.

Rosina began to refuse, but her hostess insisted. They sat in her office eating from cheap, brightly colored bowls.

"I don't know what they did to him at that Church," said the woman. "I thought that was all supposed to be superstition, but they're allowed to do what they like to people. We use science, and people criticize us."

Rosina nodded. She felt a shiver of fear—*what they did to him*—though her head told her that Cheng's condition was unlikely to be the result of anything at New Tianjing, being either genetic or caused by something much earlier in life.

Unlikely, but not impossible. Something latent could have been released. . . .

They heard the klaxon of the motorbike at the bottom of the drive.

Rosina got up and, reaching into her shoulder bag for a wallet, gave a couple of ten-yuan notes to the woman. "Buy him something," she said.

Wang kept on reading his way through the reports that Guan had sent over. Bureau Agent Ping had infiltrated the Church last year and attended a number of meetings. The agent had obviously lost interest after a while, failing to detect anything sinister. He was beginning to wonder if the report was actually a fake and, if so, how he could prove it, when the phone rang.

"It's Da here," came the voice. "I've news about your bank inquiry."

He felt a moment of elation.

"D'you want to come up and talk about it?"

No. Elation was misplaced. There was something in the tone of the old man's voice.

"Yes. Of course."

The moment he walked into Da's office, Wang knew his suspicions were right. The veteran fighter had a distant, evasive expression.

"Xiao Wang . . ." The voice was hesitant, too. "The truth is . . . we seem to be experiencing some difficulties."

He knew at once what he should do.

For a moment, he rebelled against that obligation. He would challenge Da; he would force the old man to use more *guanxi* and kick down more doors. He *could* do it: Da was a proud man, and if that pride were used against him . . .

"For a man in his prime to do harm to the old is a sin against Dao," Lao Zi had written two and a half thousand years ago. That maxim was as deeply embedded in Wang as any teachings could be. The younger Chinese, well, maybe they were different. After the Cultural Revolution, and with Western, youth-obsessed ideas blaring at them from all sides, maybe they had lost this wisdom. But that was what the middle-aged detective knew it to be, a loss of wisdom.

"It's not important," he said with a wave of the hands.

Da looked at him not so much with gratitude as pride: he had chosen well in a protégé. Someone who understood the Chinese way.

"Drink tea with me, Young Wang," he said.

15

"His name is Guan," he told Wheels Chai, tracing the character— read as *kwan* in the West—on the palm of his hand. "I want to know about his family, especially if he has relatives in San Francisco."

"Half of China has relatives in San Francisco," Chai said gloomily.

"Relatives about his own age. A brother named Guan Zhou would be ideal. You can do it, Wheels, I know you can."

"It's easy to say that," Chai replied. "It's all the rage now, this positive thinking. *If you believe something, you can make it true.* Pig farts! Just like the Cultural Revolution: if you have enough love for Chairman Mao, you can dig an H-bomb shelter with a tooth-pick. . . . Is it just us Chinese, or is the whole world that stupid?"

Wang was angry now at his friend's mood. "Just do it. That's an order."

Chai glared at the door through which his old colleague had just left. He didn't feel angry but sad.

They didn't fucking understand. None of them did, not really. The pain some mornings; always having to look up when talking to people; the glances you got in the street; the women you wanted to flirt with and maybe even get to bed but just got sympathy from. . . .

He'd made an iron rule for himself, even before leaving hospital, that he wouldn't get like this. He'd found this rule helpful—no, essential—many, many times. Keep looking forward, it told him. It had made him study computers and become bloody good with them. Most people of his age couldn't even turn one on!

But recently he had begun to feel the technology was outpacing him. Younger people assumed everything he had struggled to learn; for them the struggle was with things about which he hardly had a clue. Java, C++ ... The image of a race had begun to haunt his dreams, of seven fit young men crouching in their starting blocks and him in this fucking wheelchair.

Chai rolled himself across to the terminal, switched it on, and clicked on his modem. Then he closed his eyes, and began doing deep *qigong* breaths. Find a solid place inside—well, *re*discover it, as he knew it existed anyway. Feel strong again.

He completed the breaths and returned his attention to the keyboard.

Guan. Family abroad. Where to begin?

Next morning, Wang found a note on his desk.

"I knew you'd do it, Wheels!" he said, even before he'd begun to read it.

It was from Ze, the fingerprint analyst, with an apology for the delay—caused, he explained, by a minor technical hitch:

Item 1. Er Guo Tou bottle. Prints—one set only. Quality: good. No match to anyone at crime scene. Matches to known criminals: poor.

Item 2. Drawer on desk. Prints, several, two separate individuals. Individual One is the same as on Item 1 above; Individual Two matches with prints taken from Wu Zhongxing.

Wang took a moment to realize who this second person was. Young Wu. He went down to see the analyst at once.

"I thought you'd lost interest," said Ze.

"I've been following another line of inquiry. You know what it's like: never enough time to do everything you want."

Ze nodded and handed him a sheet of paper with the prints.

He stared at it. He enjoyed the process of collecting prints but was glad someone else had the job of interpretation. There was an element of arbitrariness in what constituted a "match" that left him uneasy. "Bourgeois individualism," Team-leader Chen would call such doubts.

"I'll run them up on the computer for you," said Ze, crossing to a desk where one of the now-ubiquitous towers and screens sat.

"The left is the print that your colleagues took of Wu Zhong-xing. On the right is the print from the drawer. I'll zoom in to the cores, then we can work outward."

There were eighteen matches, enough for any police authority in the world.

"Is this lad on our records?" he asked.

"No."

"And is the other individual?"

"No."

"You're sure."

"Of course. The computer says so."

"What do you want this time?" said Wu.

"To ask you a few questions," Wang replied.

"I thought you'd already done that."

"I want to ask more."

"Okay."

"Do you know what the Golden Master kept in the bottom drawer in his desk?"

The young man's expression of shock was instant. "No."

"I think you do."

"*No!*"

"We've found two sets of prints on that drawer: the Master's and yours."

"Fucking dogs," said Wu. This anger was new. "You never give up, do you?"

The "dog" felt a tingle of excitement. "Why were your prints on that drawer?"

Wu screwed up his face and began to shake. Then he calmed himself. "He kept alcohol in there."

"Alcohol?"

"He used to drink it occasionally."

"Occasionally?"

"Occasionally. I know you want to drag his name down into the dirt, but you won't be able to."

"I only want to find out the truth," said Wang.

The young man gave a snort of disbelief. "Hong Er was a good man. He tried to help others, which is more than you bastards do. Okay, he wasn't perfect, but who is? Real people, I mean—not those stupid goody-goody heroes we're all supposed to be like."

The Party did insist on endlessly recycling heroes like the model soldier Lei Feng: Wang found this distasteful and embarrassing. But he hadn't come here to discuss youth education policy.

"Why were your prints on the drawer, Wu?"

"Are you going to do me for theft?"

"I'm not sure the Supreme People's Procurator has got time to worry about a few bottles of liquor. But failure to cooperate with the police is a serious offense."

"A few bottles is all I took. I promise. I feel bad enough about that!"

Wang nodded. "Do you know where Hong Er got the drink from?"

"The guy who collected the incense sticks used to give him a few bottles."

Wheels Chai sat and stared at the screen.

He was suddenly aware that he hadn't had a thought for about an hour, that he'd been so engrossed in his work that there had been no room for self-pity and anger. And that results had begun to flow. He'd worked backward, assuming there was a man called Joe Kwan in San Francisco, in his fifties, brother in Beijing. American records were hard to get into but rewarding when you did: plenty of Kwans, enough Joe Kwans. The Chinese end had been harder: easier to access but scrappy.

But now, here he was.

Guan Zhou, aged 54, deserted the motherland 1969 via Xianggang, now living in San Francisco. Brother of Guan Han, Deputy Director of the New Religious Movements section of the Religious Affairs Bureau.

Chai clicked on the printer and the machine began to spew out the information. Then he closed his eyes and imagined that race again. The starter fired his gun, and he was flying forward out of his chair and sprinting like a twenty-one-year-old.

Deputy Director Guan looked worried but wasn't sweating. Yet.

"I trust the files were in order," he said.

"They were," Wang replied. "But they didn't have accounts in them."

Guan stayed cool. "Accounts are kept by the sect themselves."

"They're not, and you know it."

Guan began to look angry.

"We know about your brother, too."

"What about him?"

"Your business connection."

"Is it a crime to have business connections with other countries? I thought we had an 'open door' nowadays."

"It depends what goes through that door."

"I don't think anything illegal goes through that door."

"Incense sticks. Made by sweatshop labor."

"Sweatshop?"

"I know how much New Tianjing gets for its produce, and I

know how much Flying Spirit pays for it the other end. And I know where the money goes."

Deputy Director Guan nodded thoughtfully. "You have a warrant for my arrest on these ridiculous charges?" he said finally.

"Not yet."

"When you have one, let me know, and I'll present myself at whatever police station you ask. With a lawyer, of course." Guan smiled. "My lawyer will insist you provide proof of criminal activity. Things have moved on from the days when people like you could just march in, drag citizens away, and force whatever story you like out of them. It must be very upsetting for you, I'm sure, but that's how it is now. It's called progress." Guan's smile grew. "And of course I shall be making a complaint to your Party Secretary. I don't think this has anything to do with incense sticks and so-called profiteering. It's all about this sister-in-law of yours."

"It's about a lot more than that," Wang began. He was about to utter the word *murder*, but Guan was speaking again.

"Abuse of police power is a serious offense. If you continue to pursue these ridiculous charges, I'll fight back. The West is looking to China to clean up its act, about corruption and about law enforcement. We need another Chen Xitong. You might fulfill that requirement rather well."

The allusion was to a former mayor of Beijing who had been found guilty of corruption and publicly shamed, the latter leading, as it often did in China, to suicide.

It wasn't Wang's courage that failed him at that moment but his conviction. Not the conviction that he was right but the conviction that he could overcome the obstacles Guan would put in his way and *prove* he was right. Did he have any witnesses to Guan's activities?

"The door is there," Guan continued. "If you have any sense, that is the last time you will pass through it."

In the old days . . . But those days had gone. Rosina said that was good, that the old powers of the authorities had been abused.

In his heart, Wang knew she was right. You only needed to look at people like "Xiao" Fei to know that. But on occasions like this . . .

"Consider yourself warned," he said, mustering all his dignity, and left. It was still a humiliating defeat—how could he have gone into the confrontation so poorly armed? He, a lifetime student of Sun Zi?

But he had.

The summons came the next day.

Team-leader Chen was sitting at his desk. "Ah, Xiao Wang . . . I'm sure you know what this is about."

The junior officer just nodded.

Chen smiled. "Secretary Wei and I have been running over the cases in hand, and we feel that this New Church investigation is costing more money and manpower than it's worth. Can you convince me otherwise?"

Wang grinned. He'd been expecting something worse than this. Chen was still clearly overcome with gratitude after that business with the Armed Response Team. He knew what he had to say.

"We have no clear leads at the moment, Chief."

"That is very wise of you, Xiao Wang."

"How could you?" Rosina said.

"There was no alternative."

"So Julie can just rot there? Slave labor, being brainwashed?"

"She made a choice."

"They got at her when she was feeling particularly vulnerable!"

"She'll change her mind. Look at Miss Hu."

"Look at all the other fools who are still there. It's exploitation! Chairman Mao would have sorted those crooks out!"

"I thought I'd never live to hear you say that," said Wang, trying to lighten the conversation.

Rosina paused. She probably hadn't thought that, either. "This is different. This isn't about politics. This is . . . Xianghua. Julie. My little girl."

And Rosina was in tears again, for her own lack of children, for all the things she'd done wrong in "bringing up" her little sister, for her own bad example, for everything wrong with the world.

The Happiness again. Still Wang's favorite form of transport, except in atrocious weather. And today the weather was good. Cold, of course, with frost glistening on the trees and a bright, low sun behind him. So no chance to let the bike rip, but the journey could still be enjoyed. Even the last section, the dirt track up to New Tianjing, now frozen solid.

A familiar figure opened the farmstead door.

"Sister Modesty!"

"Officer Wang! I thought that, now your colleagues have left, we'd not be seeing you again."

"This is just a brief visit. I want a word with Julie, if that's possible."

Modesty frowned. "Fragrant Flower knows nothing about the death of the Golden Master."

He thought of asking the sister *how* she knew that, but somehow he didn't have the passion to any more. "Did you have many dealings with Deputy Director Guan at the bureau?" he asked instead.

"No."

"You don't know how often he came here, for example?"

"No." Modesty frowned again. "He was a friend of the Church. He understood that we were helping people whom other agencies in society had failed to help. Is that bad?"

"No. But when he did come here, how did he make the journey?"

"Same as you. By motorbike."

"His own?"

"I've no idea. You haven't got *Police* on your bike: they're hardly likely to write *Religious Affairs Bureau* on theirs, are they?"

"No . . ." said Wang, adding as an afterthought: "He wasn't here the day of the Master's death, was he?"

"I don't think so," said Modesty.

"But you don't know he wasn't?"

"No. How could I know that?"

Wang shook his head. "I'd like to see Julie," he said.

"You again? What do you want?"

"To see how you are."

"That's a lie. You're here to persuade me to leave. You're wasting your time."

"I'm here to remind you that you have a choice. No one back home is going to criticize you if you return and—"

"*This* is home."

Wang sighed. "D'you have a message for anyone back—in Beijing?"

"No. Well, I do have a message, of course. *Come here! Join us!* But you lot are hardly going to listen to that, are you?"

"I'll pass it on," he said woodenly.

Silence fell.

"Have you ever seen this man here?" he asked, pulling out his wallet and producing a picture of Deputy Director Guan that Chai had gotten from records.

"No," said Julie.

"You're sure?"

"Yes."

He put the photo away. "And you definitely saw the Golden Master's body?"

"Of course. We all did."

"By daylight?"

"No. This time of year we work all daylight hours."

"So you never got a close look at him?"

"I saw all I needed to. It was very inspiring. The Master had found great peace. To die at peace—isn't that something to aim for?"

"You shouldn't be thinking about death at your age."

"Why not?" said Julie.

Wang didn't know how to answer that.

"Have you anything else to say to me, Lao Wang? If not, I'll get back to my work."

He paused for a moment. Had he anything more to say? "Don't forget what I said, Julie. Your home is still there."

"My home is here," Julie replied, then stood up and walked out.

He looked at the door she had closed behind her, then at the slogan up there on the wall.

Come to me all who are burdened down, and I will give you rest.

Why do noble ideas go so wrong?

16

Julie stood in a queue outside the Great Hall of Tranquility. As usual, she was looking forward to this evening's Gathering: because she enjoyed the words of the Master, because the Gatherings always seemed to inculcate a real feeling of unity, and because—she had to admit—these were the only times she really got warm. December, it was now—"Great Snow" in the old Chinese solar calendar.

The doors opened, and the faithful began to file in. *The faithful* was a new term introduced by the Master, to make extra clear the difference between believers and nonbelievers—a difference that was going to matter more and more as the third millennium got under way.

So soon!

Julie found a place to squat on the floor and said a prayer while waiting for the Master to appear on the stage. "Dear Brother Hong, make me worthy of the new era that is coming. May I meet its challenge, whatever that challenge is. . . ."

"My children, welcome!" The words rang out around the beams of the Great Hall. "Let us say my Brother Hong Xiuquan's Prayer of a Thousand Characters."

The Master had started referring to Hong Xiuquan as *his* brother a couple of weeks back: a few people had queried this, but the Master had said that he had been instructed to say this in a dream.

Julie began to recite the familiar phrases.

"Our Kingdom will stand on a golden mountain. Its palaces will be brilliant and shining . . ."

It was so beautiful. How had she ever lived without this vision in her heart?

"... *Cleansed and purified, the chosen ones within shall fast and bathe, respectful and devout in worship, dignified and serene in prayer.*"

The Master finished the prayer, stared out over his audience for a moment, then began his address.

"My children, I have a confession to make. I have been guilty of doubting my mission. The third millennium is nearly upon us, but the wickedness of the world seems as powerful as ever. Our beloved Golden Master has been taken from us. We find ourselves surrounded by demons; some of their vilest lapdogs have even entered our sacred home. Why? I found myself asking. Why?

"My children, I confess freely to you now that I have recently knelt every day before the sacred pictures and begged the Lord Ye Huo Hua to send me a sign that all was still right. And last night, I went to my cell and prayed deep into the night, then lay down to sleep—there, in my meditation cell. And, my children, a most wonderful thing happened. The Lord Ye Huo Hua gave me that sign!"

Several people in the audience, including Julie, burst into spontaneous applause at this point.

"My children, I was taken by a great chariot, up into the presence of Brother Ye Su, Brother Hong, and the Lord Ye Huo Hua. And their faces were stern. 'How are my people?' the Lord Ye Huo Hua asked me, and I told them that we were weary with waiting and with the tricks of the demon dogs. Then Brother Hong said to me, 'Do you think the demons have more power than I do?' and I said, 'No, of course not!' Then Brother Ye Su asked me, 'Why do you doubt our purpose, then?'

"My children, I felt so foolish that I threw myself on the floor and begged them to forgive my having doubted Heaven's wisdom and kindness! Brother Hong told me to get to my feet and to return to earth to do the duty I had been called for. And the Lord Ye Huo Hua said, 'If my people are suffering, it is in order to make them strong.' 'The third millennium is about to dawn,' he told me. 'The great challenge is about to begin. I have been preparing mankind for this moment since I threw Yan Luo and his hordes out of Heaven, since I sent my son Ye Su to preach to the Western barbarians, since I sent your beloved brother Hong Xiuquan to lead my chosen people. Are you telling me you aren't strong enough, Hong San?'

"My children, I stood up at once and told him that with his strength I could meet any challenge. And he said to me, 'Take twelve chosen ones and put them to the ultimate test, and I will give to all who pass *all* the strength I gave to my sons! I will raise them up and make them gods among men, ready for the millennium."

The Master paused, to let this information sink in, then said slowly and quietly: "My children, we are every one of us chosen, but from among us will arise twelve who will make a leap of faith so great that they shall receive *all* the strength of the Lord Ye Huo Hua! Twelve mortals, who on the eve of the new millennium will become as sons and daughters of God." He gazed around at his audience. "Twelve of you have this faith. You must stand up and name yourselves now."

There was a stunned silence.

"Listen to the voice of your own hearts," said the Master. "Twelve of you are being called!"

The silence continued, then a girl was on her feet. "I can hear the voice!" she cried out.

Then another girl was doing the same, then Young Wu, then another young man, then . . . When eleven had thus announced themselves, silence fell again.

"The Lord Ye Huo Hua is calling," said the Master.

Silence.

"I am called!"

The voice was Julie Lin's.

"Remember that you have not chosen yourselves," said the Master. "The Lord Ye Huo Hua has done this. Come forward, chosen ones."

The rest of the faithful shuffled about to make paths for the twelve to make their ways to the stage. As she walked forward, Julie expected to feel exhilaration. But instead she simply felt what she now knew she'd been feeling ever since meeting Brother Valiant: the simple impulsion of destiny.

"I don't know what was wrong with the old Dong Zhi festival," complained Wang Anzhuang as he put a Christmas card from Team-leader Chen up on the dresser. (Chen! A couple of years ago, the chief had been "standing firm against Westernization" now he was sending these things!) "Dong Zhi used to be fun. My grandmother used to make those rice dumplings with the sugar on them."

Rosina nodded. "My grandma used to draw plum blossoms— one a day, from Dong Zhi to the start of spring. Otherwise, she said, winter would last forever!"

The policeman was amused by this: go back two generations, and his and his wife's family could not have been more different. The Wang and Peng families had scraped survival from the harsh land (and even harsher landlords) of Shandong province and had celebrated midwinter with food. The Lins and Taos, cultured, urban, aspiring, and never hungry, had welcomed Dong Zhi with pictures and poetry.

"Of course, I don't see why the two festivals can't be combined," she went on. "It doesn't have to be all-out war between old and new, between Chinese and Western."

"That's fine, till we get to New Year."

"Well, yes, of course. We'll never lose our New Year!"

"I hope not," he said gloomily. "Look at all this fuss that's being made about the millennium."

"Ai, that's just a gimmick."

For both husband and wife, the millennium meant the same as had the fiftieth anniversary of the People's Republic back in

October: work. On the night of December 31, many Beijingers were planning to converge on Tiananmen Square to enjoy the great fireworks display they were being promised. The capital's police would be busy patrolling this event, and the capital's hospitals would be busy waiting for results of excessive celebration.

Rosina in particular was glad of this: she knew where her thoughts would have been otherwise.

Wang sat down next to her and put an arm around her, Western style. (Why not? Nobody else was looking.) For a moment, she tensed: she still felt somewhere inside that Anzhuang could have done more for Julie. But she was beginning to tire of this feeling. She didn't know *what* he could have done, and she suddenly felt an overpowering need to be touched and held. She relaxed into his arms. This was right; this was the way forward.

The phone began to ring.

"Oh, leave it," she said.

It kept on ringing.

And ringing.

It might be Julie, Rosina thought. She reached out for it.

"Wei? Oh, Miss Hu . . ."

The Golden Pearl Teahouse was Miss Hu's choice for rendezvous. It was an almost exact mirror image of the Y2K. Its exterior demanded attention, with a huge red lantern over its plate-glass door and bright yellow fairy lights strung out from the building to (and all around) the locust tree that grew on the pavement outside. Its interior . . . well, the management was waiting for the place to make enough money to do that up properly: customers sat beneath white walls at simple wooden tables, drinking from the same variety of stained mugs that they had used when the teahouse was a shack.

Rosina found Miss Hu sitting in a corner, reading Liu Shaoqi's *How to Be a Good Communist*.

"Mrs. Wang. Sit down." She handed Rosina a tatty green menu. "The ordinary green tea is nice, or I can recommend the Pu'er. A southern taste, I know, but they do it well here."

"Just the green for me," Rosina replied, suddenly very nervous. "Now, this news from New Tianjing..."

Miss Hu summoned a waitress and placed her order. Then she tidied Liu Shaoqi away into her handbag. "The news is not good, I'm afraid."

"Tell me!"

"The new Master seems to be becoming more and more extreme in his views. The old Master believed it would take time to get his message through to the majority of people. He used the image of those changing lines in the old Chinese yijing, the first line being the people—"

"Has something happened to Julie?" Rosina cut in.

Miss Hu frowned at the interruption. "Yes. She's been ... chosen."

"Chosen? For what?"

"I was coming to that."

"Well, come to it now," said Rosina, then, realizing how that sounded, added, "I'm sorry. What does 'chosen' mean?"

"The new Master has gathered a group of special disciples around him. Twelve: that was the number that Brother Ye Su took. They now spend all their time shut away from everybody else."

"Doing what?"

"My contact isn't sure. Meditation? Qigong? Reading the sacred texts?"

"What for?" Rosina asked with increasing dread.

"Again, I don't know. Sorry."

"No. Don't apologize. I'm very grateful...." Rosina's voice died away as a new thought struck her. "Is this something to do with the millennium?"

"I don't know," said Miss Hu, as the tea arrived in simple white mugs with lids on.

"It's days away . . ." Rosina said, half to Miss Hu and half to
herself.

"I was hoping you might be able to have a word with your husband," Miss Hu said hesitantly. "He might be able to . . . I don't know . . . do something."

Rosina grinned with embarrassment. Even when she had been at her most critical of Anzhuang's dealings with New Tianjing, she would never have admitted the fact to a stranger. "Like what? He's done all he can, and more. It's . . . political."

"Oh," said Miss Hu.

Rosina took the lid off her mug and watched the steam rising up into the air, as elegant and calm as a willow in a classic painting. Meanwhile, emotions were raging inside her. Then suddenly she felt calm, too. The complete calm of decision.

"Miss Hu, I want you to tell me all you know about New Tianjing."

"Its history?"

"No. Its layout. Its timetable. Where the entrances and exits are; what all the rooms are for; whether there are any alarm systems; what people wear; what happens at what times . . ."

Miss Hu looked puzzled.

"If Julie won't come out, I must go in," Rosina explained.

"I really don't recommend such a course of action, Mrs. Wang. Things have changed so much since I was there—"

"Just tell me, Miss Hu. Please."

Silence fell.

"Okay," Miss Hu said finally.

17

Rosina stared out of the bus window. A donkey cart! When had she last seen one of those? Then she looked down again at the first of the maps Miss Hu had drawn for her.

"Wufang village!" said the driver.

She wasn't afraid. She wondered if at some time on this mission she would be, but now she was too concerned with succeeding to feel fear. She *was* worried, however. Two problems in particular. One: how to get into the farmstead. The easiest way would have been to attach herself to a work party and just march in, but apparently there was little outdoor work going on at the moment. So . . . improvise! Problem two was, once in, how to find Julie's quarters. Julie had been in one of the dormitories, but since being "chosen" she had apparently moved elsewhere.

Then of course, there was the little matter of persuading Julie to come with her.

She frowned at the thought of these difficulties—then told herself, as she had done a hundred times already, that she would find a way to do what was necessary because she had to.

The bus began to slow down. Rosina had no baggage: the only item she had toyed with bringing along was Anzhuang's Type 77 revolver. But to do that would have involved telling him what she was doing. Also, she had no idea how to use the thing and no will to do so: it might have had bluffing value, that was all. She began to make her way down the center of the bus.

"They're mainly youngsters," she heard someone say. "Crazy, the lot of them!"

Nobody else got off.

The bus drove on, leaving Rosina alone with the cutting December wind that comes howling down from Manchuria. No time to stand around.

Miss Hu's second map was typically thorough, and Rosina reached the farmstead without incident apart from having to cross a wide, fast-flowing river by a bridge that was far too rickety for her taste. At her first view of New Tianjing, she retreated into some tall, sheltering maize stalks and simply glared at the buildings. Then she began to follow the path Miss Hu had highlighted, one that led by a winding, well-concealed way to the back of the farm. She was soon by the barns, with only a strip of open ground about twenty meters long between her and the first building. She paused to take a deep breath, to look around and listen for any activity.

Nobody.

She was about to dart across the open space when she heard a surge of singing behind her. She cursed and scurried back to the nearest maize. The singing stopped, but a minute or so later a column of exhausted-looking people trudged into view. She was relieved to see that Miss Hu's information about clothing had been as accurate as her maps. Workboots; baggy blue peasant jackets with big hoods sewn onto them to keep the weather at bay: just what she'd come dressed in.

The column burst into song again: deep, manly voices.

Now the mists begin to lift,
Heaven plans an age of heroes.

When the last singer had trudged past, Rosina got to her feet, made to move forward and join them—and tripped on a tussock of grass. For a second she lay, terrified they would hear the elephantine noise she'd made. But nobody even turned: their singing had been too loud, or they were all too tired. And then she remembered a piece of advice Miss Hu had given her: *Avoid the males at all cost.* "Segregation is strict; break the rule and you'll stand out a mile." She turned to the tussock and thanked it.

The work party disappeared into a barn, then reemerged and entered the main body of the farmstead by a door. This closed behind the last worker; she listened for the sound of a lock but didn't hear anything. So she gave them five minutes, then took another deep breath and tiptoed out into the open space.

Nobody watching.

A few swift paces and she was by the door, turning the handle. It *was* locked.

"Aiya!" Rosina felt her first moment of fear, then of anger, then of—

"Sister!"

The voice was calling from a way off, but Rosina knew it was for her. She turned to see a figure approaching.

The first real test. Stay calm.

"Sister!" the voice repeated.

"Yes . . ." Rosina replied, keeping her head lowered, as Miss Hu had said "the faithful" were required to do.

The owner of the voice was close now, and looking at her carefully. "It's Fragrant Flower, isn't it?"

"Yes," Rosina replied instinctively.

"Ah! How are things in the atrium?"

"Good," Rosina replied. "I feel—very inspired."

"You're very brave," said the woman.

Rosina smiled. "Yes. I am." It felt good.

The woman stared again. "You've changed a lot since coming here. You've become—harder, more resourceful. That's good. That's how we will all need to be in the new millennium!"

"Yes," said Rosina.

The woman advanced and turned the handle. "Aiya! I'd forgotten they've started locking this now. We'll have to go 'round the front."

Rosina's heart sank—but she had no alternative. They walked around the edge of the stead in silence, then the woman began knocking on the front door. A young man opened it.

"Let us in. I've been checking the net in the pond, and Fragrant Flower here has been—"

"They sent me out to clear my head," Rosina cut in, though with her eyes still lowered. "I got this terrible ache."

The young man smiled. "I hope it's better now. We need you."

Rosina smiled back, and followed the woman down a corridor and across a quadrangle. Miss Hu had again been spot-on with her instructions: every room was exactly where she'd been told it was. The room reserved for private prayer, for example.

"I need to reflect a little," said Rosina, and the woman just looked at her with admiration, then was gone.

Miss Hu had also given precise details of the timetable at New Tianjing. A meal at six, the evening's Gathering an hour later. Rosina's original plan had been to attend these, hoping Julie would, too, then to follow her sister and catch her on her own. Now that people were beginning to mistake her for Julie, however, this plan was becoming more risky. But she couldn't think what else to do.

So she sat in the stark little room and stared at the twin pictures of Hong Xiuquan and Brother Ye Su and began worrying, then told herself that worry was the enemy of action and that as long as she stayed confident she could pull this off.

"You are very brave," she said to herself.

The wait seemed to last forever, but finally the noise of feet and voices and the ring of a bell told Rosina it was time for the evening meal. She opened the door of her cell and tagged onto a group of people heading for the dining hall. Miss Hu had told her the procedure: stand in line; pick up utensils from the shelves on the left; accept one ladleful of rice and one of gruel; sit anywhere. (She had recommended one particularly dark corner.) Silence was observed while eating anyway; no need to worry about conversation.

Things went just as promised. Once seated, everyone around Rosina ate with the intensity of the very hungry. The few times

she dared look at anyone's eyes, they seemed glazed over. With
brainwashing or with simple hunger?

Julie, however, was nowhere to be seen. So the chosen even *ate* separately. In "the atrium"? Rosina wondered where this was— no such place existed on Miss Hu's map—and what she would do if neither Julie nor the "Master" turned up at the Gathering. Then a voice cut into the silence, intoning a prayer of thanks for this humble meal, and benches began to scrape on the floor. A short break—Miss Hu had recommended returning to the meditation cell—then there would be another chance to spot Julie.

"Are you new?" said a woman as they passed through the exit.

"I've been here a week," Rosina improvised.

"Oh. I haven't seen you about."

"I haven't seen you."

"Why not?"

"I don't know. I guess I keep my own company. After all the trouble I've been through, with the trial and all that..."

Rosina thought this might scare her off, but naturally it had the opposite effect.

"Oh, what trial?"

"Nothing really," said Rosina, backtracking quickly. "I was set up by the police. I'd rather not talk about it."

This worked. "Those bastards," the woman said. "Still, they'll pay for it in the end. They have all sold their souls to Yan Luo, you know."

"Yes..." Rosina said noncommittally.

"They, and the demon officials, and the demon whores who sleep with them, will all be committed to the flames of hell. And soon, too! Makes you feel better, doesn't it?"

"In a way."

Rosina managed to lose herself in the crowd again, then to regain the meditation room, where she settled down to wait another half hour or so.

You are very brave, she muttered to herself. Her mantra.

It didn't work. The fear caught her by surprise: it was suddenly deep in her guts, where her strongest passions of desire and love and anger came from. She tried to banish it, but it wouldn't go away.

"You must go through with this," she told herself. "The crazier these guys are, the more important it is to get to Julie away."

"And the more dangerous it will be," the fear seemed to say.

The boom of another bell and the sound of shuffling feet told her that the Gathering was about to begin.

The Great Hall of Tranquility was full, and an air of expectancy had replaced the listlessness of the evening meal. Rosina found herself a lot nearer the front of the hall than she would have wished—but the flow of incomers had taken her that way. She told herself to make the best of it, and settled down in the squatting position Miss Hu had recommended, legs akimbo, head bowed, and hands crossed on her chest. A kind of calmness came, then, and she began to wait for the next event.

And wait.

And wait.

She made herself think of Julie, of how much she cherished her younger sister. And of Mama and Baba, and how they were relying on her. Then a terrible, unwanted thought broke in, of the distress they would feel if their *older* daughter got herself killed or held hostage or something equally awful. Then she found herself thinking of the deceitful note she had left Anzhuang, claiming her parents were upset and that she was taking them out to a restaurant to cheer them up, and of how only Miss Hu knew of her plan, and knew nothing of its timing.

You stupid woman, she told herself. *Rash, irresponsible, brainless . . .*

A gong sounded. Rosina looked up at the dais: a door at the back opened, and a group of men and women in silver robes emerged from it. At their head was Julie.

She'll see me, Rosina thought at once. But Julie's eyes were lowered.

Keep it that way, Julie.

A man in a silver robe—the Master, it had to be—followed, and then two women. When the second of these stepped into the light, Rosina just managed to stifle an expression of astonishment. The second woman's face!

"That's crazy," she told herself—then glanced up again, and the likeness was even stronger. Take that face, dull the eyes, and twist the mouth a little. Harden, for we're mapping the face onto a man who does hard, open-air labor.

"My children!" The Master began to speak. "Prophets of old spoke of the new millennium. Brother Ye Su spoke of it. Brother Hong Xiuquan spoke of it. My beloved brother Hong Er led us to its brink before the Lord Ye Huo Hua called him home."

Crazy Cheng.

One of the women on the platform, right next to this bizarre orator and a few meters away from Julie, had to be Crazy Cheng's mother. Those eyes, the shape of the nose, her cheeks—everything!

So was that the solution to the murder of Hong Er? Revenge?

"Didn't my Brother Hong say, *The true doctrine is different from the doctrine of the world?*" asked the Master.

The cult *had* destroyed this woman's son, and she'd gotten her own back on the cult leader.

So what was she doing up on that stage?

Well, the answer was obvious—the same thing Rosina was doing down here. Pretending to belong, in order to fulfill family loyalties. For a moment Rosina longed to meet this woman and share her secret with her. Then she told herself, no. Anyone that obsessed could be dangerous. If Cheng's mother were still here, it was for a reason. Revenge on more Church leaders? And if she thought Rosina was going to get in her way . . .

Rosina grimaced as this new, extra fear entered her mind. As if the increasingly obvious insanity of the man center stage wasn't terrifying enough! She glanced up at Julie, and at the look of rapt attentiveness that now suffused her face, and felt appalled, help-less—and more determined than ever to get her out of the place.

The Gathering seemed to go on for hours. The Master ranted on about demons, about the forces of good and evil, about parallels between 1999 and the time of the Taiping Rebellion, about the spiritual poison of communism, about the coming millennium. This latter would bring with it a crisis unparalleled in human history, but this crisis would in turn bring forth a tiny group of iron-willed individuals who would lead the righteous to salvation.

"If we have faith, we are undefeatable!" the Master bellowed. "If we lack faith, we will be seized by the demons and dragged to hell along with the deluded ones. To fly with glory or to sink and drown in shame: we have the choice. It is a choice we must make, actively, with our whole being—but the Lord Ye Huo Hua is generous."

Here he turned to the row of silver-robed acolytes of whom Julie appeared to be a leader.

"The Chosen Ones will lead the way for us. They have faith already, but it will be multiplied ten thousandfold. They will be-come as strong as mountains, as deep as oceans—for you, my children. Theirs shall be the strength when your strength wavers; theirs shall be the depth when your faith feels shallow. The Lord Ye Huo Hua has selected them to be the iron instruments of his purpose!"

Julie was positively glowing with pride. No wonder: nobody had ever flattered her like this. Or, Rosina reflected ruefully, had ever expected as much of her as this. But this was no time for recriminations. This "Master" was obviously crazy; the woman standing next to him was probably a murderess.

The oration was followed by the singing of some hymns—the weary-looking youngsters all around her weren't able to make much noise, so Rosina just pretended to have lost her voice, and nobody noticed—and the recitation of a prayer. Then the gong sounded again, and the Master and the "chosen ones" filed out of the room, followed by the two women. Then everyone else stood up and moved slowly to the rear exit. Rosina joined the shuffling mass but, once outside, separated herself and made for the side entrance of the hall, the one used by the ceremony participants.

By the time she got there, there was nobody to follow. Rosina cursed. She looked around: there was only one way the chosen ones could have gone from there, down a long corridor that Miss Hu seemed to have missed from her map. This had to lead to the atrium. She began to follow it, aware, suddenly, of the noise of her booted feet. Then, when she quietened her footsteps, of her thumping heart.

There were some doors, but none seemed to have light coming from under it. She pressed her ear against one to check if there was anyone inside but heard nothing. The end of the corridor grew ever closer, and for a moment she thought that this was a dead end. But, no, there was a door to the left, behind which she could now hear voices. She pushed at it, and it opened into another corridor.

"The body is gross, Sister. It is the spirit that has wings. . . ."

"And the Lord Ye Huo Hua can accomplish anything. . . ."

She'd recognize that voice anywhere.

Rosina paused, then, to ponder her options. She wanted to get Julie alone. But would she get a chance? Was *this* her best chance, to walk into the room now and simply tell Julie to come with her? But if Julie refused . . . If she waited, where should she hide?

She stood, prevaricating.

Move in on her now!

No, wait.

She began to walk toward the door.

She heard the footsteps the moment before the corridor light went on. Almost immediately afterward, she felt a hand on her shoulder.

"Don't move!" said a voice. A female voice, Rosina noted with some, though not much, relief.

"Now turn around slowly."

That small relief vanished as Rosina turned to face the mother of Crazy Cheng.

"I thought it was you. I know everyone here, and your face is strange. Go and stand under that light."

Rosina was so frightened that she obeyed.

"Yes . . ." said the woman. "Not that strange. Come to see your sister, have you?"

Rosina swallowed. *You are very brave.* "You have a problem with that? A woman talking to her own sister?"

"You'd better come with me," Mrs. Cheng simply said.

"Why?"

"Don't argue. It's for your own good."

Rosina's resistance seemed to collapse. This was just too much. She found herself following this woman—this woman who'd probably killed someone and was probably planning to kill at least one other, maybe more—back down the corridor, across a quadrangle, down another corridor.

They reached a door, and the woman opened it. "Go in," she whispered.

Rosina did as she was told. As the door closed, the thought crossed her mind that she might never see it open again. But she did nothing.

"Sit down. Make yourself comfortable." The tone in the woman's voice had eased. "My name is Modesty," she added.

"Oh. I'm Rosina. Rosina Lin." This was ridiculous!

"I know. I've met your husband. He's a decent man."

"Yes. He is . . ."

"And you seem to be a decent woman. It was you who gave money for my son, wasn't it?"

"I . . ."

"No need to be ashamed, Mrs. Wang. That was a good deed. Our religion says it is deeds like that which ensure the soul's ascent to heaven. Or it used to say that, anyway."

Now it was Modesty Cheng's turn not so much to lose her train of thought as to have it swamped by emotion: she fell silent, screwed up her face, muttered something under her breath—then regained her composure. "You are wise to worry about your sister," she continued. "But I don't think this rescue plan of yours will work. Were you planning to persuade Fragrant Flower, or do you have any methods of compulsion?"

"Just persuade. She has a lot of respect for my views. And our parents are old, and very upset by this."

Modesty allowed herself a smile. "Your sister is a passionate young woman and has thrown herself into the Church's activities with great commitment."

Rosina nodded.

"But I have no better suggestions for you, Mrs. Wang. Things are going wrong here. I'm old enough to remember the start of the Cultural Revolution. There was a kind of hysteria that slowly crept over China. It was like a madness, a whole nation going mad because one man was. That is happening here now."

Another nod.

"The new Master—he's wrong in the head," Modesty continued. "He says God talks to him, but I don't believe that. But I don't believe he's deliberately lying to us, either. He believes himself. That's why he's so dangerous. I used to think he was just making it up to gain power; people did that in the old Taiping days, you know. But he believes his own delusions."

"So why are you staying here?"

"I've nowhere else to go. And I hope that one day this man will leave, and we can get back to how it was in the days of the old Master."

"D'you think he killed the old Master?"

"Maybe." Modesty smiled. "You thought I did, didn't you? I could see it in your eyes."

"No. I, er . . ."

"Revenge, for the state my lovely son is in?"

"Well, I . . ."

Modesty Cheng shook her head. "The Church did Leiming good. He was fine as a little boy, but in his teens . . . He began hearing voices; he'd have sudden fits of anger—all sorts of strange things. He was put in a home, but that closed down and there was nowhere for him to go, so he came here to be with me. And I think his time here was a happy one: a lot of things that the world thinks mad we think quite reasonable. But in the end, the illness got the better of him, and he had to go. The old Master spent time and money finding that farm for him. He even made sure there was money for him to have medicine." She paused. "Do you think ill of me, Mrs. Wang, for not looking after him more?"

Rosina found she couldn't answer.

"I see you do," Modesty continued. "But I have a calling here. The Lord Ye Huo Hua summoned me to serve him here, and I had to obey that call. Does that make sense?"

Rosina thought of her initial decision to go into nursing. On some days, that seemed crazy, but she still kept at it. "In a way."

Modesty smiled. "My advice to you is to return to Beijing and get your husband to come here with some other police and simply arrest your sister. It's the only way you'll get her out of here."

"No. You know that won't work. He can't—and I must talk to her, anyway. Getting her out by force won't change anything."

"No," said Modesty.

Silence fell.

"Will you help me?" Rosina asked.

"There's little I can do," Modesty replied. But she took out a pen and began to draw a map in a slow, delicate hand. "They sleep here. Men in this room, women here. I don't know who has which bunk. I have a key to the atrium, too," she added. "I'm not meant to, but I kept a copy."

She went to a shelf and took down a Thermos with a picture of a kitten on it. From inside it she pulled a metal key that she presented to Rosina.

"If anyone asks you where you got this . . ." Modesty began.

Rosina spotted the real fear in her voice and nodded. "I'll say my husband took a copy when he was investigating."

"And the map . . ."

"I'll memorize it." Rosina stared at it, then handed it back.

"Thank you," said Modesty. "Give them an hour to put their lights out and go to sleep. Wait in the meditation room till then. You know where that is?"

"Yes."

"You've come well prepared. Miss Hu's doing?"

Rosina didn't reply.

"You should go now," said Modesty. "I wish you good luck."

One of the worst hours of her life later, Rosina made her way across the quad to the atrium door, inserted the key in the lock, and turned it. It opened noiselessly. Down the first corridor; through the door she'd been through before; twenty paces; door on the right. A door that opened at a push. Bunk beds made a lattice outline against the faint moonlight of the window.

She and Julie had shared a bedroom as kids, and even the shape her little sister assumed when asleep was instantly recognizable. And comforting: the New Church of the Heavenly Kingdom hadn't totally changed her personality.

She reached out and touched the sleeping young woman. Julie stirred; stirred, then sat up.

Rosina hissed at her to be quiet.

"I want to talk," she said.

For a moment, Julie was confused. Then she understood and got out of bed and followed her sister out into the corridor.

"What do you want?" she whispered the moment they were there.

"For you to come home. Mama and Baba are going crazy."

"That's because they don't understand. When they do . . ."

"No. *You* don't understand. Hua, there's danger here."

"No. There's danger outside. In your world."

"It's not *my* world. It's *the* world. This place is dangerous." Rosina paused. Should she report what Modesty had said? "I've seen documents about this Master of yours," she lied instead.

"They'll be forgeries. By demons."

"There aren't any demons!"

"There are, Sister. I've seen them. And your husband is a slave to them." Julie shook her head. "I'm not saying he's a wicked man, but—he's been misled."

"Oh, Julie . . ." Rosina was at a loss for words. "You must come. Please come home!"

Julie said nothing for what seemed like ages, then she broke into a big smile and threw her arms around her sister.

"Dear Rosina!"

Rosina's heart exulted. Of course it had worked! She'd known that once she and Julie were face to face, the young woman would know how much she was loved and see sense.

"I can't leave here," Julie went on. "But you can leave Beijing. Come and join us! That would be so lovely. So much is happening! I can't get you chosen, of course, but all the faithful will be saved from the catastrophe when it happens. Oh, Rosina, I'm so happy for you!"

"No," Rosina said. "No! You're coming with me. Now." She began tugging at Julie's nightgown, and Julie called out, "Let go!"

A voice rang out at the end of the corridor: "Who's there?"

"It's me. Fragrant Flower."

"Who with?"

Suddenly Julie pushed Rosina away. "Run!" she hissed, then called out, "Nobody."

"Yes there is."

For a second, Rosina stood her ground.

"Run!" Julie hissed again, with even greater emphasis. Then she began to shout "Help!"

"It's a demon!" someone shouted.

Rosina turned and ran. Through the first door. Through the second. (She was halfway across the quadrangle before she realized she should have locked it behind her.) The fear was master now.

There was a way out that Miss Hu had shown. In the back quadrangle, a huge earthenware tub stood against a wall. You

could use it to scale the wall, then jump down onto the other side.
Rosina ran into this rear quad and spotted the tub at once, despite
the feeble moonlight. She was across to it in a moment, up on it
in another moment, then up on the wall, then over the other side,
rolling in the mud, then on her feet and sprinting. To the road.
Where was the road?

Behind her, lights were going on all over the farmstead.

"It's escaped!" cried a voice.

"Don't let it get away!" cried another.

It, she had become.

"Kill the demon!"

A rectangle of light appeared in the angular silhouette of the
farmstead. People appeared. Rosina heard the sound of an engine
being started.

She glanced at the maps, but they suddenly made no sense.
She had to use intuition. There was a path ahead, which she took.
It ended almost at once in a maize field, which she began blundering through, the maize poking at her, like little imps armed
with pikes.

Then she was out in open land again; she stopped for a moment to get her bearings; those vehicle headlights must be the main
road. They seemed a world away, but at least she was headed in
the right direction. How far away were they? A kilometer? Two
kilometers?

"It went that way!" someone shouted.

It.

Get across this field before they see you!

Rosina began to run again, mud now grabbing at her feet.
She was almost halfway across the field when she realized that at
the far end there was a ditch.

I'll jump it, she told herself—till she reached the bank. It was
the river she had crossed on her way here. At least five meters
wide. Five meters of swirling, busy liquid darkness, darkness that
would be near freezing—and that she couldn't have swum even
if it were warm and lazing along.

So where was the bridge she'd come by? Nowhere.

Rosina began running along the bank till she came to another ditch, at right angles to the first one but just as wide, boxing her in. Should she follow this new ditch, or should she admit her error and return to where she'd first hit the river and try the other way? Her mind was made up by the sight of a torch flashing in the night and the sound of people entering the maize. This new ditch would take her straight back to them. So she ran all the way back to where she'd first hit the river, and on—but still no bridge. Then she saw another dike ahead of her, and her confusion began to turn to despair. Boxed in on three sides by water and on the fourth by people who thought she was a demon.

She ran up to this new obstruction anyway. And stood and stared at it. And told herself that it was narrower than the other two dikes, which it clearly was, and that it if she put everything into it, she could jump it.

No time for doubt. Rosina retreated five or so steps, then a few more: she took a deep, deep breath—"Over there!" someone cried—and ran. And slammed her foot into the dike bank; and threw herself into the air, willing herself to fly. Time seemed to stop. Then the bank was rushing toward her, then her feet were hitting the earth and her hands grabbing fistfuls of grass, then she was scuffing the water with one of her flailing boots, then scrabbling up the bank, then dragging herself to her feet, then running again. Running, along the bank of that vile river that still cut her off from the road, but at least free from that terrible three-sided trap.

And then she saw the bridge.

Thank you, she said. (To whom? To Marx? To Ye Huo Hua?) But then that gratitude evaporated, as she saw it wasn't a bridge but a pipe. A round metal pipe.

For a moment Rosina gave in to despair. It would be covered in ice, she would slip and fall and—

"Kill the demon!"

She walked up to the pipe and put a hand on it. It didn't feel cold, and certainly was not icy. Something must run through it that kept it warm. The surface was rough, too. She *could* walk on it.

She glanced up at the road ahead—headlights and safety—then scrambled up on to the pipe and took a first step.

Then another.

A third step, and she was over the water. The moon was down there, fixing her with its rippling, cold white eye.

Sometimes drowned people were brought into the hospital, from Beihai or Houhai or the Tonghui River. They were cold and white, too.

Another step.

"Kill the demon!"

Rosina walked on, deliberate step after deliberate step.

Over halfway.

"There it is!"

"Ha! It'll fall!"

How many more steps? Four? Five? Asking this question broke Rosina's concentration for a moment, and she wobbled. Then steadied herself. Only when she was totally still did she move again.

The moon looked up at her.

Step.

Then suddenly only a couple more were needed, and Rosina was half stumbling, half leaping clear and landing on the bank. She lay there for a moment, delirious with relief, then heard more shouts. "The bridge!" "Head it off!" She didn't even turn to see what bloody bridge they were talking about, just ran.

Across another bare patch lay another maize field: Rosina ran for it and gratefully plowed into its shelter. Not that this gratitude lasted for long: she found her feet grabbed by the vegetation and whipped from under her, and as she fell more imp pikes jabbed into her. Soon she was blundering forward, with one hand over her eyes and the other thrashing at the maize plants. More tumbles, more jabs in the guts and thighs and arms and breasts and face. And the voices sounded suddenly nearer all around her, it suddenly seemed.

"Kill the demon!"

Then her feet were kicking at air and she was tumbling forward into emptiness.

After a moment, she got to her feet—on the grass verge of the road. Safety! At exactly the same time, a stream of people emerged from a field break a hundred meters up the road, spotted her, and began running.

Rosina began to run from her pursuers, but they seemed to be gaining on her. The voices grew louder and louder.

"Kill! Kill!"

Her sides gave a spasm of pain. Her legs suddenly felt weak. And still there was no traffic on the road. Had she so nearly gotten away, only to be—

Light stabbed through the night. Rosina weaved out into the middle of the road. An air horn wailed, brakes squealed. A square shape loomed out of the dark ahead of her and slewed to a halt a few meters ahead. A door opened and a stream of oaths issued from it, followed by a man, whose expression suddenly changed.

"Help . . . me . . ." said Rosina.

"Are you all right?" said the driver hesitantly. The accent was *dongbei,* Manchurian, a voice that many people who had flats near Tiantan Park associated with degeneracy and criminality. Rosina had always despised such prejudice. She was about to either reap the rewards of her magnanimity or pay for her naïveté.

But right now, she just burst into tears.

They stopped at an all-night stall just short of where the suburbs begin and ate noodles; the trucker made a long detour from his planned route to take Rosina to Tiantan Park. When asked in to eat and drink by way of thanks, he looked up at the modern apartment block and grinned nervously. So much for a classless society. . . . She said thank you, put her arms around him and gave

him a big kiss on each cheek, then walked back to the compound
gates, where she stood and watched the lorry drive off into the
night.

Then she turned and made her way across the compound and
up the stairs, knocked on her own front door—heaven knew
where she had lost her keys—and fell into the arms of the bleary-
eyed policeman who opened it.

18

"Come in."

Team-leader Chen was at his desk, a pile of papers in front of him. He was staring at one, a report on drugs being smuggled into the capital, and shaking his head.

"If it's about this cult . . ." he began, in that intimidating voice he used for keeping people where he wanted them.

But Wang was not to be put off. He simply repeated the story Rosina had told him last night and added at the end that he assumed he could get an arrest warrant that morning.

"No actual violence was done," said Chen.

"If my wife says the threat was there, that's good enough for me."

Since the Red Mandarin affair, Chen had had a grudging but real respect for Rosina's judgment. But he still didn't want trouble. Not now.

"There are political implications," he began.

"They've gone crazy in there."

"You don't *know* that."

"I do."

"And you really want to stir all that up again?" Chen asked.

"Yes."

Chen said nothing for a while. "Take Lu, Wei, and Fang," he said finally. "Sort these fucking people out for once and for all."

"Thank you, Lao Chen."

"We must expect hostility," said Wang, as the Beijing Jeep turned off the main road on to the track that led to the farmstead. "Maybe even physical resistance. We must respond with gentleness. Think of bamboo that bends with the wind but doesn't break."

Lu, eager for action after his long voyage and a brief spell in a Caracas jail—both with only Dostoevsky for company—looked disappointed: at the beginning of the boss's statement, his hand had flown to his shoulder holster. Detective Wei felt a flutter of excitement: she'd not seen much action since joining the force and was half longing for it, half dreading it. Only the veteran Fang was truly unmoved. All in a day's work.

"So stay calm," Wang added as the buildings came into view. "This could be tough, but I know we can carry it off."

Detective Wei gave a grin.

They arrived in the little parking area by the front door and began to get out of the vehicle. Then the door of the farm flew open.

Lu's hand went to his gun again.

"Calm!" Wang whispered. Though inside he, too, felt a sudden tremor of fear. How many of them were there inside that place? A hundred? Two hundred? Did they have weapons?

Modesty Cheng emerged, waving her hands in the air. Nobody else. She began running toward them.

"Thank heaven you've come!" she called out.

"So they've gone? The Master and the twelve?" Wang asked as they walked across the still-beautiful front courtyard.

"Yes. After, well, last night . . ."

"D'you know where?"

"No."

"She's lying!" said Lu.

Wang ignored this. "Have you any ideas, Sister?"

Modesty shook her head. "No."

"Get everyone together in the hall," he told her. "We must interview everyone."

———

"What's your name?"

"Bei," the young man replied. He was thin, and shivering, whether from cold or fear Wang wasn't sure.

"Given name?"

"Tuoxin."

"How long have you been here?"

"A year."

"Tell me about the new Master."

"He's a very good man. A patriot."

"I'm glad." Wang put gentleness into his voice; he wanted voluntary help if possible. "When's he coming back?"

"We don't know. Soon, we hope."

"Why?"

"Because he is our inspiration. In the new millennium we will need his leadership even more."

"What did he tell you when he left?"

"That he was going with the chosen ones, to strengthen their faith."

"Where?"

"I don't know."

Silence.

"What were they going to do?"

"Make a great leap of faith and receive the strength of God."

Wang winced at these words. "What did he mean by that?"

"I don't know. We're ordinary folk here. Many of us led bad lives before finding the Church. Yet we believe that human perfection is possible. Have you heard of Hong Xiuquan?"

"Did he make a Great Leap of Faith?"

This was not the right question to ask, as the young man began relating a history of the Taiping Rebellion.

"Stop! What is this 'leap'?"

"I don't know."

"You're lying to me!" No gentleness now.

Bei Tuoxin went white with fear. "No . . . No . . ."

"Damn you." Wang got up from his chair, advanced toward

the dais, then saw Sister Modesty sitting among the people waiting to be interviewed and strode across to her.

"What is the 'great leap of faith'?" he asked.

"I don't know," she replied. She looked as scared as Bei.

"Come with me," Wang ordered.

The sister obeyed, following him out into the quad.

"I don't like the sound of this," he told her. "Is there a cliff or mountain that the Master talked about?"

Modesty shook her head, then said, "There's Golden Mountain, of course."

"What's Golden Mountain?"

She looked surprised. "It's not a real place. But it's in Brother Hong's prayer. *Our Kingdom shall stand on a golden mountain.* That's how it begins."

Wang grimaced and stared around at the buildings, as if inspiration was waiting there. He began to think out loud.

"Sacred mountains. Huangshan? No, that's a thousand li away. Taishan . . . Emei Shan . . ."

"They'd never get to any of those places, anyway," Modesty cut in.

"Why not?"

"Beijing's as far as we normally take the van. It's very old."

"The van! What's the registration?"

She paused. "I can't remember. *H* something. Nine nine zero on the end. The documents should be in the Master's office."

"Show me!" He followed her across to the office, where, with great embarrassment, Modesty pulled back a picture of Hong Xiuquan to revel a small safe.

Two minutes later, he was on his mobile, cursing the appalling signal but at least in contact with HQ.

"I want an alert put out for a minibus. White, Hino, registration (Bei) Jing H890990." He had to repeat the number several times, then was asked what area he wanted the alert to cover.

"Everywhere."

"Sorry. This signal's appalling. The whole city, did you say?"

"The whole of China."

"What?"

They were being obstructive: there was probably nothing wrong with the signal. "All mountainous areas within a three-hundred-kilometer radius of the capital."

"You know what the manpower situation is like at the moment, Lao Wang."

"Do as I say! And get someone checking maps for a Golden Mountain."

Officer Deng Weimai was sitting in his patrol car watching the busy Beijing-to-Chengde highway. He was angry, as he was down to be doing this again in two nights' time, on December 31. A friend was planning a millennium party, but priority for time off that evening was being given to married officers with families, "so the youth of China could welcome in the new era in the company of their parents," according to the Party Secretary.

Why, for fuck's sake? Weren't there too damn many people anyway? People who had no kids ought to be rewarded, not given all the pig-shit jobs.

His radio came to life, and told him to look out for a white Hino minibus. Registration . . . Officer Deng noted the details out of habit rather than any real belief that the vehicle would appear, then went back to scanning the highway. Any drunks? Any foreign trucks he could flag down and get a few yuan off? Traffic duty was for wooden-heads, but it had some perks.

The Hino almost passed him unnoticed. But then he remembered the call, double-checked the registration, and radioed HQ.

"You're to follow it discreetly," the orders came back.

Deng frowned; he wouldn't even get a decent chase out of these bastards. Still, it would look good if he caught them. He gunned the accelerator and moved down into the traffic.

The Beijing Jeep swung off the dirt track and onto the main road.

"We've got two or three hours of daylight," said Wang. "Use it."

Lu nodded eagerly and put his foot down.

Wei and Fang had been left at New Tianjing to complete the questioning. Wang would rather have had Wei with him—this situation would probably call for brain, not brawn—but he needed her back at the farmstead.

"You do understand, don't you?" he had said to the young detective, and she had simply nodded and said yes. Wang consoled himself with the thought that she was probably not eager to get involved in physical action, anyway.

"Shall I put the siren on, sir?" said Lu.

Wang hated sirens. They had an arrogance about them that went against all his ideals of public service.

"If it makes you drive faster," he replied, and at once a great wail broke from the roof of the vehicle, causing an old cyclist to wobble onto the side of the road.

Anything to speed the journey.

The snow began falling after an hour and a half. They'd left the plain and were in mountain country, where the road, despite its modernity, had to fit itself to the erratic shape of the land.

"Slow down a bit," Wang told Lu, then took the radio and had another go at contacting Police HQ in Xiaoshi, the town ahead. Another unsuccessful go.

Wang swore. Where was the place that Officer Deng had called in from? Still many kilometers to the north, he reckoned. He glanced across at Lu, concentrating on the road with almost crazy intensity. Another advantage of taking Lu: simple youth. Driving in these conditions was in many ways a purely physical task. Stamina, that was what it was going to take.

Then a lorry came looming out of the snow, horn blasting, and Lu seemed to wait an age before taking evasive action. The monster thundered past, spraying the Beijing in slush.

"I'll take a turn, Lu."

"I'm doing fine, Chief."

"No, it's best to alternate. Get some rest."

Lu protested vigorously, but Wang made him pull in at the next possible lay-by and they swapped over. Soon after he glanced across at the young man and noticed he was asleep.

"No stamina, youngsters," Wang told himself. Another truck thundered by, and his mind filled with the horrible image of an accident, not to the Beijing but to a white Hino minibus, with twelve young people and a middle-aged man on board. . . .

Officer Deng cursed as the snow began to fall. Up till now, it had been easy to follow the Hino: its driver liked to keep an exact speed, and he just did the same. At one point it had pulled into a petrol station to refuel: Deng took the chance of following it in, refueling, too, and getting a look at his quarry. The bus seemed to be full of youngsters—well, people in their late teens or early twenties, soberly dressed and quiet in their behavior. He wondered what they were wanted for. The authorities seemed very worked up about it. Political stuff? He stayed well clear of politics.

Then as the snow worsened, following became harder. Soon only the taillights of the Hino and its vague outline were visible. Deng tried to commit these to memory: the brightness of the lights, their exact color, their exact distance apart. But nothing stays constant in snow.

The bus slowed down as the road began another climb—not many more of these; soon it would head down onto the great Manchurian plain. He slowed, too. But not enough: he realized he was getting too close. He put his foot on the brake and felt the car begin to slip from his control.

"Pump the brake, steer into the skid," he told himself. The

police car began to spin, and he stabbed his foot to the floor and whirled the wheel around to correct...

No damage done. Lucky, really. Deng just sat in his seat and calmed his breathing. Then told himself he must get back to his task.

It didn't take him long to catch up. The lights were ahead, moving slowly through the snow, which was falling ever harder. Sensible. He dropped his speed; seventy, sixty, fifty-five.

"Deng, come in, please." His radio was yapping at him. "How are you getting on?"

"No problem. I have them in sight."

"Good. Beijing is sending an officer to interview these people."

"D'you want me to pull them over?"

"No. Just keep visual contact."

"Okay."

The radio fell silent again, leaving him with the noises of the car: the engine, the slush beneath his wheels, the whining wipers. Familiar, reassuring sounds.

"Ai!" The lights ahead were getting closer again. Deng braked, doing it properly this time. The vehicle ahead was stopping. Now what to do?

Drive past and radio for instructions. He put out an indicator to announce he was passing the vehicle, then noticed someone was getting out, waving a torch, flapping arms about. Curiosity overcame him, and he pulled in...

...behind a heavy old Red Flag limousine, as wide as a Hino minibus but a lot less reliable in bad weather.

"So we've lost them?"

"Sounds like it," replied the radio operator back at HQ. In the storm, even the police radios were acting up.

"Do we know approximately where?"

"Somewhere in the mountains."

"Where in the bloody mountains?"

"We don't know, Lao Wang."

"Aiya!"

More cracklings.

"And you've not come up with a Golden Mountain?"

"Not yet."

"Keep looking."

HQ made another comment that was swallowed up by the storm, then the radio went dead, leaving just the noises of the Jeep: slush hissing under the wheels, the plop of the great snow-flakes landing on the windscreen. Wang suddenly hated those noises.

"Fuck it to hell and back," he said.

Lu, who believed that a good Communist avoided such language, looked a little shocked. "Do you want me to take over again, Chief?"

"Maybe you better had," Wang replied, an odd languor suddenly in his voice. "But no need to hurry. We don't even know where we're going now."

19

Julie huddled up tighter under the simple blanket she had brought with her. She gave another shiver, then glanced again at the clock that had been placed beside her. Twenty past. At four-thirty, she was to get up and kindle the morning fire. *That shouldn't be too difficult a task,* she told herself. They had collected brushwood the day before, out there on the mountainside, then had dried it by the big fire they'd had last night and stacked it in that horrible altar room.

Another gust of wind. She should get up now, start work now: that way warmth would be brought to them all sooner. But right now it was so cold . . .

Cold shouldn't matter. Men and women had died for the faith. She was balking at the thought of a little discomfort. On this of all days!

She pulled off the blanket, lit a lantern, and got to her feet. The cold sliced through her, but she concentrated on walking, one step at a time, down the aisle of blankets along the center of the old monks' refectory. The dull eyes of her colleagues followed her: it had been too cold for them to sleep, too. And too exciting.

The altar room was at the end of a long, murky passage. Guarding the lantern carefully—there were drafts all over the old monastery—Julie made her way to the carved doorway and went in. Here she shivered not with cold but with distaste: weird, violent images glared at her from the walls. Demon images from the demon religion that had enslaved China for so many centuries. Demon faces with demon boggle-eyes and satanic grins; demon bodies with grasping claw hands and stunted legs; human bodies, naked and broken, being shepherded into various regions of the

Kingdom of Yan Luo. And the defacements, as if the demons had turned their own malevolence against themselves, scratching, gouging, daubing slogans in now-fading blood red: *Death to the Four Olds! May Chairman Mao Live Ten Thousand Years!*

Will this be how the world will look when we come down from here? she asked herself.

A hundred demon eyes watched as she picked up a bundle of sticks under her free arm and plodded across the stone floor to the entrance, then turned into the corridor.

"Fragrant Flower!"

The voice shocked her so much that she nearly dropped the sticks. But it was only the Master, up early, too.

"You are getting ready?"

"Yes, Master."

"So am I!" he said, with a low, coiled excitement in his voice. "Carry on with your work, my sister."

The fire was blazing. Smoke billowed up into the rafters of the old refectory and out through a hole in the roof. With it went showers of sparks: Julie caught herself wondering if one of these wouldn't set light to the place, but this was what the Master called *old thinking*. The Lord Ye Huo Hua was protecting them. He would never allow such things to happen.

The visitors sat around the flames, warming themselves. Nobody felt inclined to speak, maybe because of the cold but more likely because of the momentousness of the day. Several pairs were holding hands—same-sex pairs, of course. Outside, the wind gave another howl, and a flurry of snow blew in through the smoke hole.

The Master cleared his throat. "Brothers and sisters! I have had the dream I desired. All is as it should be. Even this foul weather is all part of the plan."

He smiled. "Remember, we are here to test our faith, to temper the steel of our souls in the icy furnace of this holy place, so we can enter the third millennium as sons and daughters of the Lord Ye Huo Hua. Soon we shall head out to the testing ground. Tonight we shall return here like gods, pure and steel-strong, and celebrate the arrival of the millennium. Then, on January first, 2000, we shall descend and enter the new world that the Lord Ye Huo Hua has promised us. I do not know how much of the old world he will spare, but I do know it will be a world crying out for our leadership, just as it cried out for the leadership of Brother Ye Su and Brother Hong."

A twig on the fire burst into flame.

"Are we ready to put our faith to the test?" said the Master.

"Yes!" said the twelve, as one.

"Let's go, then. Fragrant Flower, smother the fire. We will build an even higher one tonight, and in the third millennium we will build a fire from the words and artifacts of the demon-slaves, so high it will reach the gates of heaven itself!"

The youngsters began to applaud and shout agreement. The Master let this rise in volume, then bade them be silent.

"Come. Follow," he said, adding as they traipsed out into the freezing morning of December 31, 1999, "and may we all return new, pure and full of the power that the Lord Ye Huo Hua is waiting to grant us."

The fire and the Master's words had, between them, made Julie forget about the cold, but the moment she was out on the mountainside, it filled her thoughts again.

Have faith! she hissed at herself—but her feeble boots were soon sodden, her inadequate clothes damp through, and the wind was lashing at her face like the clawed hands of one of those wall-demons. In addition, the Master was leading them upward, ever upward, and the worn old steps were slippery. The thought came into her mind that if she lost her footing . . .

She glanced around, then wished she hadn't. The weather blotted out much of the view, but all around her were sheer faces of rock.

This is crazy! she told herself. *Crazy, crazy, crazy—*

No.

This was right. Absolutely right. This was a test, and the harder the test, the greater the reward.

At that thought, she felt a wave of wonder flood through her. She was helpless, half frozen, terrified, lost—and the Lord Ye Huo Hua was putting her through this. A last reminder of human frailty.

She had no idea how long the climb took. It was arduous and step and seemed to go on forever, then suddenly they were there, on a kind of plateau. The summit.

The Master walked to the highest point of this plateau and stared around with pride. "This is the place! From here we can see to the end of the world. And beyond . . . Brothers and sisters, let us pray."

Julie closed her eyes, and the Master began to recite Brother Hong's Prayer. *"Our Kingdom will stand on a golden mountain . . ."*

Of course! This was all part of the prophecy. They were here, now, fulfilling it. God's prophecy, told through his second son. Julie's sense of amazement grew.

". . . Cleansed and purified, the chosen ones shall fast and bathe, respectful and devout in worship, dignified and serene in prayer. Praising the Lord with fervor, we shall seek and we shall be granted happiness, love, and joy!"

"Happiness, love, and joy . . ."

She had been granted them already. They were filling her body to the bursting point, so much so that she wanted to leap up in the air and shout and scream about them, to let the whole world know.

The Master began to preach.

"Brothers and sisters, the soul is light. It is lighter, even, than one of these." Here he caught a flake of snow—the storm was abating now, the snow falling in occasional fat flakes—and held it out for everyone to see. "It is the human body that is gross. The body weighs us down with desires; the soul lifts us up with longing toward heaven. So we come to places like this, to be near to the Holy Ones. But we are still not near enough. We are still weighed down by our sinful bodies, while they, pure spirit, can soar to heaven in the blink of an eye. How can we bear the weight of this sin, my dear ones? How can we bear it?"

He paused. "We cannot, that is the answer. Not on our own. But we do not have to. Brothers and sisters, I have been to this place before. Many years ago, when I lived a sinful life as one of those Red Guards. It was here that I had my first vision, of Brother Ye Su. He was walking on air, on the very clouds you now see before you. And he spoke to me. Brother Ye Su asked me to walk out to him, to walk on air as he had once walked on water."

The Master paused, to let this awareness sink into the minds of his listeners. "Brothers and sisters, I was afraid. He told me that all I needed was faith—did I not think he would support me?—but I was still afraid. So he told me that when the time was right, I would have enough faith, and that *all* the truly faithful would have enough faith, and that he would then receive us and lift us up. Lift us up all the way to his Father Ye Huo Hua."

Another pause. "I asked him when this would be, and he told me I would know, that a messenger would tell me. Brothers and sisters, that messenger was our dear Golden Master, and that time is now. The birth of the third millennium. A new era in human history, which we must enter freed of all sin and filled to perfection with the Holy Spirit! For the moment we give ourselves totally to the Holy Ones, we can achieve ten thousand miracles! Just one step, just one leap of faith, is all we need to make. And we have been promised: *he will receive us and lift us up.*"

He fell silent again.

Julie looked out over the great valley ahead of them. A crow floated by. Those words came back to her, and with them the final feeling of the complete perfection of this experience: *without the chains of physicality, the soul would soar to heaven with the ease of a bird.*

She knew exactly what was required of her.

The Master began to speak again. "Brothers and sisters, I want you to close your eyes and summon in your minds the images of Brother Hong Xiuquan, Brother Ye Su, and the Lord Ye Huo Hua. I want you to hear their voices and surrender your will to them. Not to my words, but to theirs. They will guide you."

Julie did as commanded. "Give me the strength," she muttered, over and over again. "Take me to you, Holy Ones, accept me as truly yours . . ."

Then she opened her eyes.

And they were there.

In front of her, exactly as the Master had said. Hovering above the valley, in human form, but of course pure spirit, just as she could be, if only she had enough faith. What a vision! The Lord Ye Huo Hua, in his black dragon robe and great, golden beard; the warrior Hong in turban and tunic; the gentle Brother Ye Su in white robes with a crown of thorns around his pale-skinned, round-eyed head. The Holy Ones. Waiting for her!

She got slowly to her feet. "I am called," she said.

"The Lord Ye Huo Hua is bountiful!" exclaimed the Master.

She began to walk forward, toward the edge of the precipice. Two more steps, and she could see over it: rock and snow, tumbling hundreds of meters away into mist. But she felt no fear.

"I am ready!" she said.

Ahead of her, peaks—sunlit, jagged, snowcapped, and unimaginably beautiful—thrust up out of the misty landscape. An image of her current and future life, rising proud and clear out of the dismal confusion of the past.

And in front of this image, the loves of her true soul; her destiny.

Julie knew.

"Brother Hong! Brother Ye Su! Lord Ye Huo Hua! I am coming!"

It took longer to find the minibus than it should have because Officer Deng had lied about how he'd lost it, in an attempt to cover up for his incompetence. Once the actual spot where the trail had been lost had been established, it was easy to see where the Church members were headed.

"That old monastery has been deserted since the thirties," the local Party Secretary told Wang. "And of course it got vandalized in the Cultural Revolution. What place didn't? But it's still standing. I've not heard of this place called Golden Mountain, though."

It no longer mattered. Wang tried to hurry the conversation on. Was there a helicopter available? How easy was it to climb up there?

The secretary looked at him with puzzlement. He'd thought city police were streetwise and sophisticated, but this guy was plain stupid. "No helicopter will fly in this weather. As for the climb—you can do it if you want, but I'm not sending my men up there. If you want to arrest these people, wait till they get hungry."

"I can't wait."

The local man shrugged, a rude gesture in China. "We can. I've enough trouble getting men to do essential work at the moment, let alone getting them to climb mountains in pursuit of crazy kids. When we've all recovered from the celebrations, we'll launch a proper raid. First big action of the year 2000!"

Too late, Wang thought, but he kept the words to himself, as he suddenly knew what he had to do and knew that it could really be done only by him.

"Give me your best maps of the mountain," he said.

Wang and Lu pondered a night ascent, but the weather was too bad. So they spent the night in the deserted pilgrims' huts at the foot of the mountain and set off early next morning.

"You don't have to join me, Lu," Wang told him. "If there's a millennium party that you've been invited to—"

"If you need me, I'll be with you," the young man cut in.

Wang clapped him on the shoulder. "Good" was all he said, but the gesture said a lot more.

They reached the monastery by about nine. There didn't seem to be anyone inside, so they entered: a fire had been put out by a fall of snow, but its heart was still warm.

"They could be anywhere," said Lu.

Wang shook his head. "They've gone to the summit. We must hurry Lu, this bit of the mission I must do on my own. Wait here for me. They mustn't see you, or they'll think I've brought a whole load of cops with me and panic. This is about persuasion, not force. Understood?"

Lu looked disappointed, but nodded acceptance. *Obey orders in all your actions.*

Wang rounded yet another bend in the old monks' path. He paused for breath—hell, he had to; his lungs were aching, and he'd need presence of mind and composure to deal with the situation ahead.

One, he reminded himself. *Don't assume things. It's still possible they've just come here to see the sun rise tomorrow morning.*

The words *a great leap of faith* echoed in his mind again.

Two. Talk. They've been shut away with a madman, bombarded with his weird ideas. Just let reason in.

He had to press on.

Three. Stay calm.

He rounded the next bend and could see them now. As expected, right on the summit. Mad bastard!

Then he heard voices. Including one he recognized.

"Brother Hong! Brother Ye Su! Lord Ye Huo Hua! I am coming!"

And the speaker was on her feet, walking toward the edge of what looked like a sheer drop. Wang broke into a run, or rather a crazy stumble up the mountainside.

"No!" he shouted. "Julie! *Stop!*"

She did stop, and turned to gawp at him—just like the other twelve people up on the mountaintop.

"What are you doing?" he called out.

Nobody replied.

He panted the last few meters to the summit—from where he could see for the first time what lay beyond it.

Stay calm.

"This is not a safe place to be . . ." he continued breathlessly. "I've orders from Mountain Rescue. . . . You must come down."

No answers. He sought out the Master and fixed him with a stare. "Okay. I assume you're in charge here. First we must get everyone away from the cliff edge, then we have to—"

The Master stared back, appeared to consider his words for a moment, then said with great deliberation: "You are a demon."

Wang tried to finish his own sentence, but there didn't seem much point after that.

The Master began shaking his head. "I knew this would happen. Who sent you? Yan Luo? Or are you . . . ? Yes! You *are* Yan Luo. What's happening here has so much spiritual power that you have come yourself to sabotage it!" The Master turned to the youngsters. "See how important we are! The King of the demons has entered the body of a mortal and come to stop us! But he won't succeed."

"I don't know what you're talking about. I'm a policeman, and I'm here to get you all off this mountain. Weather conditions are set to deteriorate within—"

"You are a demon!" The Master's look was growing in hatred by the second. "Kill the demon!" he shouted suddenly.

Several of the young people got to their feet.

"Go away, Lao Wang!" Julie called out. "You don't understand. You're meddling with things you don't understand. Run!"

"No," he replied, gathering himself. "No one's running anywhere. We're all coming down off this mountain, slowly and sensibly."

"Destroy the demon!"

The youngsters were all on their feet now and walking toward him.

"Run!" Julie shouted.

Suddenly Wang felt fear. "I'm a policeman!" he called out, but the youngsters kept on coming.

The idea came to him instinctively. "And that man's a murderer!" He pointed as dramatically as he could at the Master. "He killed your old Master!"

It worked, for the moment anyway: the oncoming tide of fanatics halted.

"He put poison in the old Master's drink!" Wang went on, putting all the authority he could muster into his voice. "Weed killer, from your stores. Into bottles the Master drank from."

The youngsters suddenly looked confused. Wang eyeballed the nearest one, a thin, frightened-looking woman, and challenged her. "Go on: ask him if it's true!"

She said nothing.

"You're lying!" somebody called out.

"Ask him!"

For a moment nobody moved, then the woman turned to her Master and said, "Is it true?"

"Of course it's not true!"

"Prove it!" Wang riposted at once.

"How can I prove it?"

"If you're innocent, it should be easy."

"What, up here?"

"Down there." Then summoning his authority again, "I require proof."

Silence.

In that silence, Wang could hear his own heart thumping. He knew he couldn't keep this up much longer. He had no idea what anyone would do next, including himself. Lu wouldn't have followed; he'd obey orders. . . .

Then a voice was speaking. Young Wu.

"Our Master is telling the truth, policeman. I know what really happened."

"No!" exclaimed the Master. "Wu, you don't have to say that! This is not a man, this is a demon."

"I have done a very bad thing," Wu continued. "My conscience insists that—"

"You did no harm!" the Master cut in.

Wang wheeled on him. "So what *did* happen, Master?"

"What I said. The Lord Ye Huo Hua called Hong Er to—"

"No!" said Wu with a groan. "Lying is a sin, Master," he added, and began to walk toward the edge of the cliff.

"Stop!" Wang cried out. He started to run forward but knew he could never reach the young man in time.

Wu paused at the edge and turned to his transfixed audience. "I must be judged by a higher power than policemen and courts, higher even than the people I love. If I am to be pardoned my sin, Brother Hong Xiuquan will take up my body."

"Don't be so bloody stupid," Wang cried.

"You've done no wrong!" the Master called out.

"If my sin is too heavy—" said Wu. Wang tried inching toward him. A meter more, and he'd be able to make a grab for a leg, or even a piece of clothing—

The rock began crumbling.

Wang had to step back: at the same instant the ground centimeters ahead of him cracked clean away and slid from view.

Wu made no cry as he fell. Instead, there was a pattering of soil and rocks, then a thudding sound as his body hit the rock face, then more thuds and patterings as rocks and body rolled on, ever faster, down into the fog below.

Then there was silence.

Then echoes of all those noises from the far-off faces of the mountains, cold, white, and uncaring.

And silence again.

"Let's get away from here," said Wang.

"No," the Master replied at once. "He was not worthy. The Lord Ye Huo Hua did not choose to receive him."

"What do you mean, 'choose to receive'?" Wang asked, incredulous.

"You have no faith," said the Master.

"In what?"

The Master began to laugh.

"The truly faithful will step out over that cliff, Lao Wang," said Julie. "The Holy Ones will take them and raise them to heaven. They will become like gods."

"That's crazy! You saw what happened to Wu!"

"He was not worthy," the Master repeated.

Wang was furious suddenly. "Who is worthy, then?"

"The Lord Ye Huo Hua knows. He will gather up those who are *truly* chosen—"

"And let the rest fall to their death!"

"We have all agreed to test our faith."

"We? All? Good. As you're in charge, why don't you go first then?"

He hadn't wanted it to come to this. His job was to get everyone down and then to quiz them about the death of Hong Er. But it *had* come to this: He could see no other way out.

The Master fell silent, then stared around at his disciples, who were looking at him with new, needy glances.

"I want to pray first."

"Fine," said Wang.

The Master began to intone a prayer, and the youngsters, to join in.

"Our Kingdom will stand on a golden mountain . . ."

Then silence fell, as massive as the valley below them. The voice that broke it was Julie's.

"Let me go first!"

Wang was about to frame an objection, when the Master spoke.

"No, Fragrant Flower. I can see it now; it must be me. There is purpose to this demon's arrival. The world needs a true messiah for the third millennium. I am to be that messiah, the third in human history. Those of you who are worthy must follow me." He turned and looked Wang in the eye. "Policeman, you are about to see something so remarkable that in the future you will fall to your knees and thank heaven that you were here to witness it." Then he looked away, out across the huge valley ahead of them. "My father, my brothers—I am coming. Receive me, and return me to this world pure and ready to lead all mankind to the destiny you have prepared for them."

He began to walk toward the cliff face. Wang watched, impassive now.

"I am coming," the Master said again, his eyes still cast heavenward. Then he glanced down.

And stood stock still.

He took another pace, so he was right at the edge of the cliff. And again he looked down, then began to sway from side to side.

"Brother Hong!" he cried out.

He put a foot over the edge, then retracted it.

"Brother Ye Su!"

Julie watched, horrified.

"Father!" the Master cried out. He began to sway forward, out over the void, then back again.

"You promised..." he called out. Then he paused, as if to steel himself. A look of conviction came over his face; he seemed about to take that final, decisive step—then his legs gave way beneath him and he fell back in a faint.

His disciples stared at each other in disbelief.

Wang sprang forward and rolled the Master to safe ground before putting a set of handcuffs on him and then slapping him on the face.

"*Now* can we get away from this place?" he said, as the "third messiah" regained consciousness, blinked, then filled with shame as he remembered where he was.

The kids were already making their way back down the path.

The weather began to deteriorate almost at once, and by the time they reached the old monastery it was so bad that further progress was impossible. They would have to spend the night there: the last night of the second millennium A.D. Julie built a fire, and she and the other youngsters all fell asleep long before midnight, so exhausted and demoralized were they. The Master, who had not said a word since his failure to leap off the cliff, just sat and stared into the flames. Wang did the same. There would be plenty of time to hear the Master's story and find out exactly what *had* happened to the unfortunate Hong Er.

Then Wang felt a tug at his shoulder.

"It's nearly time, Lao Wang," said Lu, pointing at his watch.

"So it is." In fact, it might have been the year 2000 already, as the fake Rolex that Lu had bought in Liulichang was notoriously unreliable. "Happy millennium, Xiao Lu."

"Thank you, Chief. The same to you."

The two policemen walked out into what was now a cold but clear night and were reduced at once to silence by the stars shining with a clarity Wang hadn't seen for years. Kuixing, the pole star, the source of literary inspiration; Tianhe, the River of Heaven, the star bridge between the parted lovers Vega and Altair.

"The year 2000!" he said. He wondered what thoughts and images would come into his mind as he said those words: what did come to him was a picture of Rosina, coming home from the millennium night shift and undressing for bed.

"China will be a great power in the new millennium, won't it?" said Lu.

"Of course," Wang said tetchily.

Bourgeois individualism, Team-leader Chen called it.

The two policemen stood and stared for a while more, awed
back into wordlessness by the extravagant brilliance of the night
sky, then a gust of wind came howling up from the eastern valley,
and Wang suddenly felt cold and completely exhausted.

"I must go back," he said.

Lu went with him, and was the first one into the refectory.

"Where's the Master?"

Wang rushed in, then back out into the hallway, pausing at
the front door.

"Aiya!" There was still a dusting of snow on the ground.
There were Wang's prints, and there were Lu's, and there was a
third set.

"He's headed up the mountain again!"

"Should we follow?" Lu asked.

"Of course we follow!"

The tracks led, as expected, to the summit. To the very edge of
the cliff where they had all been standing earlier that day.

This time, the third messiah had made no hesitation.

20

"You threw him over," said Julie, wiping her red, tearful eyes again.

"No we didn't. You know we didn't."

"I don't know anything," Julie replied. She went back to staring out of the window.

They were driving back to Beijing in the Jeep: Julie, Wang, and Lu. (The rest of the chosen ones would follow soon in a police van.) Lu pulled out to overtake a truck crawling up the mountain pass.

At the top of the pass there was a parking place, and they pulled in to admire a fine view over the plain.

"Beijing's down there," said Wang.

"So?" was Julie's reply.

"It's your home,"

"They hate me."

"No, they don't."

Julie began to cry again, and Lu, who wasn't too keen on all this emotional stuff, glanced at the Rolex. It seemed to have stopped, but Lu said, "We ought to be moving on, boss," anyway.

They took Julie to her parents' place in the hutongs, where Mama, Baba, and Rosina were waiting by the old stone gateway to the home courtyard. For a moment they all stared at each other, then Rosina walked up to Julie, put her arms around her, and gave her a long, enveloping hug. Then she took her hand and led her across to her parents. Mama put an arm around her, and Baba assumed a pained expression that showed he was trying to prevent himself from being moved by the situation.

Wang felt a strange mixture of embarrassment, relief, and pride—Rosina was so good at this sort of thing! Lu hastened back to the Jeep cab, to check that there were no messages on the radio.

Lu began signaling to his boss.

"See you tonight," Rosina told Wang with a big, and decidedly flirtatious, grin.

Then she turned, and she and Mama took Julie back into the yard—the usual Beijing courtyard mixture of potted plants, old machinery nobody could bring themselves to throw away, washing lines, wood, sheets of metal: so different from the tidy but sinister world of New Tianjing. Old Mrs. Li, who lived in the rooms opposite and had never ceased spying on the Lins since August 8, 1966, appeared and watched with her usual superior silence.

Once inside the family rooms, Julie just sat on a chair and stared around her. She accepted a mug of green tea from Baba.

Rosina sat down beside her. "Tell me all about it," she said.

Julie began to cry.

Wang sat in his office, had a last read-through of his report, then took it through to Team-leader Chen.

"We made the right decision there, didn't we?" said Chen.

"Yes we did." Chen was immune to irony.

"But I'm afraid the investigation must end here," the team-leader went on. "We all deserve a lot of credit—but with two key witnesses dead and no body, it's definitely one for the files, Xiao Wang."

"I know."

Chen let the briefest of smiles cross his face. "I shall be mentioning the matter at the Party meeting, of course."

The team-leader kept his word. In a packed room, Team-leader Chen told the first section meeting of the new millennium how

his team had foiled a plot by a crazy suicide cult, how this was
an example of both teamwork and initiative, of backing intuitions
with careful planning and decisive action. Secretary Wei had com-
plimented him personally on his achievement.

As Chen spoke, a tattered banner hung over his head.

MAKE A CLEAN AND BEAUTIFUL CITY FOR THE
21ST CENTURY!

Sergeant Ye was looking around, noting things down in a
book, oddly (to an outside observer) overcome with pleasure.

January passed. Julie's first days of the new millennium were
spent at home, weeping a lot, sleeping a huge number of hours,
saying little. It was a week before she ventured out of the courtyard, taking a walk to Houhai Lake and back. A few days later,
she started telling Mama about the cult, all about it—suddenly
she couldn't stop telling her about it, and the whole story came
out.

"You think I'm stupid, don't you?" she said, many times, and
Mama just replied that she didn't, and that her generation had
been just as misled by Mao Zedong.

"Baba thinks I'm stupid, though. I know that."

"He doesn't mean it. He's gotten more old-fashioned as he's
got older. Lots of people do. That doesn't mean he doesn't love
you."

The next day, the Five Rams went missing. Mama tried not
to worry about it, but couldn't hide her relief when Julie returned.

"Where have you been?" she asked, trying not to sound nosy
or patronizing.

"Riding around the town," Julie replied.

"Anywhere in particular?"

"The south. Fengtai. To see some friends."

"That's nice."

"They weren't there. The flat's boarded up."

"Oh. Well, if they're real friends, they'll be in touch with you."

"Yes," Julie replied, unconvinced.

It was Rosina's idea to get Julie and Yuchang together. She organized a meeting at the Y2K café; Julie nearly turned and ran as she entered the place, but didn't, and Yuchang sat her down at a terminal and summoned a search engine. After visiting a number of sites, including the home page of a young and rather handsome (according to his photo, anyway) Chinese in Vancouver, several movie sites, a site about horror comics (Yuchang's personal favorite), and a site run by a man who claimed to enjoy being spanked on the bottom with a copy of the Little Red Book, they signed off and sat at the bar talking.

"It must have been really weird," said Yuchang, as they drank their imported beer.

"Yes," said Julie. Then she said nothing for a while, then added: "It was."

Adding the *guo* particle that makes verbs past suddenly made Julie feel a whole lot better.

Yet two days later, she rode off on the bike and didn't reappear for dinner. Mama phoned Wang at his office, where he was working late, back on a more conventional case.

"I think I know where she is," said Wang. He gave his desk a quick tidy and walked briskly down to the bike park and the Xingfu motorbike.

He caught up with Julie about twenty kilometers out of the city. She was sitting on the verge, clearly exhausted.

"I'll take you the rest of the way, if you like," he said.

"No. I just wanted to look and say good-bye."

"We'll go, then. Another time."

Wang Anzhuang, hero of the Golden Mountain rescue, was allowed to borrow the Beijing Jeep for a weekend.

That Saturday, he, Julie, and Rosina drove east. For the first part of the journey Julie enthused about this "ku" means of transport. As they left the suburbs, however, she became quiet; when they passed through Wufang village and turned onto the dirt track, her face had become death-pale.

The buildings came into view. Julie was shaking now and squeezing her sister's hand.

Wang parked, and they slowly got out. Rosina squeezed Julie's hand back: she had memories, too. *"Kill the demon!"* They crossed to the door, now without its slogan, and knocked. No reply.

"So they've all gone," said Rosina. The vehicles certainly had. There was an air of desolation and abandonment.

Then the door of New Tianjing swung open to reveal a man in a Western suit.

"Good morning!" he said unctuously. "You must be from the F.I.E."

"The what?"

"The Foreign Investment Enterprise. The prospective new tenants."

Wang shook his head. "What happened to the old ones?" he asked.

The man, who belonged to yet another of the new professions emerging in modern China, estate agency, grinned. "They moved to cheaper premises farther from the capital."

Wang produced his police ID.

"Oh," said the estate agent. "Well, they left. I don't know where to. The Religious Affairs Bureau came and told them to go. If you want to contact them, talk to Deputy Director Guan—he's handling the reletting."

Wang just laughed. "Now that we're here, may we look around?"

"Well, I . . ."

He held out the ID again, and the estate agent nodded. Wang even asked for the keys, and was handed them: the same huge bunch. As he felt their weight in his hand, he wondered what had happened to Sister Modesty. Did she still believe in Brother Hong and Brother Ye Su? Would her strange, all-knowing, helpless God have to send another messenger now, the way he had in 1836? He also recalled Rosina's mentioning that Modesty had a schizophrenic son, and reminded himself that some provision would have to be made for the boy.

They began a slow, nervous tour. Rosina and Julie stuck together; he wanted to wander off and look in the Masters' study again.

The room was bare: no books, no posters, just the desk, now empty. He thought of the bell on it. How had it got broken? He'd probably never know. Whatever the means of its demise, it had been of no help to his investigation. He crossed to the window and looked down at the latch. That hadn't been much help, either, though here he still felt curiosity. It *had* to be a part of the story, he felt.

He had one last try at imagining someone standing outside, priming a piece of wire to break in with. Whose face did he see? Nobody's. He told himself it no longer mattered. Julie was safe. And Wheels Chai's library was full of files of unsolved cases: what was one more?

Wang left the Masters' study and wandered along to the waiting room, where he stood and stared at the slogan on the wall. *"Come unto me . . ."*

For a moment, a terrible thought struck him—that this place was a kind of image of his own land, which had been so full of passion and noble intention but that had ended up on the brink of self-annihilation.

When he rejoined the women in the front quadrangle, Julie was in tears again.

"I think it's time to go," said Rosina.

Wang was not sorry to leave.

The estate agent showed them out. "If you see a silver Mercedes driving around looking lost, I'd be grateful if you'd give them directions."

And he shut the door of New Tianjing behind them.

Julie dabbed her eyes and broke into a smile. "Walking out of that door was wonderful," she said. "I opened my eyes again!"

Wang wasn't sure what she meant by that, but her expression certainly showed enormous relief. They crossed to the Jeep, got in, and bumped off down the driveway. Only on the main road did they relax: until they rounded a corner to find a traffic jam. A farmer was herding a flock of goats across the road.

"When I visited the police station here, an old guy came in and thought I was one of the locals," Wang said, trying to lighten the atmosphere with an anecdote. "He started going on about this goat . . ."

Halfway through his narrative, he suddenly fell silent.

"What happened?" Rosina asked.

"Nothing . . . Sorry. It's a stupid story."

A few kilometers on, he turned to his wife and said, "What was it you said about Anming? Something about not having love . . ."

"I don't remember."

"I said it was all to do with the past, and you said no, he drinks because he can't find love."

Rosina nodded. "I don't remember saying it—but it sounds the truth. But of course, you men would consider that silly."

"You know I'm not that stupid!" he said defensively. "Except that I *am* that stupid. Aiya!"

When he got back home, Wang made straight for the Beijing telephone directory.

"Who are you looking up?" Rosina asked.

"Anyone called Hong Yi."

"Why?"

"I need a witness! The whole case depends on it!"

"What case?"

"This whole story..."

Anzhuang usually got like this when he was near to solving a case. She let him get on with it. He was already scribbling down numbers. Then he paused, troubled again—till a smile returned. He dialed a number. "I'd like to speak to Master Shen please..."

Rosina went off into the kitchen. She would hear the whole story in the fullness of time.

A couple weeks later, Wang rode the Xingfu out to Jiuxian again. The "Master" was expecting him.

"You were quite right," said Shen.

"I know," said Wang. "If I'd been right a little earlier, a near tragedy could have been averted."

"You averted it anyway," Shen replied with his usual calm.

They went through to Shen's "healing room," and Wang struggled into the robe that the Master had provided for him. The false beard felt silly to Wang, but Shen assured him it made him look the part.

"He's been on time for the first two sessions," Shen said when the strange, robed figure glanced at his watch. And sure enough, at five to seven, the receptionist phoned through to announce the client's arrival.

A minute or so later, the door of the healing room opened, and Hong Er, former Golden Master of the New Church of the Heavenly Kingdom, walked in.

Wang, standing in the corner of the room, could hardly look at the man, but had to when Shen gave a great flourish in his direction and introduced him.

"This is my assistant, Fu. He's a great expert on shamanic mysticism."

Hong Er smiled nervously. Wang thought a bow would be appropriate, so made one.

"He has a particular affinity with the Phoenix energy which you so greatly need to cure your drinking," Shen went on.

Hong Er said nothing.

Shen smiled at him. "Well, come on. Tell me your story again."

"Must I?"

"You know you must. With every repetition, your negative karma diminishes. Have you not felt the effects already over this week?"

The former Golden Master nodded, then pointed in Wang's direction.

"Mr. Fu is sworn to discretion," said Shen. "Your story, please, Mr. Hong. Right from the *very* beginning."

Hong Er sighed and began to relate.

"I guess the very beginning is my name. Hong Er, the Second Hong. My family didn't give us proper names. My elder brother was Hong Yi, my little brother Hong San. One, two, three. I was the clever one and studied hard at school. I loved history—all of it, but the Taiping Rebellion was my favorite. The name of its leader, of course. Hong, just like me. I used to imagine I was he, astride a horse and leading an army across China—only I wouldn't stop at Nanjing. The Second Hong would conquer all under heaven!

"The teacher at our school knew I was bright and wanted me to go to university—but those all closed down during the Cultural Revolution, and I ended up working in the same danwei as the rest of my family, out in Chaoyang, making plastic bottles. The work was so boring that to take my mind off it, I'd prop a book up by the machine I operated and read as I worked. Nobody noticed; nobody cared. One of the first books I read there was Lin Li's book about the Taipings, and the dreams began soon after that. Well, my one dream, as it was the same night after night."

Here he gave a snort of self-disgust. "I dreamed that I met Hong Xiuquan in the flaming ruins of his capital, Tianjing, and that he took me into his throne room and handed me his Bible, and told me to read it and carry on his work. So I got hold of a Bible—they were still illegal then, but I found a way. And I read everything I could about the Taipings, too: New stuff, not just the books I'd read at school. Most of the Taiping material was Marxist, about how Hong failed because he was before his time; and I remember wondering when his time *should* have been. Then, years later, people started talking about the millennium, and I realized *that* was the time. The night after I realized that, I dreamed more vividly than ever.

"In this dream I saw the Lord Ye Huo Hua, exactly as described in Hong's writings: a big black hat, a golden beard. And he told me to find a group of Christians—an unofficial house group, not one of these government Three Self organizations—and join it. Then wait for instructions. There was a woman in the factory whom I knew to be Christian, so I made myself known to her. When she was sure I wasn't a bureau spy, she let me join her group. And I went along to the meetings, and waited for my next dream. And after a while it came, as my dreams did in those days. This time, it was Ye Su, explaining why he had chosen the Middle East rather than China, and telling me to announce myself to the group, and that I was to go on to complete his mission.

"At the next meeting I stood up and did as Brother Ye Su bid. I was a little scared, but I believed in my dreams. One man accused me of all kinds of blasphemies, but I persisted. And I'd brought some books with me about the Taipings, which I showed to everyone. They hadn't known about the Heavenly Kingdom—here in China!—and were amazed. By the end of the meeting I had many of them believing, including the woman from my work unit and the person who let us use their flat. Even the man who had made the blasphemy accusations agreed to take one of the books. Next meeting he came back, fell on his knees, kowtowed, and begged me to forgive him."

"After that, things just grew. There was a young man in the group, and he said he'd had a vision, too, that it was his duty to go out onto the streets and talk to people. At first I was doubtful—

we were a respectable group, and he wanted to bring in beggars
and thieves and all that sort. But he was insistent on his vision, so
I let him follow it, and of course he was right. These were exactly
the people who needed guidance.

"The idea for New Tianjing came in another dream. I
dreamed that Hong came to me and told me to found the city
here on earth, ready for the millennium. I asked him where, and
he said I would be told. I told this dream to the group, as I always
did, and a few weeks later a man got up and said he would
organize everything for us. He was an official, and I think his job
was to spy on us, but he said that he had been convinced by my
words. Some of the group counseled me to distrust him, but I am
not that way: I believed his sincerity, and I was right to. He was
a wonderful man, Master. He found us the farmstead; he gave us
money for things we needed; he got us making produce to barter
with; he even bought it off us. Millions of joss-sticks, we made,
and he bought them all. Such kindness! And he offered us protection from official interference. Thanks to him, I was soon in a
living, God-worshipping community that was self-sufficient and
under the protection of a senior official. It was perfect!"

For a moment, Hong Er smiled, and in that moment, he
looked almost like one of those beatific Buddhas Wang remembered from the old pagoda near Nanping.

"Then, of course, the dreams stopped happening. . . .

"I don't know why," the old "Master" recommended finally,
"but they did, as unexpectedly as they'd begun. I'd lie awake at
night, willing myself to connect to God again, but when I did
sleep all I'd dream of was—well, things of the flesh. Lust, the sin
that Hong Xiuquan had most expressly preached against! And of
course by that time, community members were asking me for
guidance—questions to which my dreams had once given answers.
But now what did I have to offer them? So I began making things
up."

He hung his head in shame. "It worked for a while, but I
hated it. I wanted God back! I'd been promised, you see. *You will*

always have the guiding hand of my Father to show you the right course of action, that's what Brother Hong had told me. So what was he telling me now? *Go forth and sleep with every woman in the community?"*

"It had to happen sometime: someone else began claiming that they had holy dreams. And it had to be Sheng, too—the man who'd accused me of blasphemy at that first meeting, then had begged my forgiveness, and who had then worked his way so much into my favor that by now he was my Silver Master. I was pleased at first: at least *someone* was in contact with God. I even admitted to him that I had stopped dreaming, and was worried about the fact: he said he would offer me his dreams. I must announce his dreams as my own. What difference did it make who the Lord Ye Huo Hua used as a channel? It seemed so easy."

He shook his head again. "It did work for a while. But his view of things began to change and his dreams to become stranger and stranger. . . . He had this obsession about flying. I began to doubt that his inspiration really was divine. I started to pray for a sign—any sign—from the Lord Ye Huo Hua about this. None came. Just more bodily desire.

"I admit, I couldn't take it. It was too much. I began to drink alcohol. It was easy to get hold of: the man who collected the sticks used to bring me bottles. But that was a fool's way out: I knew that. One day, I got talking to a supplier of ours, a local farmer, and he started talking about women who would, well, do what I wanted, if I paid them. Then he said there was such a woman in Wufang. . . . Brother Hong talked of quenching desire, and I thought that if I could do that, my dreams would come back. . . ."

He fell silent, then glanced at Wang again.

"Carry on," said Master Shen.

He did so: "I began to climb out of my office window, while all those people were in their hall praising God and promising to serve him all their lives, and to walk into the village, to her house, and to pay her—with the community money!—to do all the things

I wanted . . . and of course, the Holy dreams still stayed away. I
began to go more often, hoping that if I quenched my lust enough,
the Lord Ye Huo Hua would forgive me.

"It had to end. When I went into the village, I always left the
window open a crack: one night, I came back to find someone
had shut it. To keep the heat in, I suppose. Very wise. But of
course, I then had to break in. Into my own community! Somehow
that was too much. Standing outside that window, fiddling with
a piece of wire I'd found by the tractor . . . I went to the Silver
Master next morning, told him the truth, and begged him to let
me leave. I said I would hand over all power to him, and tell
everyone that I'd been told to do so in a dream. He took the news
very calmly: he seemed to think it was natural. He told me to
carry on as normal until he was told how best to effect this. Then
a few days later, he said he'd been told. I should pretend to die
in the night. That way, I'd remain a hero at New Tianjing. Just
like Mao up there on Tiananmen. It would be my last contribution
to New Tianjing: to give them a martyr, the beginnings of a new
mythology.

"He had it all worked out. He and Young Wu would pretend
to find me dead. I even had to act the death out, in case anyone
was up and about unusually early. Then I had to lie in a coffinlike
thing for an evening while prayers were said. I was scared about
that, but Wu and the Master made a cage around my body out
of the hoops we used for plant protection, and laid rugs over it:
it looked very dignified, and I could breathe without being noticed.
The hall had respectful, low lighting—just a few candles. It
worked perfectly. I remember thinking as I lay there, that if I
sprang out of the coffin, I could have them all in my power forever. Back from the dead! But I didn't want that any longer. I
just wanted to be out of that place, to escape, to run back to my
old life, to see my real family again and beg their forgiveness.

"When I'd gone, they had a cremation. I heard they built a
huge fire, put petrol over it, and had such a blaze that nobody

could tell what had been burned in there by the end of it. I think they put a dead animal in the coffin—I don't know the exact story, but the deception worked."

Wang fought back the desire to tell Hong Er that the creature had been a goat. And that he could even describe its former owner.

"I suppose you think I'm a wicked man," the cult founder said, looking at Master Shen with pleading eyes.

"I do not," Shen replied gravely.

"I was abandoned," Hong went on, just as if Shen had answered "yes." "I was abandoned by God. But he does that to everybody, Master. Everybody he truly claims to love. Brother Ye Su died nailed to a piece of wood, screaming about being forsaken. The Taipings were butchered by foreign mercenaries. What kind of creator is that, Master? What kind of being presides over the world, that he can do that?"

Hong Er stared around the room, with a look of awful despair on his face. Wang felt a pang of sympathy: this man reminded him of his brother Anming (if one were to substitute Chairman Mao for the dreamed God).

Master Shen began a lecture on the precise nature of Phoenix energy. Hong Er listened like a child. Wang watched and pondered the frailty of people's beliefs, how often they were driven by desperation, not reason.

"That was a very good plan of yours," said Master Shen once Hong Er had gone. "I'm delighted to be able to play my part in it."

Wang smiled. "It does seem to be working . . ."

"Of course it's working! You don't believe in Phoenix energy, but he does. You heard what he said about his drinking. You will get your witness, sober and upright and happy to testify because he's been saved from his own weakness. He will be able to forgive himself. I shall have another success to add to my long list." Shen grinned. "I think this calls for a celebration. Some wine? It's foreign, the best . . ." He reached down behind his lacquer desk and produced a bottle and two glasses.

.

Wang took a glass, let Shen fill it, raised the glass to his lips and sniffed the strange, foreign liquid. *Ya pi* were idiots. But it was rude to decline an offer.

"Ganbei!" said Master Shen. Cheers!

"Ganbei!" Wang replied, a word that always filled him with cheer, laden as it was with associations of conviviality.

He drank. Ai, maybe this stuff wasn't too bad after all. Well, for something Western . . .

21

The peasants stood by the statue of Colonel Sanders and grinned. One of them put an arm around the white plastic waist; another tickled the Colonel's white plastic beard. The one with the camera stepped back, fiddled with the machine—he'd just bought it today, from a shop in Qianmen Main Street, and still wasn't sure how it worked.

Julie Lin looked out at them and laughed. Not a cruel laugh, but an affectionate one: she knew the kind of hard physical work these people probably did and that they deserved their spot of fun in the nation's capital.

Her gaze moved on, to the busy evening traffic on Qianmen West Street. Life was going on all around her: something she felt a part of, something she belonged to, something she no longer had to delve for the meaning of in strangeness and suffering.

She still wondered about the people at New Tianjing: about Valiant, about Modesty, above all about Qingai. But that all seemed a long time ago; the wondering no longer hurt. Her brother-in-law had, after all, saved ten of them from suicide. Wherever they were, they should be grateful to her. And if they weren't, that was their problem.

She finished her chocolate shake—after a period of weight-gaining, she was back on the low-fat stuff again—and allowed herself a smile at the thought of those strange people she had known. It was, she reflected, good to wonder. To wonder about other people meant to belong, not to the dreams of a hurt child or to a self-appointed elite of perfectionists, but to the human race.

It felt good.

She finished the shake—so what about the noises? everybody

else made them—and walked out into the sharp, exhilarating late-spring twilight of Beijing, her home. Leaves were budding on the plane trees; the evenings were getting warmer; back at the hutong there were summer clothes to take out of storage and to air.

And it was the start of a new millennium.